VIOLET FORSTER'S LOVER

BY
RICHARD MARSH

CHAPTER I
The Card on the Floor

Tickell turned his cards.

"A straight." The men all bent over to look. "King high--there you are, nine, ten, knave, queen, king; a mixed lot, but they'll take some beating."

Something on Beaton's face seemed to suggest that the other's hand was unexpectedly strong. He smiled--not easily.

"You're right, they will; and I'm afraid----" He turned his hand half over, then, letting the five cards fall uppermost on the table, sat and stared at him, as if startled. It was Major Reith who announced the value of the hand.

"A full and ace high--he's got you, Jack; a bumper, Sydney."

He pushed the salver which served as a pool over towards Beaton. Obviously it contained a great deal of money; there were both notes and gold, and cheques and half-sheets of paper.

"What will you take for it, Sydney?" asked George Pierce.

Anthony Dodwell interposed.

"One moment, before Beaton takes either the pool or--anything else. Perhaps he won't mind saying what is the card that he dropped on the floor."

They all looked at him--Beaton with a sudden startled turn of the head.

"What do you mean?" he asked.

Dodwell met his eager gaze with a calmness which, in its way, was almost ominous.

"I'm afraid that question is quite unnecessary; I fancy you know quite well what I mean. Will you pick up the card you dropped, or shall I?"

"I dropped no card." He drew his chair a little away from the table so as to enable him to see the floor. "I didn't know it, but there does seem to be one down there."

"Unless some good fairy removed it since you dropped it, there was bound to be. Draycott, would you mind picking up that card?"

Noel Draycott, stooping, picking up the card, showed it to the assembled players, in whose demeanour, for some as yet unspoken reason, there seemed to have come a sudden change.

"It's only the nine of spades."

"Exactly, which was possibly the reason why Beaton dropped it; with the nine of spades he could hardly have made a full."

Beaton rose to his feet, his face flushed, his tones raised.

"Dodwell, are you--are you insinuating----" The other cut him short.

"I'm insinuating nothing. You are the dealer; there's a pack close to your hand; you gave yourself three cards; I saw you glance at them, then drop one on to the floor, and take another off the top of the pack--in the hope, I presume, that it was a better one. It clearly was; the card you dropped was the nine of spades; the hand you have shown there consists of three aces and a pair of knaves; I can't say which was the card you took from the top of the pack, but it was one of them, and it certainly gave you the full."

There was silence, that curious silence which suggests discomfort, which presages a storm. It is not often that an accusation of foul play is made at a card-table around which are seated English gentlemen. These men were officers in one of His Majesty's regiments of Guards; they were having what they called "a little flutter at poker" after the mess dinner--it had gone farther perhaps than some of them had intended. Considerable sums had been staked, and won and lost. Sydney Beaton in particular had punted heavily. For the most part he had lost--all his ready cash and more. For some time he had been betting with I.O.U.'s scribbled on odd scraps of paper. There had just been a jackpot. Five men had come in, dropping out one after the other until only Beaton and Tickell had been left. Tickell's last raise had been a hundred pounds; Beaton had covered the bet with an I.O.U. for £100 to see him; the hand he had exposed was, of course, the better one; there was a large sum of money in the pool, much the largest which it had as yet contained; if it was his, then it would probably more than set him on his feet again. It was the fact that there seemed to be an "if" which caused those present to stare at each other and at him as if all at once tongue-tied.

Beaton had gone red, then white; and now one felt that something must have happened to the muscles of his face, its expression seemed to have become so set and rigid. Major Reith, who was the oldest man present, broke the silence.

"Dodwell, please be careful what you say. Come, Sydney, tell him he is mistaken."

What Beaton said was gasped rather than spoken.

"It's a lie!"

Dodwell's manner continued unruffled. He turned to Draycott.

"Noel, I fancy I caught your eye. Am I wrong in supposing that you also saw what happened?"

"I'm afraid I did."

"You saw Beaton drop one of the three cards he gave himself, and take another off the top of the pack?"

"I'm afraid I did."

As Draycott repeated his former words, Beaton, still on his feet, swinging round, struck him with such violence that the man and the chair on which he was seated both went together to the floor. The thing was so unexpected that it had been done before anyone could interpose. Frank Clifford, who was on the other side of him, caught at Beaton's arm.

"Sydney! That won't do!"

Beaton, instead of heeding his words, was endeavouring to thrust the table away in order to get at Dodwell, who was on the other side. The others were able to prevent his doing that.

"If I get at him," he gasped, "I'll kill him."

But they did not allow him to get at his accuser, for they held him back; and they were five or six to one. Major Reith spoke.

"Don't make bad worse, Beaton, please; this is not a matter with which you can deal on quite those lines. Do we understand you to deny what Dodwell and Draycott say?"

The fact was, Beaton had not only had his share of wine at the table, he had been drinking since, liqueur after liqueur. Trifles of that kind, when in sufficient numbers, do not tend to cool a young man's already heated brain. For longer than they supposed Sydney had not been his real self; many and various were the causes which had been tending to make him lose his balance. Then, in that supreme moment, when he needed to keep his head more than ever in his life, he lost his balance altogether and played the fool.

"Do you think," he shouted, "that I'll condescend to deny such a charge coming from a beast like Draycott and a cur like Dodwell? I tell you what I will do, I'll take them on both together and fight them to a standstill, and choke their infernal lies back into their throats. Major Harold Reith, if I do get hold of you, I'll tear your lying tongue out by the roots."

He tried to get at the major, but of course they would not let him. For a few minutes there was a discreditable scene; Beaton behaved like a lunatic. Those who tried to keep him from attacking Major Reith he fought tooth and nail. Between them he was borne to the ground, then, as if he had been some wild beast, they had to drag him out of the room, and fling the door to in his face.

When, later, inquiries were made as to his whereabouts, he was not to be found. His room was empty. He had apparently paid a hurried visit to it. His mess uniform was on the floor. Apparently he had torn it off him and attired himself in something else. What he had done afterwards there was little to show. The sentry on duty, when closely questioned, said that Captain Beaton, in civilian dress, had passed him, reeling like a drunken man, and vanished into the night. The sentry was the last man connected with his regiment who saw him. Not a line came from him; nothing was heard; the place which had known him knew him no more. He had gone, a pariah, out into the world. He had been one of the best-liked men in the regiment; there were many who missed him; but there was one whose heart was nearly broken.

CHAPTER II
While the Groom Waited

Two days before that fatal night Sydney Beaton had gone down to see his brother, Sir George Beaton, head of the family, and practically its sole representative, in his old home at Adisham, in the County of Wilts. The visit had been of the nature of a forlorn hope. Sydney wanted help, pecuniary help, as he had done more than once before. He was in a very tight place. He had piled folly on to folly, and just lately he had surmounted the pile with the biggest of the lot. If he could not get money quickly matters would go very ill with him. Money-lenders and all those sort of people were not to be persuaded; he owed them already more than they ever expected to get. Nor did he know of any friend or acquaintance who would be likely to do what he required; his credit was bad even among them. He did not think he would be able to get the money from his brother; George had told him on a previous occasion that he would never let him have another farthing; there was evidence that he meant to keep his word. Still, Sydney had to try lest worse befell.

But he failed, badly. There was something very like a quarrel. Sydney confessed, after a fashion. He warned George that if he did not get the money he wanted the family name might suffer. George, in reply, said right out what he thought of him; he made it quite clear that his opinion of his brother could hardly have been a worse one. He refused to let him have even so much as a five-pound note.

"Sydney," he said with brutal frankness, "nothing can save you--certainly my money can't; I mean, nothing can save you from yourself. I mayn't be the steadiest mover; I'm not holding myself up as an example----"

"There you show your wisdom."

"But you--you're the limit. In the sense in which they use the word in the stable, you're a rogue. You're worse than an unbroken, bad-tempered colt; you're not safe either to ride or drive. You're absolutely certain to come a cropper, and probably a bad one. I give you my word that I have no intention, if I can help it, of letting you bring me down with you. You know, I'm not a rich man; I want all the money I've got for my own use----"

"That I will admit."

"If you had your way you'd make a bankrupt of me in another couple of years. But you're not going to have your own way; not another sovereign do you get out of me. That's my last word."

The younger brother seemed to be moistening his lips before answering; there was a strained look in his eyes.

"You understand that if you won't help me I'm in a hole?"

"I understand that clearly. I also understand that if I won't, what you call, 'help' you, you'll drag me in with you. In fact, what you're after is sheer blackmail. If there had been a witness of our conversation, I could give you into custody for attempting to obtain money by means of threats, and you'd be convicted. If the family name is to be dragged in the mud by you, then I shall want all the money I have to get it out again. Hadn't you better go? I don't propose to offer you a bed for the night, and if you waste much more time the last train will need some catching."

Sydney did go, after some very unbrotherly words had been exchanged; but he did not catch the last train. The last train from that part of the world left early; another interview which immediately followed the one with his brother delayed him till it was dawn. As he was leaving the house in which he was born, Ling, the butler, handed him a note, remarking, as if imparting a confidence:

"From Miss Forster, Mr. Sydney. It reached me just after you came, but I thought I had better not bring it in to you while you were with Sir George."

Without a word he tore the envelope open. Within was a sheet of paper on which were half a dozen lines.

"DEAR SYDNEY,--Why did you not let me know you were coming? How dare you not to? If I had not seen you driving from the station I might never have known. I shall be at the old place this evening at seven o'clock; mind you come. I don't know that I need give a special reason why you are to come; I take it for granted that you will jump at the chance, but there is a special reason all the same.--VI.

"Mind--I said seven! Just you make it *seven*."

Sydney looked at his watch; it was a quarter to seven. The last train left for London soon after eight. The station was nearly eight miles off; the dog-cart in which he had come was waiting at the door; he had not much time to spare if the train was not to go without him. He arrived at a sudden resolution--all his resolutions were arrived at suddenly, or he would have been a happier man. He spoke to the groom in the cart.

"Go down the village and wait for me at 'The Grapes.' I'll be with you as soon as I can."

He strode off. The groom touched his hat. He winked at Ling, who had appeared on the doorstep. The butler resented the familiarity.

"I don't want anything of that sort from you, Sam Evans; you mind your own business and leave others to mind theirs. You do as Mr. Sydney tells you, and wait for him at 'The Grapes.'"

"I'll wait for him right enough, but I wouldn't mind having a trifle on it that I keep on waiting till it's too late for him to catch his train."

Sam Evans grinned; he kept on grinning as he drove off, although the butler had done his best to keep him in his place. But the groom was right; the dog-cart waited outside the village inn till it was too late for Sydney Beaton to catch the last up train.

Autumn was come. The nights were drawing in. It was dusk. Sydney Beaton pursued his way through gathering shadows, through trees whose foliage had assumed the russet hues of autumn. There had been rain earlier in the day; a northerly breeze had blown it away, the same breeze was bringing the leaves down in showers about him as he walked. He went perhaps a good half-mile, taking a familiar short cut across his brother's property on to the neighbouring estate of Nuthurst. He came to a ring of trees which ran round a little knoll, on the top of which was what looked to be an old-fashioned summer-house. His footsteps must have been audible as they tramped through the dry leaves; that his approach had been heard was made plain by the fact that a feminine figure came out of the building and down the rising ground to meet him as he came. What sort of greeting he would have offered seemed doubtful; something in his bearing suggested that it would have been a less ardent one than that which he received. Moving quickly towards him, without any hesitation the lady placed her two hands upon his shoulders and kissed him again and again.

"Sydney, you are a wretch! Why didn't you let me know that you were coming?"

"I scarcely knew myself until I was in the train."

"You might have sent me a telegram before the train started."

"I'm only here for half an hour; I shall have to hurry off to catch the last train back to town."

Something in his words or manner seemed to strike her. She drew a little away from him in order to see him better.

"Sydney, what's wrong?"

He smiled, not gaily. To her keen eyes his bearing seemed to lack that touch of boyish carelessness with which she was familiar.

"What isn't wrong? Isn't everything always wrong with me? Aren't I one of those unlucky creatures with whom nothing ever does go right?"

"Have you quarrelled with George again?"

"He's told me he couldn't give me a bed for the night, which doesn't seem to point to our being on the best of terms."

There was a momentary pause before she spoke again; and then it was with quizzically uplifted eyebrows.

"More money, Sydney?"

He was silent. His hands in his jacket pockets, his feet a little apart, he stood and looked at her, something on his handsome face which seemed to have obscured its sunshine. When he spoke it was with what, coming from him, was very unusual bitterness.

"Vi, what's the use of this? I didn't want to let you know that I was coming; I didn't mean to let you know that I had come, because--what's the use of it?"

"What's the use of my loving you, do you mean? Well, for one thing, I thought that you loved me."

"An unlucky beggar who is always in a mess, and only scrambles out of one hole to get into another--what does his love matter to anyone?"

"I cannot tell you how much it matters to me. And, Sydney, doesn't my love matter to you?"

"Vi! you mustn't tempt me."

"How do you mean, tempt you?"

"If you only knew how I longed to take you in my arms, and keep you there. But what's the good of longing?"

"You can take me in your arms--and keep me there--for about ten seconds."

"Yes, I know; I know that you're a darling, the sweetest girl in the world, but what right have I to do it? What prospect have I of ever making you my wife? All debts, and nothing to pay them. What would your uncle say if he came upon us now? Wouldn't he warn me off the premises, as my brother has done? You know, my dear, you're not for such as I am. I don't want to say anything unkind, but don't you see, can't you see, that the only thing left for me to do is to withdraw and leave the field open for a better man?"

"Sydney, this time you must have come a cropper."

There was that in the girl's tone which, in spite of himself, brought a real smile to the young man's lips.

"I have. You're right. One which is going to make an end of me."

The girl shook her head gaily.

"Oh, no, it won't. I know you better. You've been coming croppers ever since I have known you, and that's all my life, some of them awful croppers; there must have been quite twenty from which you were never going to rise again. But you've managed, and you'll manage again. Only, really, I do wish you'd get out of the habit, if only for a while."

"Vi, you don't understand, this time you really don't. I'm done. I went to my brother as a last resource--you may be pretty sure it was a last resource--for the money which was the only thing that could save me. I am quite serious. He told me he would not give me so much as a sovereign; he even refused me a night's lodging. That means, as I tell you, that I'm done. I don't know quite what will happen to me, but something not pretty. When you and I meet again it is quite possible it will not be as equals; I shall be in a class of which you do not take social cognisance."

Again the young lady shook her head; if again it was with an attempt at gaiety, there was something which looked very much like tears in her eyes.

"What a cropper you must have come; it makes my blood run cold to hear you talking. Have you been robbing a bank?"

"I might as well have done. I'm likely to be in as awkward a position as if I had."

The girl looked at him steadily; his eyes met hers. Each might have been looking into the other's soul.

"Sydney, do you still love me?"

"Wouldn't it be better for you if I were to tell you straight out that I don't? Think, wouldn't it?"

"No, it wouldn't; it would be much worse. It would be a cowardly thing to say, and also, I happen to know, an untrue one. I know that you do still love me. I only asked you for the sake of hearing your answer. You do."

"It has become a habit."

"And habits are not things which are easily rooted up."

"So it would seem."

"I don't flatter myself that your love for me is such an important a factor in your life as I should like it to be, or you would keep clear of croppers. I don't think you are capable of very strong and enduring emotions where a woman is concerned; nowadays men aren't. But, in your own fashion, you love me all the same, and you'll keep on loving me. I know you. And it's a fashion with which I should be very well content if----"

"Yes, if; that's it--if! So what's the use?"

"You're frightfully selfish."

"Is that a new discovery? You've told me so--how many times? And now, when for the first time in my life I'm really generous, you say it again."

"But you're not generous; you're only considering yourself. You're more selfish than ever. You love me in your fashion, but you must remember that I love you in mine. I don't see myself how I'm going to marry you just yet awhile."

"Just yet awhile!"

"Yes, I said just yet awhile. But then, are you thinking of marrying someone else?"

"I shall never marry any other woman if I don't marry you. I'm not that kind of man."

"Precisely. I believe you. Nor am I that kind of girl. As I say, I may not be able to marry you just yet awhile, nor may I ever be able to marry you at all, but--it's you or no one. Sydney, whatever becomes of you, you will always be the only man in the world for me. You may come badly to grief; you may do things I would much rather you didn't do; you may make me suffer more than the average man makes the woman who loves him suffer; but I'd rather anything than lose you. Whatever may become of you, whatever you do, wherever you may be, be sure of one thing, always--that I love you. I'll make open confession. Sydney, I'd marry you to-morrow if you wished me. I don't think you're likely to, nor do I think that it would be good for either of us if you did, but--there's the truth. And that confession stands for always. In whatever plight you may find yourself, penniless and in rags--I'm only talking to suit your mood, you know--you have merely to say so that I can hear you, 'Come, let's marry,' and I'll be your wife, your glad and loving wife. Here's my hand on it, and my lips to boot if you'd like them, as soon as the thing may be."

CHAPTER III
"Stop, Thief!"

Since his brother had refused him hospitality; since Violet Forster had spoken such sweet words to him by the summer-house; since he had been thrown by his brother officers out of the room which he had regarded almost as his own--these things, to Sydney Beaton, seemed how many years ago? It was as though the Sydney Beaton that had been belonged to one world and the Sydney Beaton that was to another. And indeed that was the case. He had in truth passed from one world to another; out of a world in which it was all joy, into another in which it was all misery. But, instead of being divided by years from one another, it was only by days. It seemed incredible that so much could have happened to him in so short a time; but in cases such as his it is the incredible which happens. Scarcely more than four weeks ago, twenty-eight days, and already he was brought to this. During the last few days he had been practically penniless; now he was literally without a farthing, or the prospect of getting one, and it was November in London, one of those damp, cold, foggy, uncharitable Novembers which Londoners know well. Never since the night when he had been thrown out of the room could he be said to have had all his wits about him, to have been, in any real sense, himself. It was as though a cloud had settled on his brain and dulled it; which was, perhaps, an explanation why from that last moment of his crowning degradation he had behaved like an utter fool. He had left the barracks with, as his whole fortune, the suit of clothes which he was wearing, his watch and chain, his studs and links, and about three pounds in money. All the rest of his cash, which had been little enough, was in that last pool. His account at the bank was overdrawn; no one owed him anything; and, placed as he was, there was not a soul to whom he could turn. His first idea, if he could be said to have had a really clear one, was to get out of England--it generally is the first idea of men placed as he was; they are to be met all over the English-speaking colonies. In his case it was impossible. He had heard vaguely of a man working his passage, but he had no idea how it was done. When he found his way down to the docks, and began to have some glimmering of an idea of the state of things that obtained there, it was borne in upon him that he had as much chance of working his passage to any place worth going to as he had of getting to the moon. For him there was only London, the seamy side of it.

His money lasted about a week. Then he pawned his watch and chain for £10, and had fooled that away before he knew it. He got five more for his links and studs, and that went. There was nothing left but the clothes he stood up in. They were already in a state in which he had never dreamt that clothes of his could ever be. It is unnecessary to enter into details, but his full wardrobe was in what, a very short time ago, would have been to him an unthinkable condition. He had to get money somehow, or--he could not think or what. He had contemplated suicide during the first few days; vague thoughts in that direction still passed through his mind; but--he still lived. If he was to keep on living, food was necessary. The less chance he had of getting food the more he seemed to crave for it, with a craving which became sheer agony.

That November night hunger seemed to be driving him mad. He had lived during the last week on two or three shillings, but he himself could scarcely have said how. He had come to look upon a common lodging-house as a desirable haven, of a Rowton House as positive luxury; he had slept two nights running in a Salvation Army shelter, and had been thankful for that. The last three nights he had slept--if he could be said to have slept at all--out of doors, under the November sky, in mist and mire, cold and gloom. To-night he found himself in Hyde Park. No man knows of what he is capable until his whole being cries out for food, and gets none. When a man who has been nurtured as Sydney Beaton had finds himself on the verge of starvation, his plight is much worse than that of the man who has fared hardly all his days. His powers of resistance are less, in more senses than one. Let so much be urged in excuse of Sydney Beaton, because that night he went to Hyde Park with some idea of asking for alms. Darkness, he thought, might shelter him; in some sort hide his shame. He would not be able to see clearly whom he accosted; what was much more, they would not be able to see him. But almost at the outset he had a shock which drove all notion of playing the beggar from him.

He was on the path on the Knightsbridge side of the Ring, under cover of a tree. A fine rain was falling; it was the only shelter to be had. Two men same swinging along the path. Something in their gait told him even in the darkness, while they were still at some distance, that they were well-to-do. He made up his mind that he would try to get out of them at least the price of a loaf of bread; the mere thought of a hot crusty loaf fresh from the oven made his brain reel. If he could only get the wherewithal to purchase one from the men who were coming towards him! Nearer they came, and nearer; they were almost on him. He was just coming out from under the tree when one of them spoke and the other laughed. He shrank back against the friendly trunk trembling, shivering. He knew who the two men were; in the other world which he had left behind they had been his brother officers: one was Anthony Dodwell, who had accused him of foul play, the other was Noel Draycott, who had supported the accusation! And he had been about to ask them for the price of a loaf of bread! If he had!

They went on. Dodwell's voice came back to him again, and Draycott's laughter. His heart was thumping so against his side that it seemed to be shaking him to pieces. He felt sure they had not seen him. He had noticed particularly that they never turned their heads; they were too anxious to press on to look his way--but if they had! It was some time after they were out of both sight and hearing that he recovered himself sufficiently to venture out into the open. Then, like a frightened cur, he slunk across the roadway towards the remoter portions of the park on the other side.

What a night that was, almost the worst of all the nights that he had had. Something, he knew not what, kept him in the park. When the hour for closing approached, he was cowering under a clump of bushes not far from the Serpentine. No one saw him. A policeman tramped along the path, but did not trouble himself to search for stragglers either on his right or left, seemingly taking it for granted that on such a night even the most miserable wretch would not choose such quarters.

Towards morning the weather improved. When the tardy light came back into the sky, Beaton ventured to show himself--a rain-sodden, half-frozen, shivering, weary, hopeless, starving wretch; his hunger seemed to be tearing at his vitals like some wild animal. A keeper eyed him suspiciously.

"What are you doing here? Where have you been all night? Have you been in the park?"

"In the park! Why, man, I spent last night at Claridge's Hotel, where I've just had breakfast. You haven't got a crust of bread about you, have you, something which you were going to give to the ducks?"

"No, I haven't. You had better take yourself outside of here. You're up to no good, I'm sure."

The keeper passed on, leaving Beaton to obey him or not as he chose. Sydney, aware that the park was now open to the public, did not choose. The morning grew brighter; positively the sun began to appear in the sky, a faint, uncertain sun in a watery sky. Riders began to come upon the scene, for the most part masculine; those victims of too much work, or perhaps too good living, who for various reasons are unable to take exercise in any other form, and are ordered by their doctors to take a regular morning ride in the park, no matter what the season of the year or the weather. Possibly because the morning, for November, was a fine one, the equestrians became quite numerous. Sydney stood up against the rail to watch them. There had been times, not so very long ago, when he had taken his morning canter in the park. As he watched the riders come and go, it seemed incredible--now. In spite of his physical distress it still tickled him to notice how badly some of them rode; the "Liver Brigade" always had been famous for its bad riding. But what did it matter how they rode? The world went very well with them; they had slept on spring mattresses, between linen sheets, had come from luxurious homes, were returning to an excellent meal, which they probably lacked appetite to enjoy; while he----! He was rapidly approaching that state of mind in which the anarchist throws bombs; if he had had one handy he might have thrown it at one of those well-fed looking persons there and then. If he were to stop one of them and ask him for the price of a loaf of bread? Was it not probable that, instead of giving him what he asked, he would summon the police? He knew them, ignorant, stupid, selfish to the backbone, thinking that no one could be hungry because they themselves were too well fed. The pangs of hunger seemed suddenly to grow more intense; he would have to get food somewhere, somehow, soon.

Two pedestrians came down the path, an old and a young man. They hailed a passing rider. He stopped; they drew close up to the rails as he came towards them. They were within three feet of Sydney Beaton. He could hear distinctly what was said. The elder man drew out a sovereign purse, and from it two gold coins. He said to the equestrian:

"You were right, Buxton, and I'm the loser. Here are your ill-gotten gains."

He held out the coins towards the man on the horse. Always a creature of impulse, Sydney Beaton gave way to the worst impulse he had ever had yet; in other words, he all at once went stark, staring mad. The old gentleman's umbrella was under his arm, in his left hand were the two coins, in his right the sovereign purse, still open. A heavy gold chain stretched from pocket to pocket across his waistcoat unguarded. Probably there was a handsome gold watch at the other end of it. No thought of anything of the kind had been in Beaton's mind one instant; the next he stepped forward and, snatching at the unguarded chain, had it in his possession before he himself clearly realised what he was doing. The act was so audacious, so instantaneous, so unexpected, so astounding, that for three or four seconds even the victim did not appreciate what had happened. Then he shouted, so that he might have been heard outside the park:

"The scoundrel's taken my watch and chain!"

Then his companion became alive to what had occurred, and the man on the horse to whom he had been about to give the coins, and presently everyone within sight and earshot. It is conceivable, and even probable, that Beaton did not understand what he was doing till he had done it; it was only when he saw the watch and chain in his own hand that understanding really came. He knew he was a thief; and the first instinct of a thief was born within him, the instinct of self-preservation. In a moment all his energies were centred in an attempt to escape. He rushed across the path, vaulted over the railing, tore across the grass as fast as his feet could carry him, with the chase at his heels. The old gentleman could not do much in the way of chasing, but seemingly his companion could, and there, were others who joined him who plainly were still capable of running after such a quarry. Swift-footed though he knew himself to be, before he had taken many steps Sydney knew that he would owe not a little to fortune if he escaped scot free. His impulse was to hurl from him the incriminating watch and chain, but that was an impulse to which he did not yield. It would do him no good; everyone would see him throw it, just as everyone had seen him take it. The watch would certainly be damaged, perhaps ruined; there would be nothing gained by treating it in such brutal fashion. So he crammed it into his jacket pocket, and set himself to move yet faster. The victim's companion was uncomfortably close behind him.

It was plain that he would have to reckon with more pursuers than one. People were coming towards him from all sides, even from the front. A crowd was gathering, all bent on capturing him. He saw a keeper hurrying down the path which bounded the stretch of grass which he was crossing, possibly the keeper who had already accosted him. A constable was advancing from the other side. If he shook off the amateur thief-catchers, he would have to reckon with them. The pair would probably be more than a match for him, but he would not be taken if he could help it. That would be indeed the end.

As he neared the opposite railing three or four persons were already there to meet him, others were rapidly approaching, including the keeper and the constable. He swerved to one side, ran rapidly along the railing, vaulted over it a dozen yards lower down, alighting within a few feet of the constable. That official halted, seeming to take it for granted that the criminal had delivered himself into his hands. He was premature. Nothing was farther from his intention. Sydney charged right at him, as he had learnt to do in his old days of Rugby football. The policeman, taken unawares, went over like a ninepin; he made a vain grab at the other's legs as he fell. Sydney sped triumphantly on.

But, although he had sent the policeman sprawling, he knew that he had almost shot his bolt; the next fence would bring him down. His breath was failing him; the world seemed spinning round; a few more steps and he would be able to go no farther; they would have him; all would be ended.

At the very moment when already his pace was getting slower something happened which, if he had had his wits sufficiently about him and time enough to use them, would have seemed to him very like a miracle. He was coming into the road which leads through the park from the Corner to the Marble Arch. He had still sense enough to see that a motorcar was coming along the road, slowing as it came. It came to a standstill just as it was abreast of him. The sole occupant of the body of the car was a woman, who all at once opened the door, stood up, and beckoned to him. He did not pause to think what the gesture might mean, who this fair owner of a motor-car might be who had fallen from the skies. There was not time, nor had he wit enough; his senses were fast leaving him. He was so conscious that this was so that he made a last desperate effort, scrambled pantingly over the railing, got somehow to the side of the car. When he had got there, unless the woman inside had given him a helping hand, he would have been hard put to it to enter.

The moment he was in the door was slammed, the car was off. For Sydney that was the end of the chapter. He just managed to drop back on to the seat, but almost before he reached it his few remaining senses fled; he was as unconscious of what was happening as if he had not been there.

CHAPTER IV
The Good Samaritan

The thing was successful because so unexpected. The car was started, quickened its pace, and was out of the park before, probably, any of Beaton's pursuers understood what was being done. It was a triumph of impudence. The car had joined the other traffic, and was running along Piccadilly, without anyone lifting so much as a finger in an attempt to stop it. It turned up Bond Street, crossed Oxford Street, and began to thread its way among the maze of streets which constitute Marylebone.

The unexpected passenger continued unconscious throughout the entire run. The night and morning had completed the havoc wrought by the last few weeks; the works had run down at last. On his seat sat the chauffeur, a youngish man, clad in immaculate livery; he had apparently paid not the slightest heed to the incident of picking up in such strange fashion so singular a passenger. Although he had received no instructions as to the route he was to take, he drove steadily on without the slightest hesitation, as if carrying out a prearranged programme. By Sydney's side sat the woman who had opened the door, beckoned to him, and assisted him to enter. In spite of its being an open car, she was scarcely dressed in what is generally known as a motoring costume, but was rather attired as a lady might be who is taking the air in the park, or paying a morning call. It was not easy, from her appearance, to determine her age. Where a woman is concerned it seldom is, but she was certainly not old; she might have been anywhere between twenty-five and thirty-five. Nor was she ill-looking. At times, as she glanced at the man beside her, her face was lit by a smile which made it even more than pretty, then the smile went, and was succeeded by an expression which had in it something hard and cruel and even sinister; but even then, after some uncomfortable fashion, it was a handsome face, though scarcely one which one would have chosen for a friend. Her immobility was striking. Although she had been guilty of such a quixotic action as to rescue a man, a vagabond, who obviously was flying from the police, so soon as she was in the car her interest in him had seemed to cease. One might have supposed that this was a sentimental person, whose emotional nature was prone to lead her into what she supposed to be acts of kindness which afterwards she would have reason to regret, but there was nothing suggestive either of sentiment or emotion as she sat by Beaton. He presented such a pitiable spectacle, huddled there in the corner of the car, limp and lifeless, that the average woman would surely have shown some sign either of interest or sympathy. Not only did she do nothing to relieve his position, which was a more than sufficiently uneasy one, but she made no effort, even by speaking to him, to win him back to consciousness.

She regarded him almost continually, but rather as if he were a lay figure than a living man. One wondered if she proposed to use him as a model for a picture; she seemed to be studying him with so curious an air. She was observing him closely enough; one felt that nothing about him escaped her scrutiny--that she noted the well-cut clothes as well as the state that they were in; the hand which dangled helplessly by his side, that it was not that of a man who had done much manual labour; the face, which, unshaven and unwashed though it was, was not only a handsome one, but also the face of a man of breeding. Possibly she was putting these things together, and from them drawing her own conclusions.

Whatever her conclusions were, she kept them to herself. Clearly, instead of being the prey of her own emotions, this was a woman who kept her own feelings in the background; whose face was a mask; who was mistress of herself; who, to judge from her bearing, was as cool and calm and calculating as if she had been thrice her years. Which made this thing she had done seem all the stranger.

The car drew up in a short street of dull, old-fashioned houses, with stuccoed fronts, tall, narrow, dingy. The moment it stopped, before the lady had the chance to alight from the car, the door of the house flew open, and a tall, clean-shaven man appeared on the doorstep who might have been a servant. Crossing the pavement, he opened the door of the car; the lady got out. As she moved towards the house she made one remark, which seemed an odd one:

"I've got him."

That was all she said. Moving easily--one noticed as she did so what a charming figure she had--she passed into the hall. The chauffeur sat still; he did not so much as glance round at the man who had come out of the house. That individual shared the general calmness of demeanour. He exhibited no surprise at what the lady had said or at the sight of the figure which was huddled in the car. He said nothing. Leaning forward, he put his arms under Beaton and raised him as if he were a child, carried him into the house, up a flight of stairs, into a room at the back, and laying him on a couch which it contained, looked down at him with an air of detached curiosity without showing any sign of having turned a hair. Beaton had grown lighter of late, but he had nearly six feet of bone and muscle, and still weighed something. The man must have been possessed of unusual strength, as well as knack; it is something of a feat to lift a big and unconscious person out of a vehicle and carry him up a steep flight of stairs as if he were a baby.

Presently the woman entered. The man was still standing by the couch, with a watch and chain and sovereign purse held in his hand. He was examining the watch. He nodded towards it as the woman appeared.

"What does this mean?"

He spoke quietly in a not unmusical voice; his accent was that of an educated person; his tone, though respectful, was that of one who addresses an equal, not that of a servant who speaks to his mistress.

"What's what?" She glanced at what he was holding. "It looks as if it were a watch and the usual appendages. Where were they?"

"In his jacket pocket. There's a name on the watch--Charles Carter--and a crest, and there are a couple of sovereigns in the purse."

"So that's why they wanted him."

"Who's they?"

"I was coming through the park when I saw that something interesting was taking place on one side of me: one man was trying to get away from a number of others. When I saw the way he bowled over a policeman I said to myself, 'That's the gentleman I want,' and here he is."

"I presume that watch and chain and sovereign purse explain the interest the crowd was taking in him. I imagine that they are articles that have only very recently come into his possession. He's a gentleman."

"I felt sure he was from the way he handled that policeman."

"There's his name on the jacket." He picked up the garment in question, of which he had relieved the still unconscious Sydney, and which was hanging over the back of a chair. "Here it is on the tab. The jacket was made in Savile Row, and here's his name: Sydney Beaton."

"It might, of course, have been made for someone else and come into his possession; he alone knows how."

"No; it was made for him, it fits too well. His name is Sydney Beaton, and he's a swell who's down on his luck."

"That's the kind of person we want, isn't it?"

For the first time the man's and woman's eyes met. In hers there was a gleam as of laughter. In his there was no expression at all. His was one of those square faces whose blue cheeks and chin show how strong the beard would be which is not allowed to grow. He glanced from the woman to the unconscious figure on the couch before he spoke.

"Perhaps. When will he be wanted?"

"By to-morrow morning. I ought to write at once to say that he is coming; it will be safer."

"Safer!" The man's thin lips were parted by what was rather a sneer than a grin, as if the word she had used had borne an odd significance. He continued to survey the unconscious Sydney, as a surgeon might survey a body which he is about to dissect. "He'll have to be ready."

"There's time; and no one can do that sort of thing better than you."

Again the lips parted in that curious substitute for a smile, as if the woman's words had conveyed a compliment.

"Oh, yes, there's time; and, as you say, I dare say I'll be able to make a decent job of him."

When the woman left him it was to remove her hat and coat. Then she went into a good-sized apartment, in which there was a blazing fire. In a corner was a bookshelf filled with books; she took one down, it was Burke's "Landed Gentry." She took a case out of some receptacle in her bodice, and lit a cigarette. Settling herself in a big arm-chair before the fire, she put her feet upon a second chair, and set to studying Burke. She found what she wanted among the B's.

"There it is: 'Beaton, Sir George, seventh baronet,' and all the rest of it. 'Seat, Adisham, Wilts; unmarried; next heir, his brother, Sydney, D.S.O., the Guards, captain, twenty-eight years old.' If that coat was built for him it looks as if that ought to be our man."

She closed the book and let it fall upon the floor. She inhaled the smoke of her cigarette, staring with a contemplative air at the flaming fire.

"I wonder what's his record? One can, of course, find out, but there will be hardly time before he's wanted. An heir to a baronetcy, a captain in the Guards, and a D.S.O. hardly comes to snatching watches and chains without good and sufficient reasons. And yet, in spite of the state he's in, he hardly looks it, and by this time I ought to be a judge of that kind of thing. He must have had some queer experiences, that young gentleman. I wonder if any of them have been queerer than the one he'll have to-morrow. And what'll become of him afterwards? It seems a pity, but so many things are pitiful which have to be."

As she indulged in the expression of that almost philosophical opinion she expelled the smoke of her cigarette from between her pretty lips, and she smiled. Then she sat up straighter in her chair, and threw her scarcely half-consumed cigarette into the fire.

"And there are those who pretend that this is a very good world that we live in!"

CHAPTER V
Dreaming

"Will you have all the apollinaris, Sir Jocelyn?"

Sydney Beaton looked up. He was vaguely conscious of having been roused from slumber by someone, possibly by the person who was standing by his side. He was still very far from being wide awake; his eyes, limbs, body, all were heavy. He had not a notion where he was. There was a real bed, in striking contrast to the makeshifts he had known of late; there were soft sheets, a soft pillow, and there were hangings. It was not really a large room, but, compared to the kind of accommodation with which he had recently been made familiar, it was palatial. There seemed to be some decent furniture, and a carpet on the floor. It was not well lighted; there was only one not over large window, on the other side of which was the November fog. What had happened to him? Where could he be? He put his wondering into words.

"Where am I? Who are you?"

The man at his bedside did not answer. He was holding in one hand a tray on which was a glass; in the other was a bottle, out of which he was pouring something into the glass. He repeated in another form his first inquiry:

"Will that be enough apollinaris, Sir Jocelyn?"

"I'm not Sir Jocelyn, if you're talking to me. What's in that glass?"

"A good pick-me-up. I think you will find it just about right, Sir Jocelyn." Sydney took the glass which the man advanced. Whatever its contents, they were pleasant to swallow.

"That's good, uncommon good. My word!" He had another drink. "I haven't tasted anything as good as that since"--he hesitated--"since I don't know when."

"I thought you'd find it refreshing, Sir Jocelyn?"

"Why do you call me Sir Jocelyn? Who are you? Where am I? How did I come to be here?" The question was again ignored.

"Her ladyship wished me to say that if you felt equal to it, Sir Jocelyn, she would be glad if you would join her at breakfast."

"Her ladyship! Who's her ladyship? Didn't you hear me ask you where I am?"

Perhaps it was because the man was busy with certain articles of the gentleman's wardrobe that he did not hear what was said.

"I thought you might like to wear this suit to-day." He was placing three garments over the back of a chair, which Sydney felt, hazily, were certainly not his. "Everything is quite ready, Sir Jocelyn."

Why did the fellow persist in calling him by a name which was not his? What had happened to him? What did it all mean? What was the matter with his head that he felt so incapable of collecting his thoughts? He had never felt so stupid before. Before he clearly understood what was occurring, the bed-clothes were being removed from the bed, and he was being assisted on to the floor as if he were a child or a sick man; indeed, as his feet touched the ground he felt as if, literally, he was a sick man. The room swam round him; his legs refused him support; had not the other had his arm half round him he would have collapsed on to the carpet.

"What," he asked, with a sudden thickness of voice, "what is the matter?"

Had he been clearly conscious of anything he could scarcely have helped but notice the keen scrutiny with which his attendant was observing him. His manner almost suggested a medical man; it was so suave, yet he treated Sydney as if he were an irresponsible patient.

"You've not been quite well, Sir Jocelyn. You've had rather a bad night. I think you'd better have another pick-me-up."

Sydney was placed in an easy chair. Presently he found himself drinking the contents of another tumbler. How good it was. And it did him good; it seemed to relieve some of the heaviness which weighed down his limbs and to render the confusion in his head less obvious, but it was very far from restoring him to himself. The other dressed him, slipping on garment after garment with a curious deftness, for Sydney seemed incapable of giving him any help at all. Beaton was dressed actually before he knew it in garments which he realised were not his, but which somehow seemed to fit him. How he had come to be in them he could not have told; yet so skilful was his valet that in a surprisingly short time his costume was completed, even to his collar and his tie, yet he had not once moved out of the arm-chair in which he had originally been placed.

The other took a final survey of his handiwork, standing a little back to enable him to do so. He gave audible expression to his candid opinion; he was plainly aware that the other was not in a condition to resent anything he might either say or do.

"You look very well indeed, Sir Jocelyn, quite remarkably well, considering. You want one more pick-me-up, made a trifle strong, then I think we'll take you downstairs, and breakfast with her ladyship may be trusted to do the rest."

For the third time Sydney Beaton emptied the contents of a tumbler which was insinuated into his hand. Possibly because it was more potent it had a more visible effect upon him than either of the other two. The other watched the effect the liquid made on him with about his thin lips that not quite agreeable something that was half a sneer and half a grin.

"Now, Sir Jocelyn, how are we feeling? Do you think you could manage to stand up?"

Sydney proved it by standing up there and then, but there was an unsteadiness about the fashion with which he managed to keep his feet which the other could scarcely fail to notice.

"I'm all right," he said; "pounds better; sound as a roach; if this----" He held out the glass with a hand that was shaky. "What was the stuff you gave me? It's first rate, a regular corpse reviver."

"It is rather effective, under certain conditions, in its way." The man's tone, in spite of its suavity, could hardly have been drier. "Now, Sir Jocelyn, I think you'll find that her ladyship awaits you."

"Her ladyship? Why will you keep calling me Sir Jocelyn? That's not my name. And who's her ladyship?"

Once more the questions were ignored. The other placed his fingers lightly on Sydney's arm, and Sydney found himself moving towards the door. But whether he was moving of his own volition or in obedience to the other's behest he would not have found it easy to say. The man opened the door, led him through it, walked beside him down the stairs--always with his fingers on his arm. At the foot of the stairs he paused:

"Now, Sir Jocelyn, how are you feeling?"

For the moment Sydney really could not say; he was feeling very queer indeed, incapable of expressing himself in articulate words. Had it not been that the other's arm was again half round him he might have found it difficult to retain his perpendicular.

"Another taste, Sir Jocelyn?"

It seemed that the man had brought the glass with him down the stairs refilled. Sydney had it between his fingers without his quite knowing how it came there. He took another taste; it had on him the same effect as before, seeming to steady his limbs and to clear his brain. Before the effect could pass away the man had led him to a door, had opened it, and was ushering him into the room beyond. Someone advanced to him, a woman, whom even in his hazy state he was aware was good to look at.

"I am so glad to see you; you can't think how anxious I have been. I hope you're feeling better, quite yourself again?"

Sydney knew not what to say. The woman's voice was a pleasant one, and was grateful to his ears; her face was lit by such a delicious smile, it was grateful to his eyes. He had a feeling that this must be some old and very dear friend. Yet he could not place her, he had not the dimmest notion who she was; his memory must be playing him a trick. It was part of the general haziness through which he was looking out upon the world. But she did not seem to wait for an answer or to be hurt by his silence.

"Come," she said, "breakfast has been waiting quite a while. Will you have the seat by the fire, or will it be too much for you?"

"I'll sit wherever you please."

He managed to get out that much. She laughed, as if he had been guilty of a joke. She had quite a musical laugh.

"Then you shall sit by the fire, and I will do the honours. For once in a way I'll wait on you. I don't think you'll be required." The last words were addressed to the man who was still standing in the open doorway. They exchanged glances, of which Sydney was oblivious. The man made a significant gesture with the empty tumbler which he was holding in his hand, then touched his finger to his forehead. "I quite understand," said the lady. "But I tell you again that I don't think you'll be required. If I want you I will ring. In the meantime you may go."

The man went. Outside the door he paused; an odd look came on his face; he knit his brows; he glanced about him quickly, back and front; then he drew himself up straight and grinned.

"It's a ticklish game she's got to play, but there's few can play a ticklish game better than she can."

CHAPTER VI
His Wife

To Sydney it was all as if it were part of a dream. He had not dreamed--he did not know since when. This was like one of the dreams he used to have when he was a boy; a delightful dream. The sense of comfort which filled the room, the charmingly laid breakfast table, glorious with pretty china and shining plate; the charming woman who, with the most natural air, was treating him as one who not only had an assured footing, but who was both near and dear. Whether in this matter it was he who dreamed or she, he could not make sure. He wondered if he had been ill. He had such a strange feeling that he very easily might have been; he might have been ill for quite a long time; all sorts of things might have happened, and he might have forgotten all about them. It was the more possible since he could remember nothing; all he could remember was that he had awakened and found the man at his bedside with a tray on which was a tumbler. Before that, beyond that, his mind was a hazy blank.

But there seemed nothing hazy about his hostess, if she was his hostess; he supposed she was. If she was not his hostess, then who was she? She was ministering to his creature comforts in a manner which made the dream seem still more delightful, and such a very real one, too.

Through the haze which served him as a mind there seemed to gleam something which troubled him. The breakfast was excellent, the coffee, the food, everything. Was that not, in part, because at some remote period he had gone without breakfast, without-- anything? He was frantically hungry. There was a fragrance about the hot rolls which recalled something. Was there not a time when he had wanted a hot roll very badly, or something like it? The effort of recollection caused him to stop eating, a fact on which the lady commented.

"Of what are you thinking? You looked as if your thoughts were miles away. Won't you have a little more bacon?"

He had a little more. There was an exquisite flavour about that bacon which made it seem fit food for a god. He ate and ate, while she sat by, putting more food upon his plate as soon as it was empty or replacing one plate with another. At last he ceased. How much he had eaten he had no notion; he could eat no more.

"Now," she said, "you must have a cigar and a liqueur."

It did not occur to him to ask if it was usual to follow such a breakfast as he had had with a liqueur; he was too full of physical content to care. He watched her as she brought a box of cigars to the table, choose one, cut it, put it between his lips, and, striking a match, held it up to him. The first puff at that cigar was ecstasy, so great as to be almost painful. What was the flood of recollections which it brought back? How long ago was it since he had tasted such a cigar as that--a cigar at all? What dreadful things had happened to him since? She had poured something out of a bottle into a glass. She had spoken of a liqueur; but it was not a liqueur glass which she held out to him and from which he sipped.

It was curious how willing he seemed to be to have everything done for him; to eat and drink what was given to him; to have no taste of his own; to behave almost as if he were a puppet, moving when she pulled the string. And it seemed to amuse her to observe that it was so. One felt that she was curious to learn how far in this direction she might go, to what extent she could pull the strings and he would move. She put almost the same question to him as the man had put to him upstairs:

"Now, how are you feeling?"

"I'm feeling--well, I can't tell you how I'm feeling. I'm feeling just right. But do you know--I hope you'll forgive my saying so--but do you know, it's a fact that I can't make things out at all."

"What sort of things?"

"Why--everything; all sorts of things."

"Explain just what you mean."

"I'll try; but somehow, you know, it doesn't seem easy." He took the cigar from between his lips and had another sip from the glass which was not a liqueur glass. Something in his manner seemed to be tickling her more and more; each moment the smile on her face seemed to be growing more pronounced; it was, apparently, only with an effort that she could keep herself from bursting into a roar of laughter. He was looking her straight in the face with something in his eyes which seemed to cause her profound amusement. "Have I been ill, or--or queer, or something? I don't quite know how it is, but I feel so--rummy, if you'll excuse the word, that I feel as if I had had something."

It was some seconds before she answered. She sat with her elbows on the table looking at him with twinkling eyes.

"Well, you have had something; indeed, I should say that you had something now."

"That's how I feel. You know"--he put his hands up to his forehead--"it seems as if there was something wrong with the works. I can't think nor understand. As for remembering--I can't remember anything at all."

"I should imagine that that might be awkward."

"It is; you've no idea. For instance--you laugh--but I can't make out where I am, or how I got here, or--and that's the worst of it, it does seem so ridiculous--but I can't remember who you are."

"I'm your wife."

She said it with a face all laughter. That the statement took him aback was evident. He started and stared as if he could not make out if she were in jest or earnest.

"My--what?"

"Your wife."

"I suppose you're joking?"

"Not at all; I've seldom felt less like it. Being a wife is a very serious thing. Aren't you conscious of your weighty responsibilities as a husband?"

"I know you're joking." A strange something came on to his face which might have been a smile, but, if it was, it was a pathetic one. She smiled back at him. Into her smile there came, upon an instant, a something which was hardly genial.

"But I'm not joking. You are Sir Jocelyn Kingstone, and I am Lady Kingstone, your lawful wife."

"Now, I do know that you are pulling my leg, in spite of the something wrong up here." He touched his forehead with his finger. "I do know that my name is not Kingstone, and I'm just as sure that I'm not married--no such luck."

"Can't you regard yourself as married for, say, a few hours, perhaps even less? Can't you act as if you were?"

"What do you mean?"

"Nothing much. But, you see, I've done you a favour--I don't want to mention it, but I have--and couldn't you do me one in return?"

"I feel you've done me a favour--I've a sort of consciousness of it in my bones--but for the life of me I can't straighten things out."

He presented an odd picture as he sat there endeavouring to get his wits into working order; he seemed to be gradually collapsing under the strain. Instead of being touched by his obviously piteous plight, it seemed to add to her amusement.

"Don't let's go into details; don't try, it will only worry you. I have done you a service, and that's enough. Now I want you to do me one, and as you're a gentleman, and all that sort of thing, I don't think I shall need to ask you twice; you'll do it the first time of asking."

"What is it you want me to do? I'll do what I can, but there's precious little I can do; I'm so--well, you can see for yourself how it is with me."

"I've told you already what it is I want you to do. I want you to consent to regard yourself as my husband for--probably only a very few minutes."

"But I don't understand. I don't see what good you're going to get from my pretending to be your husband. A very poor sort of a husband I should make."

"You'll only be my husband *pro forma*--I think that's the proper term. You see, I'm in a position in which I've got to have a husband, just for a very few minutes; it doesn't matter what sort, so long as he's fairly presentable, and you know you're quite nice looking."

If he heard the compliment, it went unnoticed.

"It may be my muddled head, but I still don't see what you're driving at."

"It's like this--I'll try to make it plain: There's a large sum of money which is due to me, but I can't get it without my husband's assistance. He's got to come with me to the banker's, and sign papers, and things like that."

"Sign papers, and things like that?"

"That's all."

"That's all?" Again he echoed her words, as if, by dint of doing so, he was trying to get at their meaning. "But, signing papers, and things like that, isn't that rather a deal? What sort of papers would he have to sign?"

"Oh, nothing very dreadful." The smile with which she regarded him was a bewitching one. "You're not drinking your liqueur." She took up the glass and put it into his hand. He sipped at it with that docility with which he seemed to do all things. "You'd merely have to sign your name."

"Yes; but to what?"

"I really can scarcely tell you. I'm not a lawyer or a banker. I don't know what the forms are on such occasions, but I guess--mind you, it's only a guess--that you'll have to say you are my husband, and sign for the money after you've got it."

"Wouldn't that be forgery?"

"Forgery? How?" The smile did not fade, but a gleam came into her eyes which hinted that the question had taken her a trifle aback; it is conceivable that she had not supposed that he was sufficiently clear-headed for it to occur to him. "What an extraordinary thing to say! My dear man, it would be done with my authority, at my wish, and in my presence."

"Yes; but where is your husband?"

"At this moment he is not easily accessible, or I shouldn't want to worry you. I'd no idea that you'd have made such a fuss."

She made a little grimace, which became her very well. There was nothing to show that he observed it. He seemed to be struggling to follow out the line of thought which had come into his head.

"Is the money to be paid to your husband or to you?"

"Nominally to him, but really to me."

"Does he know about it?"

"How do you mean, does he know?" All at once she rose, and came and stood in front of him. "Young man, you're not to ask curious questions. This is a very private matter; there's a lot about it which I don't wish to explain, and which I don't think you're quite in a state to understand if I did. I'll tell you exactly what it is I want you to do. I want you to drive with me in, say, half an hour to the banker's. There I shall take you into a private room, and I shall tell them that you are my husband, Sir Jocelyn Kingstone; that you have not been very well, and cannot stand much worry, so that they're to get matters through as quickly as they can. If you like, you need not speak at all; you can leave all the talking to me, and, I may add, all the responsibility, too. Then, I imagine, they may ask you to sign a paper of some sort--I don't quite know what, but it won't be very much--then they'll hand you the money, and you'll sign for it, and then we'll come away. You see that the whole thing won't last more than five or, at the outside, ten minutes. We'll drive back here together, and in return for the service you've done me I'll do anything you like--mind, anything you like--for you. You'll find in me the best friend you ever had."

She knelt beside him on the floor, cajoling him, whispering things which he barely understood, but which were pleasant to hear. Somehow the feeling of physical well-being seemed to dull his senses still more. The dream became more dream-like; the woman's hands softly smoothed his hair; her lips were close to his; her eyes bewitched him; her words charmed his ears. She refilled the big sherry glass, and, even unwittingly, he sipped the insidious liqueur. In short, she played the fool with him, which, after all, was easy. At the best, after what he had lately gone through, he was little more than the husk of a man; but they had taken care that he should not be at his best. Her male accomplice had, as they put it, "readied" him. It was true that they had fed and washed and clothed him, but it was also true that they had dosed and drugged him. Being helpless in their hands, they had played tricks with him of which he had no notion and against which he had no defence.

After awhile the woman went out of the room. Without, suspiciously close to the door, was the man. They exchanged a few hurried sentences. She asked: "Is the brougham outside?"

"It's been there ever since I brought him down."

"I'm going to put on my hat. Give me his; I'll put it on for him. He's in a state in which he's more in my line than in yours."

The man grinned. He rubbed his chin as if considering.

"How long shall you be?"

"I ought to be back inside an hour. I shall come straight back."

She began to ascend the stairs, the man watching her as she went.

"I'll take care that you come straight back. You may have a card up your sleeve which you mean to play; but I have another, which will perhaps surprise you."

These words were not spoken aloud; they were said to himself. He looked as if he meant them, and as if they had a significance--an ominous significance--which was a little secret of his own.

CHAPTER VII
Among Thieves

She sat very close to him as they went through the streets in the brougham. She had persuaded him to have still another taste of the liqueur before they started; the world seemed more dream-like than ever. When the vehicle drew up, she helped him out into the street. The air of the misty November morning seemed to add to the fog which was in his brain. Nothing could have been more gracious or graceful than her solicitude for his seeming incapacity to take proper care of himself; no wife could have taken more tender care of a delicate husband. He did not know what place this was at which they stopped, and she did not tell him. When presently he found himself seated in an arm-chair, he had only the vaguest idea of how he had got there, and no knowledge whatever of the room in which he was. There was a gentleman who occupied a seat behind a table who he had a dim feeling was observing him with considerable curiosity. Something was said to him which he did not catch, possibly because his hearing was unusually dull. The woman at his side repeated it.

"My dear Jocelyn, this gentleman is asking if you are my husband, if you are Sir Jocelyn Kingstone."

Sydney said something. He did not know what he said; he never did know; but it seemed to be regarded as an efficient answer. Shortly something else was said to him, which the woman again repeated. He had a misty notion that she was doing a good deal of talking; that notion became clearer in the days that were to come. She put her hand lightly on his arm.

"Come, Jocelyn." She led him nearer to the table, placing him on a chair which was drawn close up to it. "This is what you are to sign. They have given me the money; here it is."

She held up what, although he did not realise it, was a bundle of bank-notes.

"Is it all right?"

He did not know why he asked the question, but he asked it. It was the first thing he had said consciously since he was in the room. He had had an odd feeling that she wished him to ask the question. She smiled.

"Quite all right. I will count it if you like, but I assure you it's right. Would you rather I counted it, or would you like to count it yourself?"

"No; it doesn't matter, so long as it's right."

He was conscious that a piece of paper was on the table in front of him, and that he had a pen between his fingers, though he was not sure how either of them had got there. She pointed to the paper with her finger.

"Sign here. Just put your name--Jocelyn Kingstone. My dear boy, how your hand does shake!"

He was aware that it shook, but he was not aware of the glance that the lady exchanged with the gentleman who was on the other side of the table, to whom, when he had made an end of writing, she handed the sheet of paper.

"What a scrawl! Jocelyn, your writing's getting worse and worse." Then, to the elderly gentleman: "I'm afraid my husband's signature is not a very easy one to read."

The elderly gentleman surveyed the performance through a pair of gold-rimmed pince-nez smilingly.

"It isn't very legible, is it? Your signature is not very legible, Sir Jocelyn; it would take an expert to decipher it. Would you mind, Lady Kingstone, witnessing the fact that it is your husband's signature?"

"Do I mind? Of course I don't." She laughed as if she appreciated the joke of the suggestion. "There--'Witness, Helena Kingstone,'--I think you will be able to read that."

"That certainly is legible enough. You write a good bold hand, Lady Kingstone, the sort of hand I like a woman to write."

When the pair had left the room the elderly gentleman said to a younger one who was seated at a table to one side:

"That's a sad case, a very sad case indeed. That is quite a charming woman, and not bad-looking; while he--he's the sort of person who, in a better ordered state of society, would be consigned to a lethal chamber at the earliest possible moment. Upon my word, I often wonder what makes a woman marry such a man. Fancy, at this time of day, drunk."

The younger man seemed to consider before he spoke.

"It struck me that he was something else as well as drunk. He didn't carry himself like an ordinary drunken man. He seemed to be under the influence of some drug. She says that he's been ill; he looks it. I wonder if they've been drugging him to bring him up to concert pitch."

The elder man shook his head. He seemed to be weighing the other's words.

"It's a sad case, a very sad case, whichever way you look at it. Poor woman! She may have had her own motives when she promised to love, honour, and obey him, but it's a long row she has set herself to plough."

When the pair in question were back in the brougham, and the horse's head was turned the other way, they had not gone very far before a distinct change took place in the lady's manner. She was no longer solicitous; she no longer sat close to her companion's side; indeed, she seemed disposed to give him as wide a berth as possible, to ignore him as completely as the exigencies of the situation permitted, and she never spoke a word. She was, possibly, too engrossed with the singularity of her proceedings to pay any attention to him. On her lap was a pile of bank-notes which she was dividing into separate parcels; these parcels she was bestowing in distinctly surprising portions of her attire. She slipped one parcel in the top of one stocking, a second into the top of the other; she took off her shoes, and placed a wad of notes in each; she turned up the sleeves of her coat--into the lining about the wrists, in which an aperture seemed to have been purposely cut, she inserted quite a number. Loosening her bodice, she slipped several into the band at the top of her skirt. With the residue she performed quite a surprising feat of legerdemain. She produced a small bag which was made of what looked like oil-skin, into which she crammed the notes; raising it to the back of her neck, she gave her shoulders a sort of hunch, it slipped down the back of her dress; one could see from the movements she made that she was trying to get it to settle in its proper place. Then, for the first time, she turned towards Beaton.

Some of her performances had been hardly of the kind which the average woman would care to essay in front of an entire stranger. She had been as indifferent to her companion's presence as if he had been a mechanical figure; and, indeed, when she looked at him, one perceived that he might just as well have been. He seemed to be as devoid of intelligence, as incapable of taking active interest in what was going on about him; it was probable that he had been quite oblivious of what she had been doing. But this time the spectacle he presented, instead of amusing her, seemed to fill her with quite different feelings. She addressed him all at once as if he had been a dog, her voice hard, cold, strident, even a trifle vulgar:

"Hullo--over there!" He remained still, clearly not realising that he was being spoken to. She went on in the same tone: "Now then, wake up! Haven't you been ill quite long enough? Try another sort of game. Do you hear me speak to you?" Apparently he did not. "Don't you, or won't you? Are you drunk? Now then, this won't do. I'm very much obliged to you, but I've had quite enough of it."

Leaning towards him, taking him by the shoulder, she began to shake him with considerable vigour, considering he was a man, and a big one, and she was a woman. The effect was, in its way--a grim way, ludicrous. His hat first tilted forward over his nose, then dropped on to the floor; his head fell forward over his chest. It seemed as if, if she kept on shaking him, he would come to pieces. Perceiving this, she stopped, eyeing him more closely, but still with no show of amusement, rather with contempt and annoyance.

"What's the matter with you? Are you ill, or is it the liqueurs and--the other things? Anyhow, I've had enough of it; I'm not going to have you ill in here. The time has come when we must part. Do you hear? Wake up!"

He did seem to wake up, in a kind of a fashion. He raised his head with an effort, looking at her with lack-lustre eyes.

"What is it?"

"What is it? It's the key of the street, the same key you had before."

A thought seemed all at once to occur to her. Stooping, she took off her right shoe, from it the wad of notes; selecting one, she replaced the others and the shoe.

"When I first made your acquaintance you had nothing, and rather less. Now, you've had a good night's rest, a bath, and other luxuries; you've had good food and drink; you are rigged out in decent clothes from head to foot; you've not done badly; but here's something else, as a sort of tit-bit."

She held out the note. He not only paid no heed to it, but seemingly he had no idea of what it was, or of what she was talking. This time she did seem to be amused; she laughed right out, as if his grotesque helplessness tickled her.

"Here, you're a pretty sort; I'll put it in your waistcoat pocket for you. Mind you, it's a ten-pound note--do you hear, it's a ten-pound note--for goodness sake do look as if you were trying to understand--and it's in your waistcoat pocket; I've put it there; take care, and don't you lose it; you'll want it before you're very much older."

She slipped the note into his waistcoat pocket without his showing the slightest sign of interest in what she was doing; he seemed to be mumbling something, for his lips were moving, but it was impossible to make out what he said.

"Now then, my funny friend, you'd better pull yourself together; we're going to part--try to look as if you were sober, if you aren't."

She tapped at the window; the carriage stopped; she opened the door and descended.

"This way, please." Taking him by the arm she drew him towards her, he yielding with the old, uncomfortable docility. Somehow he joined her on the pavement. "You've left your hat behind you, you can't go about London without a hat." Picking it up from the floor of the carriage, she placed it on his head. "That's not straight; there, that's better. What a helpless child it is! Sorry I can't stop, but I've another engagement; pleased to have met you; glad to have been able to do you a good turn."

She was re-entering the carriage with a smile again upon her face, when the man who had acted as Beaton's valet came round from the back and stood beside her; at sight of him her smile vanished. He raised his hat to Beaton.

"I also am pleased to have met you." He turned to the woman. "I think, if you don't mind, or even if you do, that we'll keep that engagement together. After you into the carriage."

Evidently she found the sight of him by no means gratifying.

"What's the meaning of this? What are you doing here? I thought it was agreed that you should wait for me till I came back."

"I had a sort of idea that I might keep on waiting; it even struck me as just possible that you might never come back at all. After you into the carriage."

She hesitated; looked as if she would like to refuse; then, with a laugh, which was hardly a happy one, she did as he suggested. He followed her; the door was shut; the carriage drove off. Sydney Beaton was left standing on the pavement; oblivious of what was taking place, of where he was; as incapable, just then, of taking care of himself as any inmate of an asylum. He remained standing where they had left him, swaying to and fro. The fog had thickened; a drizzling rain had begun to fall. It was not easy to make out where he was, but he was at the corner of a street, in what seemed to be an old-world square, which in that moment was as deserted as if all the houses round about it had been empty and it was miles away from anywhere.

But presently his solitude was broken; two men came round the corner, doubtful-looking men, shabby-genteel looking men, in some queer way the sort of men one would expect to find prowling about in such a place at such a time. At sight of Beaton they paused; they exchanged glances; one nudged the other. Then one spoke to him, with what he possibly meant to be an ingratiating smile.

"Nasty day, captain; looks as if we were going to have a real London particular." When Sydney seemed to be unconscious even of his presence his tone became a little insolent. "Waiting for anybody, guv'nor--or are you just a-taking of the air?"

The other spoke, with a glance at his companion which had in it something which was evil:

"Can't you see that the gentleman's taking of the air? What he wants is someone to take it with him; what do you say to our offering the gentleman our society?"

Sydney remained speechless, motionless, save that he continued swaying to and fro. They again exchanged glances. The first man said, with ostentatious impudence:

"I say, old cock, can you tell us how many beans make five?" Sydney was still silent. The first man went on. "Here, Gus, you take one of the gentleman's arms and I'll take the other: what he wants is a little bright, cheerful society, and he'll get it if we take him along with us."

Each of this most unpromising-looking pair took one of Sydney's arms; and without his attempting to remonstrate, or to offer the faintest show of resistance, they led him away.

CHAPTER VIII
The Sandwich-man

A bitingly cold afternoon towards the end of January. Six sandwich-men trudged along the Strand, urged by the cutting wind to more rapid movement than is general with their class. On the board of the last man which was slung over his back were the words, "Look at the man in front." On the board which was at the back of the man in front, to which your attention was directed, was "for Warmth And Sunshine Try Cox's Bitters." The legend was repeated all along the six. It almost seemed as if it must be a joke, of a grim order, to compel such unfortunate wretches to stare for hour after hour at such advice, on such a day. One had only to glance at them to see how much they stood in need of both warmth and sunshine; yet the chance seemed extremely slight that they would have an opportunity of trying Cox's bitters.

Some of the passers-by, who were in better plight than the six in the gutter, seemed to be struck by the fact that a jest might be intended, and where there were two of them together, they commented on it to each other.

"Poor beggars!" said one of the passers-by to the acquaintance at his side. "It's pretty rough on them to make them carry about a thing like that, when they're pretty nearly at death's door for want of the very things which, according to their own showing, are so easy to get."

The words were heard by someone who happened at that moment to be passing them--a woman. Possibly, as is easy in London, the sight is such a common one, she had been unconscious that the sandwich-men were there. When she heard the words she glanced at them to see to what they might apply. As she did so she started and stopped, as if she had seen something which had amazed her. The sandwich-men passed on, none of them had noticed her; they were probably too far gone in misery to notice anything, each kept his unseeing eyes fixed on his fellow's back.

The woman stood still, seemed to hesitate, went on, then turned and looked after the retreating sandwich-men. She seemed to be asking herself if it would be possible to catch them up, they were already at a distance from her of perhaps fifty yards. Then, as if arriving at a sudden determination, she moved quickly after them. Yet, although she walked so quickly, it was some little time before she caught them up, so that she had an opportunity to consider whatever it was that was passing through her mind. At last she was abreast of them again; was passing them; she scanned the last man, the fifth, the fourth, and, with much particularity, the third. Behind the others was probably all of life that was worth having, if it had been worth having to them; it seemed scarcely likely that the scanty, broken fragments of what remained of it could be worth anything to them. Theirs would probably be a continual tramp through the gutter, or its equivalent, to the grave.

But with the third man in the line it was different. He was young. In spite of the grotesqueness of his attire--he was clad in ill-assorted, ragged and tattered oddments of somebody else's clothing--there was something in his bearing which suggested that he was still a man. These others were but torsos. And although the hair beneath his greasy cap stood in crying need of both a barber and a brush, and there was an untrimmed, unsightly growth upon his cheeks and chin, a shrewd observer might have ventured on a small wager that if his hair had been cut and trimmed and he had been shaved and washed, he would not be altogether ugly.

One thing was noticeable, that though the woman stared at him he took no heed at all of her--he did not take his eyes off the man in front of him; and that although the woman kept step beside him in a manner which the others began to mark. All at once, as if moved by an overmastering impulse, she stretched out her umbrella and touched him on the shoulder.

"Hullo!"

That was all she said, but it was enough; he turned his head. At the sight of the eyes which glanced at her out of that dreadful face she started again, not without excuse. This was the face of one of those men of whom society has good reason to go in terror. Desperation was in every line of it; something like madness was in the eyes. This was the face of a man who had suffered much, and who, if opportunity offered, would stick at nothing to get even with those who had made him suffer.

He looked at the woman with, at first, no sign of recognition in his glance. Then, a muscle moved; something came into his eyes which had not been there before; all at once the fashion of his countenance was changed. He stopped, bringing those behind him to sudden confusion. He turned, the better to look at her; beyond doubt this was a woman of nerve, or she would have shrunk from that which was on his face. One felt that if, in that first wild moment, he had not been impeded by the boards which bound him, he would have laid violent hands upon her, and she would have fared ill.

But the boards did bind him. With them there he could do nothing but stand and stare. She met his gaze unflinchingly. Not only did she show no sign of concern at the threat which was in it, something in the expression of her own face suggested that it occasioned her positive pleasure. Certainly she could not have been more completely at her ease.

"Take those things off and come with me."

The man glared at her as if he wondered if his senses were playing him a trick.

"Come with you?"

It was an interrogation conveying, it would seem, a world of meaning. She smiled; at sight of the smile the gleam in his eyes grew more pronounced, his face more threatening. But she was in no way troubled.

"You heard what I said; you're not in the state in which you were when I saw you last; but in case you didn't quite hear I'll repeat it. I said, 'Take those things off and come with me.' And be quick about it, please, if you don't want to have a crowd collect and mob us; you see they're gathering already."

There was a momentary, very obvious, hesitation, then he did what she requested--he took the things off, meaning the boards which were suspended from his shoulders. When he had them off he put a question:

"What shall I do with them--shall I bring them with me?"

From the purse she took out of her handbag she chose a coin, speaking to the man behind him:

"There are five of you, there's half a sovereign; that's two shillings apiece. Take these articles back to their owner, and explain that the gentleman who was in charge of them has been called away."

She hailed a taxicab; at her suggestion he got in first, she followed, and the cab drove off towards a destination the driver alone had heard. The five remaining sandwich-men followed it with a chorus of thanks; one of them exclaimed, "Good luck, old pal! I wish I was in your place." He was a very old man, quite probably in the seventies, small in stature, nearly bent double as if shrivelled by the cold. For some cause his words, uttered in shrill, quavering tones, seemed to amuse the bystanders. A crowd had gathered, a heterogeneous crowd which so quickly does gather in a London thoroughfare; the five remaining sandwichmen were explaining to the people, as best they could, what had happened. In the taxicab nothing was said; the passengers were a queerly assorted pair, offering even a more striking contrast than when, on that first occasion, they had been alone together in the motor in the park. Then it was she who looked at him; now it was he who looked at her.

She sat in her own corner of the cab, her glance kept straight in front of her, so that she never looked his way. He, on the other hand, never took his eyes off her; it was perhaps as well she did not see them, they were unfriendly. His grimy hands were clenched in front of him; to judge from his expression they might, in fancy, have been clenched about her throat; no one watching him could have doubted that he was capable of such an action; this was rather a savage animal than a civilised man.

The cab crossed Brompton Road into a street on the other side, and after one or two turnings drew up in front of a small house which formed one of a terrace of old-fashioned villas. The woman paid the cab, opened the door with a latch-key, ushered the man into a room of fair size, comfortably furnished, a bright fire made it seem a veritable haven of refuge after the inclemency of the weather without. For the first time she spoke.

"Come to the fire and warm yourself; I should think you must be cold."

He echoed her last word with a very different accent.

"Cold!" He said it again in a tone of voice which was indescribable; in the word as he uttered it there was a whole dictionary of meaning. "Cold!"

"Have a drink?"

She was moving towards the sideboard on which there were bottles and glasses.

"The last time I saw you I had a drink at your expense, though I'm always paying for it."

"The world doesn't seem to have been using you very well since I met you last."

His speech was not a reply to hers.

"At least you have courage."

"Women of my sort have to; experience gives it to them. Without courage where should we be?"

"I wonder where you are sometimes even with it. Do you know that you've scarcely ever been out of my thoughts more than an hour or two at a time since we parted?"

"That's very nice of you."

"You think so. I've told myself over and over again that when I did get within reach of you--that's just the trouble, I've never quite been able to make up my mind what I'd do to you. I've told myself I'd kill you; in some of my happiest moments, in imagination, I've been wringing your neck; it was a delicious sensation."

"For you?"

"For me."

"Very well, then, give yourself that delicious sensation in real earnest--wring it. Here I am, quite close, ready to make things easy; I promise that I'll do nothing to keep you from wringing it to your heart's content." She had gone right up to him. He drew himself up straight, with a look upon his face as if he were about to take her at her word; but he stood still. Observing his indecision, she laughed. "How long do you propose to keep me waiting? Are you going to wring it now, or--it might be rather a nuisance in such a matter to have one's moment chosen for one--would you rather wait?"

"I'll wait."

"Good; then while you're waiting won't you come closer to the fire and have a drink? That's whisky and soda."

She held out to him a tumbler.

"Don't you give me that."

"Why not? It's warming."

"Last time you gave me something which was--warming."

"I see." She laughed. "You're thinking this is the same as that. I understand; or--are you very hungry?"

"Don't you ask me questions; I'll take neither food nor drink from you. I'll pay my debt and then----"

He left his sentence unfinished. If his bearing was more than a little melodramatic, hers was easiness itself.

"Before we go any farther--and we are going farther, so you needn't glare at me--we'll clear that up about what you call your debt. You think you owe me one?"

"Think! I've been in hell because of you; I'm in it still. Now I've a chance I'm going to make it my business to give you a taste of it too."

"There's nothing so silly as using extravagant language. I found that out long ago; and I'm a woman, and women are supposed to be inclined that way, and you're a man."

"You're a woman? A woman!"

"Yes, I'm a woman, a woman, a woman, and all the vitriolic bitterness you can get into your tone won't alter that. Now just you keep still and let me talk. You've your own point of view--of course, you would have, being a man--and I've mine; before you start paying that debt which weighs so heavily on your chest, you'll listen to what it is. I'll be as brief as I can, and while I'm talking I'll lay the table; I'm acting as my own maid just now. I may remark that you and I are quite alone in the house, so that if you do feel like wringing my neck you need fear no personal interference. I'm going to put some food upon the table, because I'm going to eat something, if you aren't."

Out of a drawer in the sideboard she took a tablecloth.

"Now about that debt you were speaking of; but before I talk of it, I'd better go and see what there is in the pantry that really is worth eating. Wouldn't you like to come and help me? There will be a tray to carry."

She had laid the table, and now stood at the open doorway looking at him with a smile on her face. Plainly he was in more than two minds as to what to do; this woman was, so far, proving more than a match for him. His tone was surly.

"I'm not coming with you."

"Aren't you? Very well, don't; stop there. I may as well go upstairs and take off my hat and coat and make myself look decent, even if I am to have my neck wrung directly afterwards. And then I'll go and forage in the pantry. Until we meet again."

With a saucy little nod she paused out of the room and shut the door.

A student in pantomime would have been interested by the man's proceedings when he found himself thus left alone, he was so evidently at a loss. He stared, or rather glared, at the door through which the woman had vanished; he seemed to be in doubt as to whether to go through it and out of the house. Then his eyes moved round the room, and stayed; as if it were all in such delightful contrast to what he had been used to that he had to stay. He made a half-step towards the fire, then drew back, with clenched hands and knitted brows; he would not warm himself beside this woman's fire. Then he saw the tumbler on the table, which she had left on the snowy tablecloth invitingly beneath his nose; his hand moved towards that--it was harder to keep that back, but he did. He saw, for the first time, the mirror above the mantel; as if unwillingly he went to it; the action was significant, a mirror had not been a necessary adjunct to his toilet for a considerable time.

He stared at the face that looked back at him as if it were that of a stranger, as if he found it difficult to realise that it could by any possibility be his, as if it were incredible that the man who had been could be the man who was now. He took the greasy cap off his head, as if the mirror had made him conscious that it was there. No woman could have shown keener interest in a tale told by the mirror; so absorbed was he by his own image that apparently he could not tear himself away. He became aware that the fire was just beneath; he stretched out his hands to the grateful blaze, then, remembered, glanced round him shamefacedly, moved away towards the window. How cheerless it was without, how cheery it was within. He twisted his cap as if he would have torn it; his jaw was hard set; his eyes looked this way and that. He moved from the window, this time towards the door, as if he were trying to bring himself to the sticking point, to retreat in time. He was nearly there when the door reopened and the woman appeared.

"Now then, you really must come and help me carry this tray; it's perfectly absurd to suppose that I can do everything while you do nothing. My maid is out; I only keep one, and it's her day out. You needn't eat anything; the fates forbid that I should press my food on you or my anything. But surely you can help me to get something to eat myself. Do you hear?"

"Yes, I hear."

"And you're not coming?"

"No, I'm not coming."

"You won't help me to carry the tray?"

"I won't."

"Then thank you very much. You know, you used to be a gentleman."

She passed out of the room with her head in the air. He let her go, waiting, grimly, for her return, the greasy cap between his hands. Presently she was back, bearing a well-filled tray.

"Won't you sit down? I should think even my chairs would not do you any serious injury; but, of course, stand if you prefer it; I suppose you can wring my neck better standing. I'm going to have some tea, the kettle's boiling, and I feel like tea. I suppose it's no use suggesting tea to you, but I've brought a second cup, which you can throw at me if you care to use it for nothing else. It might amuse you to throw things at me before you wring my neck, including the teapot and the tray."

She was laying the table while she spoke. He kept his eyes turned from her, which was perhaps the reason why she imparted to him information which he declined to observe for himself.

"That's a tongue; nothing of your tinned or glass things, but a Portland and Mason; and that's a ham, a small Westphalian boned ham; I like Westphalian ham, even if you don't; and that was a chicken at lunch, and it's very nearly a chicken now, and there's honey, and marmalade, and jam, and cakes, and bread, and lots of things which some people wouldn't turn their noses up at, whatever others may do. I don't know that I'm fond of a meat tea, or high tea, or whatever you call it, as a rule; though after all we do have sandwiches, all sorts of sandwiches, with tea; everybody does, so it doesn't make such a very great difference. Anyhow, I'm going to eat meat--all sorts of meat--with my tea this afternoon, and you can watch me. There are two plates, and two knives, and two forks, and two of everything for two people, and two chairs; if you should know of anyone who will do me the honour to take tea with me, I'll be very glad of--his society. I'm going to begin."

She had placed a chair at one side of the table in which she sat, making as if to pour out tea; then suddenly sprang up, turning to the man who still stood twisting his cap between his fingers.

"Do you think you're playing the noble pudding-headed hero in a Drury Lane drama? Haven't you got sense enough to get in out of the rain? Do you suppose I don't know you're starving? How long ago is it since you had a square meal?"

"Didn't I tell you not to ask me questions?"

"You didn't tell me! It will need a very different person from you to tell me things of that kind in my own house."

"Then I'll leave your house."

"No, you don't!" She interposed herself between him and the door. "I say no, you don't; and you can glare at me for all you are worth. I've been glared at by much more dangerous persons than you, and I still live on. You wouldn't lay a finger on me if I'd treated you twenty times as badly as I have done; you may think you would, but you wouldn't; you may tell yourself that you will when you're all alone, but you won't, and you couldn't; you're that kind of man. The devil may get into you, but he won't get into you enough to induce you, when it comes to the pinch, to lay violent hands upon a woman. You say you are going to leave my house, and I say you're not. I say I won't let you; there's a direct challenge. You won't touch me, but I shan't hesitate to touch you. I am that kind. You understand, you are not to leave my house without my permission; and in order that we may know exactly where we are I'm going to lock the door and put the key in my pocket."

"You shan't do that."

"Shan't I? Well, we'll see." All at once her tone changed to one of the most singular appeal. "Man, do you know that I've been starving, and not so very long ago? Why, for years of my life I as good as starved; but there have been times when I've gone without food for days together, and known what it is to feel as you are feeling now." She laid her finger-tips softly on his ragged coat-sleeve. "You're a much stronger man than I supposed, but please don't be a fool; do sit down and have some tea with me, and afterwards you can wring my neck; you'll want lots of strength to do it properly."

CHAPTER IX
<u>The Drapery</u>

He was persuaded, he knew not how; he never meant to be. The something which was in him, the craving for food which was life, was on her side; he did have tea with her, a gargantuan tea. He ate of everything there was to eat, while she showed that the necessity that she should have something to eat of which she had spoken was a fiction, by trifling with odds and ends, while she watched that his plate was kept well supplied, and kept on talking. She was even autobiographical.

"Compared with what I have gone through, with my course of training in life's hard school, what you've endured is nothing, and you see that outwardly I'm none the worse for it. I used to think that there wasn't such a thing in the world as laughter for me, that it was just as improbable that I should have a good time as that I should jump over the moon. Yet,

I've learnt to laugh at times, nearly all the time; and as for a good time, I've acquired the knack even of getting that. It will be the same with you, and more."

"I doubt it."

"Of course, all green hands do; they take life too seriously."

"Do they? When you left me I don't remember; when I remembered anything again I was in the workhouse infirmary. I'd been found senseless and practically stripped in an alley off the Gray's Inn Road. I'd been in the infirmary more than a week before I came to my senses, after a fashion; then they wanted me to account for myself. I couldn't, or I wouldn't, they were not sure which, so they put me out again into the street. I'm not certain, but I fancy that they gave me the choice of that or of being an able-bodied pauper. It was snowing on the day they turned me out; you should have seen the clothes I was wearing, and the boots!"

"I know the Christian charity of the parish and of the workhouse master!"

"It's rather more than two months ago, and since then I've never had a square meal nor a comfortable night's lodging. You know what kind of weather we've been having, an old-fashioned winter, the best skating we've had for years. I don't know how I've lived through it, but I have. And there are thousands who've been no better off than I have, men, women, and children; I've herded with them. What a world! And for what I've suffered I have to thank you."

"That's not true."

"That's a lie. I'm eating your food--I can't help eating it, I've got to that--but don't you fancy that I'm under any obligation to you because of it. I owe everything I've had to bear to you, and I'll pay you for it. I've told myself that I would over and over again, and I will."

"You talk nonsense; would you rather I had let you go to gaol?"

"What do you mean?"

"Have you forgotten that when I first had the honour of meeting you I saved you from the police? I came on the scene in the very nick of time. In another minute they'd have laid you by the heels and marched you to the station."

He laid down his knife and fork.

"So I was right."

"About what?"

"It's all been a haze; something must have happened to me, something must have cracked in here." He laid his hand on his head. "I don't seem to remember anything beyond a certain point. I don't remember how it was I came to meet you. I know you took me to your house, and dosed and drugged me, and dyed my hair and painted my face, and that while I was still more than half stupefied by your drugs you made a catspaw of me to enable you to bring off some swindle--what it was I've never understood--and that then you left me in the street, as if I were carrion that you were throwing to the dogs; but how I first came to get into your house I have never been able to make out."

"I have upstairs the watch, chain and purse of which you relieved an old gentleman in Hyde Park, just before I came upon the scene. There's his name inside the watch. I only have to communicate with the owner--I know all about him--and you'll be sentenced to a long term of imprisonment, during which you'll suffer much worse things than anything you've had to bear because of me."

"Is that true, that I did what you say?"

"Perfectly, honestly; do you mean to say that you can't remember?"

"Now that you speak of it I do seem to recall something; it's coming back."

"I should think that it probably was; it will all of it come back if you give it time. I know all about you. I know your name, your record, the whole dirty story; you were as deep in the gutter when I first met you as you are now, and perhaps deeper--certainly you had no more chance of getting out of it; men with your record never do, I know."

"What's my name?"

"Do you mean to tell me that you don't know?"

"Not--not clearly; sometimes I nearly know, it's on the tip of my tongue, I can see it written, somewhere; but the writing is not plain--I can't quite make it out."

"What do you call yourself?"

"They call me 'Balmy.'"

"Who's they?"

"Oh, some of them; some of the swine with whom I herd. I didn't know what 'balmy' meant before they told me; it seems that it means a man who's not right in his head--not quite mad, but very nearly. I don't think I'm mad, or even nearly, but, looking back, I can't get beyond a certain point--beyond you. What did you do to me that caused it? Can't you undo it?"

"Personally, I did nothing. There was somebody else there besides me; can't you remember him?"

"I do seem to remember someone; wasn't it a man?" She nodded. "I do seem to remember a man, a black-faced man. I suppose he was your tool, and what he did to me was done by your orders."

"He certainly was not my tool. You say they tell you that you're not in your right mind; you were not when I first met you. I should say that you were practically starving and had been living the life of a London gutter man; that bolt from the police finished you; we had to do something to get life back into you. You certainly had your senses no more about you than you say you had in the workhouse infirmary. I declare to you that when I left you you were in a much better condition than when I met you. You had your senses more about you; you had been well fed, I believe the food I gave you saved your life; you were well dressed, you had money in your pocket. I don't see how I can fairly be held responsible for what happened to you afterwards; if you were in your right mind now, you'd see I can't."

"I don't know how much of what you're telling me is true. What do you want with me now? Why have you brought me here, do you want to use me as a catspaw again?"

"Let me tell you my story, and then you'll begin to understand. Do you mind if I have a cigarette? I can always talk better when I am smoking. And won't you have a cigar?"

"I had a cigar when I saw you last."

"You remember that? Have another now that we meet again. You'll find that there's nothing the matter with those cigars, they're good tobacco."

She placed a box of cigars in front of him. He glared at them as if he would rather they had not been there, but the craving that was in him got the upper hand again. He took and lighted one, puffing at it while she talked.

"My father was a country schoolmaster; I don't remember my mother, but my father died when I was, I suppose, about fourteen. My only relative, an uncle, found me a situation in a draper's shop, where I got no pay because I was so young, but where they worked me from the first thing in the morning till the last thing at night, and gave me in return my food and lodging--such lodging and such food. When I had been there three years they turned me out because I objected to the attentions of the master's son. I knew my uncle wouldn't have me; I'd known that all along. I should have been without a penny, absolutely, if it hadn't been for one of the assistants who lent me a sovereign. With that I came to town--I had ever an adventurous spirit. I went to a big shop, a famous shop; they took me on at once. A sale was coming on, they were in want of extra hands; with people of that sort they didn't want references; the assistants there never had a chance of being dishonest, they were too well looked after. They wanted no character when you came, and they gave you none when you left; you were liable to be discharged at a moment's notice, without any cause being given, and assistants were being discharged like that continually, and they gave you no character though you had been there ten years; they never do give characters, it's a rule of the house. I was there rather more than two years. I was in the mantles when I left. One afternoon just as I was going down for tea, they called me into the office, gave me my wages, and told me I could go; trade was slack, the season was over; they gave me no reason, but that was the only one I could guess that they had for sacking me."

She stopped to knock the ash off her cigarette, smiling to herself as she did so.

"I got another berth after--well, after experiences something like those which you have lately had; I was looking a nice sort of drab by the time I got it. It was in a shop which did a cutting trade, a low-class shop, an open-to-all-hours-of-the-night sort of shop, in a low-class neighbourhood in which people did not start buying till an hour when the shops ought to be closed. What a life I had there! You talk about what you've been doing, and you're a man."

Her thoughts seemed to be harking back, but she still smiled.

"I've seen columns of gush in the papers about the woes of shop assistants; if the British public only knew--if every woman had to serve a term as assistant in some of the shops I could tell them of, things would be altered pretty quick."

She leaned towards him over the table.

"You say you'd like to wring my neck; if you only knew the number of people there were in that shop to whom I would have given almost anything for the chance of wringing theirs--I almost did wring one woman's, who was, ironically, called a housekeeper, and who was an unspeakable thing! You talk of the swine with whom you've herded; you've never had to associate with the likes of her, and be under her thumb--and that's why I left."

Restlessness seemed all at once to seize her. She rose from her seat and stood in front of the fire.

"I did some more starving, and--that sort of thing, then I got another berth, no better than the other. They said my accounts were wrong--they couldn't prove it, and I don't believe they were, but they sent me packing that very day. You've no notion for how little, for nothing at all, a draper's assistant, who may have given months and years good service, is thrown into the ditch, no reason vouchsafed, no remedy obtainable, no character to be had."

She swept out her hands, as if she were brushing from her a flood of memories.

"Oh, I had all sorts of experiences; I was in the place you mentioned for years, although I'm not an old woman now; you see, I got there first when I was so very young; that does make a difference. Oh, I saw the drapery in all its phases; to this hour I can't enter a draper's shop without feeling a chill at the bottom of my spinal column; my skin goes all goose-fleshy; I think of what drapers' shops once meant to me. But there came a time when I had done with them--I'll take care that it's for ever; that was when I reached the very lowest circle in the pit. How many circles were there in Dante's hell? I'm convinced I reached the bottom one."

CHAPTER X
The Woman Tempted Me

"I'd been out of a berth for practically a year; not all the time--I'd been taken on for a few days here, for a week of two there, as odd hand when the rush of the sales was on; but for a year I had had no regular work. How I lived I can't tell you; you know, I had to live, and--well, you talk of the things you've endured, you have no conception how much worse that sort of thing is for a woman than for a man. At last I came down to selling flowers--yes I that was a nice profession, wasn't it?"

She put her hands up to her brow, pressing back her hair; she presented a sufficiently dainty picture then, with her well-fitting gown and her look of perfect health.

"One evening--I'd had a bad day--I was hawking in the Strand, just where I met you when I saw you with those boards upon your back. How it all came back to me! My flowers had not been in very good condition in the morning, they had not grown fresher as the day went on. I offered them to a man who came sauntering along; he stopped to look at them, he soon spotted the state that they were in. 'Why,' he said, 'these things are only fit for throwing away.' Then he looked at me. 'Bertha!' he exclaimed, 'surely it must be you?'"

She laughed. Turning, she stood looking down into the fire, tapping her toe against the curb.

"If I'd only had a peep at him in time I should have let him pass; I shouldn't have tried to make of him a customer, but I hadn't. I had just seen that he was well dressed and looked as though he had money, and, in the dim light, that was all."

She paused for so considerable a space of time that one wondered if she proposed to carry the story any farther. When she did go on it was in an altered tone of voice; she spoke very quietly, very coldly, as if she wished to make a mere statement of facts.

"In one of the shops in which I had had the honour of being an assistant he had acted as shopwalker. We had been on quite decent terms, which was not the case with most of the gentlemen of his sort that I had come across. Rather than that he should have seen me, in my rags, hawking faded flowers in the streets, I would--I would have done anything. When I tried to get away from him he wouldn't hear of it. He called a cab, put me in it, and took me home with him, to his wife; they had quite a nice little house Peckham way. I recognised her as one of the girls who had been at the opposite counter to mine. It was not strange that he had married her; what was queer was that they should be living in such a house, unless one of them had come into a fortune."

Again she paused, staring at the fire as if she were seeking words among the burning coals. Then, turning, she faced the man who was still seated at the table. He had scarcely moved since she had begun her story, as if he found in it a fascination that was not upon the surface, as if he were looking forward, with eager interest, to what he felt was coming.

"Nobody could have been kinder to me than those two people. They gave food, and drink, and clothing, and shelter, and, something more, they gave me the secret of the philosopher's stone; told me how it was that, though no one had left them a fortune, they came to be living there."

Holding her shapely hands in front of her she kept pressing the tips of the fingers together, and then withdrawing them.

"A piece of silk was missing at the shop. She was charged with stealing it. She assured me that she had not stolen it, that she did not know who had, that she knew nothing at all about it; they had not the slightest real evidence that she was the guilty party, but they sacked her all the same. And because the shop-walker sided with her, they chose to assume that he was at least in part responsible for its disappearance, and they sacked him too. So they married. That's a funny sort of love story, isn't it?"

The man spoke, for the first time since she had begun her story.

"It's as good as others I've heard."

"No doubt, love stories are the funniest things. For what would you marry?"

She was looking at him with laughing eyes.

"I shall never marry."

"Sure? Nothing's ever a certainty in that sort of thing. It was only after they were married that they thought of ways and means. They had about twenty pounds between them; they tried and tried, but neither could get a berth; so they decided to throw up the drapery--probably because it had thrown them up--and try another trade. They had given honesty a trial; they decided to try the other, and see if it couldn't be made to pay. It paid uncommonly well; the house in which they were living, the way in which it was furnished, the style in which they did things, was proof enough of that. They told me all about it, quite frankly; then they suggested that I should join them in their new profession. The occasions were not infrequent on which they wanted a partner of my sex, who had her wits about her, and upon whom they could absolutely rely. I did not need much persuasion; like them, I had had enough of honesty; and--here I am--flourishing like a green bay tree."

"Do you mean that you're a thief?"

"A professional thief, exactly; just as you're a gutter-snipe--a much less creditable, and a very much less profitable profession than mine."

She spoke in the airiest of tones, as if the thing that she admitted was a trifle of no account. When she saw that he kept silent she went on.

"I'm about to suggest that you come into the business as a partner of mine."

"What prompts you to suggest it--affection?"

"Not altogether--no." Her eyes were dancing. "What prompts a woman to do anything? She seldom knows, really and truly; I don't believe there ever was a woman who was able to give all the reasons which moved her to do anything. I've had you in my mind ever since I saw you last. I did not do you anything like the ill turn you seem to imagine; I vow and declare to you that when we parted you were, if anything, better off than when we met. But sometimes--oh, sometimes--I think that I must be the very queerest woman that ever was; but then I know better, because all women are queer, and, when she's in the mood, every woman can be the very queerest that ever was."

Quitting the fire, perching herself upon the side of the table, with one foot upon a chair, she began to light another cigarette.

"Sometimes I've felt very bad about you; I didn't like to think of what might have become of you after we had parted. Then when I began to learn certain little facts about your personal history, I was conscious of feeling a sympathy for you which you might have found amusing. I told myself that if ever chance did throw us across each other's path again, I would, if I could, if you stood in need of it, do you a real good turn. When I saw you just now, in that dreary procession of six, and realised that it was you, I knew that my opportunity had come. So now I hope you understand."

"Only very dimly. I am still not so clear-headed as I might be. I want to have things made very plain."

"I will try to make them as plain as you can possibly want them. First of all, I want a partner; do you want to know why?"

"If it wouldn't be troubling you too much."

"I'm not altogether without associates, though I do miss my two first friends."

"What became of them?"

"They brought off a big coup, got bags full of money, went off with it to America, where they started a business of their own, in which I believe they are now doing very well."

"Why didn't they take you with them? Didn't you get your share?"

"Rather, and a first-class time I had with it; one of the times of my life; and I may mention, between ourselves, that, of late years, I've had some good ones. I may tell you about some of them one fine day."

She seemed to be laughing to herself, as if the recollection tickled her. He sat stark, stiff and silent, his strange hollow eyes fixed on her face. She enjoyed her cigarette in silence for some seconds before she went on.

"And as for why they didn't take me with them, one reason is that I wouldn't have gone. Why should I? I should have been in their way, and they most certainly would have been in mine. We parted on the very best of terms; we correspond; one of these days I'm going to pay them a long visit. But, from a purely professional point of view, I've never been able to fill their place, especially his. You've very nearly finished that cigar. Won't you have another?"

"No, thank you; I'm not at the end of this; I'm enjoying it--slowly."

She watched the rings of her cigarette smoke ascending to the ceiling.

"You see, in my profession, there are so very few gentlemen; and of all the professions in the world, it's the one in which gentlemen are most needed, the one in which they're sure to get the best reward for their labours. There are one or two things in my mind, big things, things involving quite possibly thousands of pounds, which I can't work alone, in which I need the co-operation of a man whose birth and breeding, whose knowledge of the manners and customs of good society are beyond question. Now, you're the very sort of person I want; Eton and the Guards; from my point of view there couldn't be a finer qualification."

"How do you come to know anything about me?"

"Your name--Sydney Beaton--was on the tab of that very well-worn coat which you had on when first I met you. I know all about Sydney Beaton; shall I tell you what I do know?"

"You needn't."

"I thought you said that you'd forgotten such a lot; that your mind, beyond a certain point, was a blank?"

She was eyeing him with a malicious twinkle in her laughing eyes; he was grimly silent, meeting her look with what seemed to be a strange defiance.

"I'd rather not remember--now."

"I see; it's like that, is it? I don't blame you. I've no wish to touch your sore places, though never so lightly; I've plenty of my own which I'd just as soon people kept their fingers off; I'm not pachydermatous quite. But there's one thing which I should like to ask, if you will let me, and it's this: Have you any expectation of getting back to where you were?"

"None."

"I don't wish to push the knife in, but--do you think there's any probability of your regaining the position you once held? I repeat the question in another form because, as you said, I want to be plain; this time I want you and me to be colleagues, not what we were before, to run no risk of a misunderstanding."

"Not only is there no probability, there is no possibility."

"Not even a thousand to one chance?"

"Nor a million to one. That side of me is dead; there can be no resurrection. There is no person of the name you mentioned any longer; some of my new friends call me 'Balmy'; I call myself James Langham."

"Then, Mr. Langham, let me put it to you as a sound business proposition, that you've everything to gain, and nothing to lose, by becoming my partner in certain delicate matters which I have in my mind's eye."

"You're proposing that I should become a thief?"

"Well, 'a rose by any other name would smell as sweet.'"

What might have been meant for a smile distorted his attenuated visage.

"The sort of thing that I've gone through turns the whole world topsy-turvy; the ladies and gentlemen with whom I have associated think nothing of stealing; they've robbed me times without number of the worthless trifles of which I could be plundered, and--I had to bear it. I've said to myself over and over again when I've been mad with misery, that I would rob a bank if I dared."

"Yes, and if you had the chance. You would not see your way, for instance, to enter, say, the London County and Westminster Bank attired as you are, with the intention of coming out of it a wealthier man."

"You're quite right, I shouldn't."

"What I'm offering you is the opportunity to do that sort of thing with perfect impunity; I'm not doing it out of philanthropic motives; at least I'm not a humbug. I'll give you the means to replenish your wardrobe, which needs it, and to live in comfort for a reasonable time, on the understanding that you'll consider seriously certain propositions that I shall make you, and, if you see your way, that you'll give me your assistance in carrying them out, on sharing terms. Is it a deal?"

For the first time he moved, withdrawing himself from the table and standing up; he was so thin, there was something about him which was so little human, that the ill-assorted, filthy rags of which his attire consisted seemed to be hanging on a scarecrow.

"You feel that you can trust me?"

"I am sure of it."

"Knowing my record?"

"Records like yours don't count in my eye. There's nothing in your record which hints that you ever played false to a woman. I know that you won't play false to me."

"You expect me to tell you that I know you'll never play false to me?"

"Not a bit of it; I know what you've got in your head quite well. I don't ask you to trust me one inch farther than you can see. But at the beginning, at any rate, the confidence will be all on the other side. I'm willing to make an investment for which my only security is faith in you. When you know what these little schemes are of which I have spoken as being in my head, you'll see that it isn't trust I'm asking for; that what I propose is merely a matter of plain and open dealing, in which no question of trust or mistrust can arise on either side. Once more, is it a deal? Are you going back to carrying sandwich-boards in the Strand at a shilling a day in weather like this; with the certainty of there being certain intervals in which you'll be even without a sandwich-board; or are you willing to get something out of the world in return for what it's done for you; to throw black care to the dogs, and laugh with me? Which do you choose--the sty and the swine, cold, hunger and misery; or as good a time as ever a gentleman had? England was made by freebooters; I'm suggesting that you should be a freebooter up to date. As things are, a man can choose no other life which gives much promise of adventure."

There was silence; although she waited for him to speak, the silence remained unbroken. Presently he turned, and looked through the window at the snow which had begun to fall fast, and was being driven here and there by the shrieking wind; then he turned again, and looked at her and at the fire. He still said nothing; but he shivered; and she said:

"I see that you have chosen."

CHAPTER XI
In the Wood

"I Don't think I need tell you that this is a very severe blow to me; it almost knocks me out, but not quite; there's some fight still left in me. There's one thing which I should take it as a very great favour if you would tell me; have you said--what you have done, because--there's someone else? I know I've no right to ask such a question, but--I can't help it."

Major Harold Reith looked as if he could not; a more woe-begone looking gentleman of six-feet-two one could hardly expect to find. The most absurd part of it was that he had been so very nearly confident. The lady had been so kind--so very much kinder, perhaps, than he supposed, but for that she had her reasons. Then her uncle, old Geoffrey Hovenden, had been not only on his side but so delightfuly sanguine. When the major expressed a doubt as to what the lady's sentiments might be, Mr. Hovenden had pooh-poohed it.

"Don't talk like a schoolboy, Reith; you know better than that; you admit that the girl likes you--you can't expect to be told how much till you give her a chance."

Now he had given her a chance, and if he had not been told how much, she had at least endeavoured to make it clear that it was not as much as he wanted. Her answer to the question he had asked put an end to the little remaining hope he had left.

The proposal had been made in the wood. He had gone for a stroll with her with the intention of finding an opportunity to ask her to be his wife; being conceivably quite aware of his intentions, she had given him one. It was the commencement of April. Spring promised to be early that year. The wood was carpeted with primroses. She had been picking them as they walked, and was arranging her nosegay as she talked.

"Of course, on the face of it, no one has a right to ask a girl such a question; she might be consumed by a secret passion which was not reciprocated, which she knew never would be, and yet which she was aware would render it impossible that she should ever listen to another; by another I mean, for instance, you."

"Is yours a case of a secret passion?" She had dropped some of her primroses; he stooped to pick them up for her; a great bunch of them she had, almost as large as her two hands would hold.

"Thanks; no, I can't say that mine is; yet all the same--I've a fellow-feeling for you."

"That's very good of you; but in what sense have you what you call a fellow-feeling, and to what extent does it go?"

"It goes all the way. There go some of these primroses again; they are such droppy things."

"If you really mean what you say then I am a very happy man."

"You may be or you mayn't; happiness is often largely a question of temperament. For example, I ought to be a very unhappy girl, but I'm not; somehow unhappiness doesn't seem to come easy to me."

"You are very fortunate; what cause have you for unhappiness? I should have thought that there were few people who had less. Has it anything to do with the imagination?"

"There's only one thing I want in this world, and it looks as if I were as little likely to get it as if it were the moon; you may call that imagination, but it's a fact."

"And what may that one thing be?"

"You were just now saying some pretty things about there being only one thing you wanted, and that was the girl you loved, meaning me. I am in the same delightfully romantic situation; there's only one thing I want, and that's the man I love."

A slight change took place in his face, as if a cloud had obscured the sun. He looked at her in silence; it would have been hard to say which was the prettier--she or the flowers. It was seen when he spoke that the change had extended to his voice.

"So there is someone?"

"Oh dear, yes; there always has been, and there always will be."

"Your uncle gave me to understand that the field was clear."

"My uncle Geoffrey Hovenden is--I'm sorry to have to say it of a relation of mine--a Machiavellian old gentleman. No one is better acquainted with my piteous plight than he is; but because he wants you, and wants me to want you, he says nothing about it. Do you mean to say you don't know who it is?"

"Do you suppose that if I had even guessed that there was another I should have said what I have done?"

"There's no telling; his own brother knew all about it, but that didn't stop him."

"Who is the lucky man?"

"Lucky! Pray do let us keep clear of the language of exaggeration, but I doubt if there is a more unlucky creature on the face of God's earth."

"You pique my curiosity; standing with you as he does I can hardly conceive of him as unlucky. Do I know him?"

"You did, if you don't now."

"You speak in riddles, at which I was never any good."

"Sydney Beaton."

He seemed to start away from her. This time not only his face, but his whole bearing, the entire man, seemed to change.

"Miss Forster, are you in earnest?"

His tone, his manner seemed all at once to have grown cold; he could hardly have held his figure more stiffly erect.

"And pray why shouldn't I be in earnest?"

"You place me in a difficult position; what answer am I to give to that?"

"I know very well what you mean. No one knows better than I do that Sydney is not all wisdom, but do you suppose a woman loves a man because he is wise? Go to!"

"I presume that there are qualities that a woman requires in a man."

"What are they?"

"Surely she looks for at least some of the primitive virtues, say, common honesty, some sense of decency, and that kind of thing."

"Well?" She paused as if for him to speak, but he was still. "Now how am I going to tie these flowers together? I ought to have brought a reel of cotton; as I haven't, you'll have to find me a nice long piece of grass. Yes, I think that will do. Now, I'll hold the flowers if you'll pass it round--so."

While together they secured the primroses she went on. The exigencies of the situation required that they should be very close together; her nearness so affected him that he found it difficult to comment upon her words as frankly as he might otherwise have done, which was a fact of which she was possibly aware.

"I know very well all about his having been supposed to have cheated at cards; but I also know him much too well to believe for a single instant that he ever did it; he couldn't, not Sydney Beaton."

"Then--forgive my saying so--why did he run away?"

"Oh, I'll forgive you anything; I want you to say just what is in your mind; that's what I brought you here for. You brought me here to propose; and I brought you because I wanted you to tell me things which I could never find out from anybody else; you've done what you wanted, so now it's my turn."

"It's beginning to occur to me that your uncle is not the only Machiavellian member of your family."

"No? Perhaps not. I wish you'd pull that tighter--what big, strong fingers you have got! Most of my information has been derived from what I call tainted sources--from his brother, for instance. George Beaton wants me to believe that his brother is an unutterable creature. He has told me tales about him which have had quite a different effect to that which he intended; it sometimes is like that when a man tells a girl tales about another man. It seems to me that between you Sydney has been very badly used indeed. His brother's behaviour has been inconceivably bad, and so I took the liberty to tell him. And I'm afraid you don't come out with flying colours."

"What have I done? I am not conscious of having even mentioned his name to you."

"All those men against one; though I'll do you the justice to admit that I think it's quite possible that you are ashamed of yourself."

"I'm afraid I don't quite follow." Again his bearing had stiffened.

"If you don't take care, all these primroses will fall, and then where shall we be? That's better--tied at last. Thank you, Major Reith. George Beaton told me all about the affair--how all you men set upon one, and actually--according to Sir George--threw him out of the room. I can't think whatever men can be made of, that you should still be walking about with your heads in the air."

"It's a subject, Miss Forster, which I'm afraid I can hardly discuss with you; there are subjects which men do not discuss with women."

"Is that so, Major Reith? And pray is that meant for a snub? That shows the kind of treatment which I might expect to receive if I consented to become your wife; because I'll have you know that this is a subject that I mean a good many men to discuss with this woman, and, to begin with, you're going to be one of them. What do you think I brought you into the wood for? Didn't I tell you? Now you're in the witness box; if you don't answer all the questions which are put to you I'll have you committed for contempt of court. Sydney Beaton is alleged to have cheated at cards; what is the exact act of which he is said to have been guilty?"

"He substituted one card for another."

"Did you see him do it?"

"No, but he was seen by others. The original accusation was made by Anthony Dodwell--you know Dodwell?"

"I know of him, Major Reith, and, thank you, that is quite enough. Was Mr. Dodwell the only eyewitness?"

"Draycott saw him also. Do you know Draycott?"

"Mr. Noel Draycott? Oh, yes, I do know Mr. Noel Draycott. I daresay Mr. Noel Draycott means well; I wish to speak ill of no one, but I've heard him make some surprising statements, and I'm afraid I shouldn't believe anything Mr. Noel Draycott said merely because he said it. Was he seen to do this thing by anyone else?"

"He was not actually seen."

"What do you mean by that, Major Reith? Either he was, or he was not, seen; surely in such a juxtaposition the word 'actually' is out of place. Explain yourself; don't convey to my mind the impression that you also are prejudiced."

"I assure you that, so far as I am concerned, it is all the other way. I should be only too glad to believe him innocent, but--Miss Forster, it's a tall order."

"Tell me exactly why; has he ever been suspected of such practices before?"

"Never. God forbid! To some extent I am inclined to excuse him as it is; he had been drinking too much. I think that had as much to do with it as anything."

"My dear Major Reith, that is not an excuse, but an aggravation. I have seen it written somewhere that when a man is drunk his real character is seen, because he is no longer able to hide it. If what you suggest is correct, then--Sydney Beaton must be past praying for. But it is incorrect. I am convinced that Sydney Beaton, drunk or sober, is a man of honour; else I could not love him as I do."

"But what has become of him? Do you know?"

"I do not, but I'm going to find out; so now you see why I ought to be unhappy. All these months I've been wondering where he was--waiting, longing, hoping to hear. Every post I thought would bring me news; every time that there was a telegram my heart beat a little faster. I made inquiries in my own way, but I've found nothing. All I know is that one night his brother officers attacked him--about twelve men to one. I have the charity to suppose that they were in a condition in which they did not know what they were doing. Sydney was always apt to do things first and think afterwards. I don't wonder that such treatment caused him to lose his head; I should have wondered if it hadn't. I can understand why he hasn't communicated with me; I know my Quixote. But now that all these months have gone, and there's still no news, I'm getting anxious."

"I don't wonder. Has absolutely nothing been heard of him, by anyone, by his brother?"

"Sir George Beaton would be the last to hear, if Sydney could help it. You can be trusted to keep a secret?"

"Where you are concerned I certainly can."

"I have been a bone of contention between those two brothers since ever. George, being the head of the family, is of opinion that he has the first claim on me; as I think otherwise, he shows what seems to me to be the most unfraternal eagerness to think the very worst of Sydney. And that seems to be the case with everyone. You all, when you come to look into the matter, seem to have discreditable reasons of your own for pretending to think ill of him."

"Am I included among that 'all'?"

"No, it happens that you're not, and that's why I'm talking to you now. I'm going to look for Sydney; I'm going to leave no stone unturned to find out where he is. I'm getting tired of waiting; and, while I'm looking, I'm going to find out the truth of what took place on that disgraceful night. You're going to tell me all you know; I'm sure that will be the truth as far as it goes, but I'm afraid it won't go far enough. I shall have to go to other sources to get at all I want, and that is what I am presently going to do."

"How do you propose to set about it?"

"I have a friend--a very, very dear friend. You know Lady Cantyre?"

"Who doesn't? Saving your presence, is there anyone better worth knowing?"

"Saving nothing, there isn't; and she's my very, very dear friend. She knows the pickle I'm in and she's going to help me; this is between ourselves, mind. I want to get at Mr. Noel Draycott under circumstances in which he will find it hard to get away. She has asked him down to Avonham, and I shall be there to meet him; before we part I shall find out a great deal more about what Mr. Noel Draycott really did see, as well as about other things, than he in the least anticipates."

"I can quite believe it; when a man like Draycott is concerned, I should imagine that you could turn him inside out like an old glove."

"I don't know about the old glove, but I do mean to do something like turn him inside out, and the process is going to begin next week. Sydney has been too long under a cloud which was none of his making; I am going to bring him out from under it into the sun. I am going to do it single-handed; and it's because I am so sure that I shall do it that I cannot be unhappy. Major Reith, I talk like a braggart of doing it all single-handed; but all the same I am conscious that occasion may arrive when I shall require some assistance; if I do, will you give it?"

"I will give you, very gladly, all the assistance which, in such a position, a man may give to a woman."

"Then--that's all right. Thank you, Major Reith."

In her left hand she had the bunch of primroses, which she held close to her face; her right she held out to him.

CHAPTER XII
"What Does it Mean?"

The night of the Easter Ball--the event of the year at Avonham.

The Countess of Cantyre, on her way to the scene of action, looked in on Miss Violet Forster. That young lady, apparently already fully equipped, seated in an arm-chair, was studying what seemed to be a small memorandum book. She looked up as the Countess entered. Her ladyship came well into the centre of the room, drew herself to her full height, which was less than she would have liked it to be, and slowly revolved in a complete circle, by way of exhibiting her plumes for the lady's inspection. When she had made an end, she prompted the criticism which did not come.

"Well?"

"Excellent."

"You think I shall do?"

"Margaret, you're a dream of delight."

"You really think so? You like the dress? I was afraid there was a little too much on the bodice."

"There is nothing anywhere which could be altered in the slightest degree for the better; the gown and the wearer are perfectly matched: they are both lovely."

Her ladyship dropped a curtsy.

"Thank you, that's just what I wanted you to say. Now you stand up, and I'll give you my candid opinion."

"Very much obliged, but I'm not sure that I want it; I'm not the Countess of Cantyre. Who cares what I look like?"

"You little humbug! It's only your conceit; it's simply that you take it for granted that you always look your best, which couldn't be improved." Her ladyship was arranging the drapery of her skirt as she glanced in the mirror. "What have you got out of Noel Draycott?"

"Nothing, as yet. I haven't tried; but I shall. I mean to drop a bomb at his feet at the moment he least expects it."

"If it's to be to-night, don't let it go off with too loud a bang. I don't know if I told you that the whole regiment has decided to come. They telegraphed this afternoon that they would all be able to get off, as I understand, to a man. You'll have a chance of dropping a bombshell at the feet of every one of them."

"I should like to. Every time I look at Mr. Noel Draycott I feel--I can't tell you what I feel."

"Any news of the absentee?"

"None; but I'm beginning to dream of him again."

"You'd better be careful what you have for dinner; eat nothing for at least three hours before you go to bed."

"Last night I dreamt that he was starving; and to save himself from starving he was doing something so awful that it woke me up, and I lay wide awake, trembling with terror."

"You poor child! You may congratulate yourself that it was a dream. Are you coming? I must be off."

"I'll follow in a minute or two; don't you wait for me."

Left alone, the girl tried to resume her study of the small volume she was holding; but the effort seemed in vain. Her eyes refused to be fixed upon the page; they stared into vacancy at something which was not there. She rose; placing the little book in a leather case which stood upon the dressing-table, she pressed down the lid, which shut with a spring.

"It's very odd, but I seem to feel that something is going to happen to-night; I wonder what it is?"

There was a tapping at the door; a maid came in. She advanced towards the girl with something held out in her hand.

"Excuse me, Miss Forster, but is this yours?"

It was a locket, attached to a slender gold chain. The girl looked round quickly; she made as if to open the box she had just now shut. Then she said:

"I don't think it can be mine, but it resembles one I have; please let me look at it."

She took the locket and examined it closely. As she did so her face changed, as if something had startled her. She looked at the maid, with in her eyes what might almost have been a look of fear. Then, turning her back, as if to hide the agitation which she could not help but feel, she touched a spring; the locket came open. At the sight of what was within she broke into a sudden exclamation; she swung right round again. There was no doubt that something had startled her now; the blood had come into her cheeks, her eyes were wide open, she trembled.

"Where did you get this?" she cried.

"If you please, miss, I found it on the floor outside your room. I was coming along and I saw it lying there, and it was so close to your door that I thought you might have dropped it."

"When was this? When did you see it there?"

"A moment ago, miss; as soon as I had picked it up, I knocked at your door."

"But it's inconceivable, incredible! It certainly wasn't there just now when Lady Cantyre went out."

"That I can't say, miss; I didn't see her ladyship."

"But if it had been there she would have seen it." The girl moved a step closer. "Who are you?"

The maid seemed as if she did not know what to make of Miss Forster's manner, which was peculiar; so peculiar that it might almost have been described as threatening.

"Me, miss? I'm Simmons."

Miss Forster was silent, not, it would seem, because she had nothing to say, but because she had so much that she didn't know how to say it. All at once she moved towards the door of the room.

"Come here; now show me, please, exactly where you found this locket, the very spot."

Opening the door, she allowed the maid to precede her into the passage. As if, as was only natural, disconcerted by the young lady's manner, the maid did what was required. She pointed to the floor.

"I can't, of course, miss, say which was the exact spot--nobody could; but I should say, as near as possible, it was just there."

"Then Lady Cantyre must have seen it as she went out; if she had she would have brought it to me; she would have done something."

"As to that, miss, I cannot speak."

"You say that your name is Simmons?"

"Yes, miss, Jane Simmons."

"Have you been here long?"

"No, miss; I'm one of the new servants who came in just before Easter when the family returned from town."

"What made you think that the locket had anything to do with me?"

"I didn't, miss. I didn't think anything at all about it; there was the locket and there was your door. I thought that someone who was the other side of the door might have something to do with the locket. I didn't know that you were in your room, miss; I thought that you might have dropped it going out."

"There's something about this that I don't understand; but, for the present, that will do. I may have some questions to put to you later, Jane Simmons. You can go; when I've spoken to Lady Cantyre, you will probably hear from me again."

Violet Forster, back in her room, stared at the locket as if it were some strange, terrible mystery; which to her, in a sense, it was.

"My locket; the one I gave him; the double of the one he gave me."

Unlocking the leather case which stood upon the dressing-table--from what was perhaps intended to be a secret receptacle at the bottom, she took a locket which was attached to a slender gold chain, comparing it with the one the maid had brought.

"It's my locket--there are my initials--my portrait inside; they are a pair--only I'm in one and he's in the other. He told me that mine should never leave him; that if it wasn't about his neck, it would always be somewhere about his person; how came it to be there, where that woman said it was? Is this the something which I felt was going to happen? What does it mean? Is it a message? From whom?--from him? I feel--I feel--Sydney, where are you?"

She swung suddenly round, gazing round the brightly lighted room with startled, staring eyes, as if she did not know for what she was looking. Then she caught sight of something which was lying on the floor almost at her feet.

"What's that?" She picked it up. "Where did that come from? Surely it was not there just now; what--what does it all mean?"

It was an envelope which she had picked up from the carpet; she was holding it gingerly between her finger and thumb as if it were some dangerous thing.

"What's written on it? 'Sydney Beaton's card'--what! There's something inside it." Tearing it open, she took out what it contained. "It's a playing-card, the ace of clubs. What does it mean?"

CHAPTER XIII
The Alcove

The ball was a great success, it was generally admitted. Miss Forster could have danced each number on the programme with half a dozen different partners if she had chosen. She danced with Mr. Noel Draycott; when it came to sitting out, he found her manner a little disconcerting. He was of the fatuous type of young man, a better dancer than conversationalist. He had a sort of cut-and-dried routine on such occasions, saying the same things, as much as possible, to each of his partners in turn. New ideas would not come to him quickly, especially when he was talking to women; if they would not keep to the subject which he felt was appropriate to the occasion, he preferred not to talk at all.

Miss Forster treated him in that respect quite badly. When he tried to make one of his orthodox remarks, which were meant to be compliments, she ignored him utterly. She not only said things which worried him--to him it always was a labour to find an answer to a remark that was unexpected--she asked him questions which puzzled him still more, questions which he felt that she had no right to ask; particularly of a man in the middle of a dance.

When he had quitted her, before seeking his next partner, he unburdened himself to his friend, Anthony Dodwell.

"She's a top-hole dancer, Miss Forster, and as pretty as paint, but when it comes to asking a man if he likes liars I draw the line."

"Did she ask you if you liked liars?"

"She asked me much worse things than that. She was just asking me, when I hooked it, what I thought was the most shameful way in which a man could treat a friend. If I hadn't hooked it, I don't know what she wouldn't have asked me next; she's taken the stiffening out of my collar, talking to a man like that, between a two-step and a waltz."

When his friend had left him, Dodwell advanced to the lady of whom they had been speaking.

"May I have the pleasure of a dance, Miss Forster?"

She had her hand on the arm of the partner who was about to bear her off; looking Captain Dodwell up and down in a fashion which, to say the least, was marked, she said, in a tone of voice which was clearly audible to those around:

"In any case, Captain Dodwell, you would have been too late." She looked him straight in the face, then she turned to her partner. "Will you please take me away?"

It was not strange that, as the pair moved off, Anthony Dodwell did not look happy; if she had flicked a whip in his face her intention could hardly have been plainer. He was conscious that while there were smiles on some of the faces about him, and while some observed him with curious eyes, there were others who kept their eyes carefully averted. On the whole, he carried the thing off uncommonly well. He strolled away, and presently was dancing with a lady whose charms were not so obvious as they possibly once had been. While he danced he was saying things to himself which would have surprised his partner if she could have heard them.

"What the devil did the little cat mean by that? What have I ever done to her? I swear I've done nothing. I expect that the tale is being told all round the room at this moment; people will be taking it for granted that I've behaved to her like--God alone knows what. I'll have an explanation from her before the night's out--and an apology. I should like to force her down upon her knees before everybody who heard her, the little----"

He left the sentence unfinished, even though he was only speaking to himself; as if he could not find words which would give adequate expression to his feelings. His partner asked him a question, he answered it; but even while he was speaking, as he steered her round the room, he was thinking of Violet Forster.

A little later Miss Forster was dancing with another of his brother officers, Mr. John Tickell, better known as Jackie. Mr. Tickell was not only still a subaltern, he was a junior subaltern; it was his habit to mention the fact, with an air of grievance, to persons of the feminine sex, after a very brief acquaintance, if they showed signs of being sympathetic. As he was quite a nice boy, and not bad-looking, as he would himself have expressed it, when he "struck" a girl, nine times out of ten, he found her as sympathetic as he could possibly have desired. He had made Miss Forster's acquaintance for the first time that night; had booked a dance with her with the brightest hopes, which were destined to be blighted. There was no mistake about her dancing, their steps went perfectly together; it was in other directions that disappointment came. He led her, when the music ceased, to a spot on which he had had his mind's eye all along. In the passage outside the ballroom there was an alcove, quite a small one; it was screened by a palm in a wooden tub, a sensible-sized palm, with plenty of leaves, which really did do service as a screen. Behind this palm there were chairs, two chairs; no more. Any two persons who sat on them would be in the midst of the crowd; there was a perpetual procession up and down the corridor; and yet as much alone as the most sensitive young man who was in need of sympathy could possibly desire. Mr. Tickell made straight for that alcove, rather hurrying the lady.

"I know a first-rate place for sitting out, if only someone isn't there before us."

No one was; they placed themselves in the two chairs. Mr. Tickell gave a little sigh of satisfaction; the young woman beside him was distinctly a find--as he would himself have phrased it, "a ripping dancer, awfully well turned out, and a dazzler to look at." He had no doubt that he was in for an extremely good time, and therein showed that the prophetic eye was certainly not his, because he had been there only a very few minutes before he began very ardently to wish that that alcove had been occupied by a dozen, or even twenty, people, instead of being left invitingly open for him.

"Are you fond of dancing?"

He also had his methods of commencing such conversations; this was one of his stereotyped openings; he liked to lead up to the sympathetic point by routes with which he was acquainted.

"Don't I dance as if I were--is that what you mean?"

This was not at all the sort of answer he had expected; from his point of view, it was not playing the game. While he was still floundering about for a suitable answer, she put a question to him on her own account.

"What are you fond of?"

He would have liked to say that he was fond of her. He had had partners to whom he would have said it without the slightest hesitation; but somehow he felt that this was a partner with whom the remark might not have the success it deserved; and before he spoke she again went on.

"Are you fond of gambling?"

"Gambling?" He stared at her with startled eyes, it seemed to him to be such a singular question to have hurled at him.

"I mean, for instance, are you fond of poker?" Again she went on before he could speak, taking an answer for granted in a fashion which he found a trifle disconcerting. "But, of course, I know you are; I have heard of some of your performances at poker."

He really did not like her tone at all; there was something in it which made him conscious of a vague discomfort. What could the girl be driving at?

"Particularly I've heard of one."

She said it while she was glancing at him over the top of her fan, which she was opening and shutting.

"Which one?"

"Weren't you playing some months ago when one of your brother officers was accused of cheating?"

Small wonder if his eyes seemed to grow rounder, the bad taste of such a remark! To say nothing of its unexpectedness.

"Really, I don't know to what you refer."

"Oh yes, you do. You know perfectly well; if you don't, I'll explain."

"Thank you very much, but if you don't mind, I'll take you back to the ballroom; there's someone whom I've just thought I ought to be behaving nicely to."

"You'll behave as nicely as you can to me before you try your practised hand on anybody else. You've presence of mind, Mr. Tickell, but it won't do. You sit still until I let you go."

Except by violence, he could hardly have got away; he saw now why she had expressly directed him to take the farther chair. He could scarcely get out of the alcove without passing her; he did not see how he could do it if she did not choose to let him.

"At the game of poker to which I wish to call your attention, right at the close, you were betting against Mr. Sydney Beaton."

"If you don't mind, I'd much rather not talk about it; I don't know how you came to know anything about it, but you'll understand that it's rather a painful subject to me. What do you think of the floor--first-rate, isn't it?"

If he hoped to get her to confine her conversation to what he regarded as proper topics, his hope was doomed to disappointment, as she at once made plain.

"There was a good bit of money in the pool, at the point on which I wish to refresh your memory--over a thousand pounds, I've been given to understand, at the moment when Mr. Beaton covered your raise--you had a straight, king high; Mr. Beaton had a full, three aces and a pair of knaves, a much better hand than yours, and yet, I'm told, you claimed the pool."

"Then you've been misinformed. Excuse me, Miss Forster, I don't know what all this has to do with you."

"It has a very great deal to do with me. You claimed the pool----"

"I did not claim the pool; really, Miss Forster, I don't think this is the sort of thing to talk about at a dance."

"You took the pool, you conveyed its contents to your pockets."

"It was adjudged to be mine. But with all possible apologies, Miss Forster, I must decline to discuss the subject with you, especially at such a moment as this. May I take you back to the ballroom?"

He stood up, his face a little flushed; if he thought that she would be overawed by his air of determination, he was mistaken. She also stood up, in such a way that without an actual tussle it would have been impossible for him to escape--that well-screened alcove had its drawbacks.

"You will not leave me, Mr. Tickell, till you have given me certain explanations which I am about to require from you. Sit down."

Nothing could have been more dictatorial than her manner, or more uncalled for; his visage sufficiently expressed the amazement he felt.

"Miss Forster!"

"You have done me a very serious injury, Mr. Tickell, a wrong which no man with any pretensions to decency would do any woman; if you decline to sit down, if you try to leave this place, there'll be a scandal, because I shall follow you into the ballroom, and wring an explanation from you there. I am not friendless; I will take care that you don't leave this house till I have it."

The young gentleman sat down, with every appearance of the most extreme discomfiture. His words came from stammering lips.

"I--I--I never heard such a thing in my life; I--I've done you a wrong? Why, Miss Forster, I never met you before. Of course, I've heard of you, everybody has; as--as to doing you a wrong, I'd no more think of doing you a wrong than--than---- Whatever makes you think I have?"

She resumed her seat beside him with an air that was much more commanding than he had ever seen worn by his colonel.

"Be so good as to answer the question which I put to you just now, Mr. Tickell: why did you convey to your own pockets the contents of the pool which properly belonged to Mr. Beaton, since he had won it?"

"I do not know why you are talking to me like this, Miss Forster--I give you my word I don't--but if you know so much you must know the chaps said he cheated."

"What chaps?"

"All the chaps."

"Do you mean to tell me, Mr. Tickell, on your honour, that all the men who were present in the room accused Mr. Beaton of cheating?"

"That's what it amounts to, but, of course, it began with Dodwell."

"I am perfectly aware that Captain Dodwell made a certain statement for which Mr. Beaton was only kept from knocking him down by the rest of you--brave men! What I want to know is if you were all in the conspiracy. Did you yourself see, with your own eyes, Mr. Beaton cheat?"

"I can't say that I did."

"You were watching him the whole time?"

"I suppose I was."

"Did you see anything in the least suspicious about anything he did?"

"I'm bound to say I didn't, at least, not to notice it."

"Had you any suspicions of him?"

"Not the faintest shadow of one, we were chums; I would as soon have suspected myself."

"So, except for what Captain Dodwell said, which was, after a fashion, corroborated by Mr. Noel Draycott, you had no reason to suppose that Mr. Beaton had been guilty of the slightest irregularity?"

"I suppose I hadn't, if you look at it like that."

"You would unhesitatingly have handed the pool to Mr. Beaton, without even the slightest feeling of having been ill-used?"

"Of course I would; he had won it; his hand was better than mine."

"He denied having done what Captain Dodwell stated?"

"Rather; as you said, he wanted to knock him down; he was as mad as a hatter."

"Would you have behaved with perfect calmness in the face of Captain Dodwell's hideous accusation?"

"I don't expect I should, especially as we were all of us pretty warm to begin with."

"Would you want to knock a man down who said that kind of thing of you?"

"You bet, I should want to kill him."

"Because Mr. Beaton felt exactly as you would have done, his brother officers, chivalrous creatures, threw him out of the room--you assisted them?"

"Upon my word, I hardly know what I did do, it was a regular rough-and-tumble; Beaton fought like ten wild cats. I daresay I did bear a hand."

"Oh, you dare say? I congratulate you, Mr. Tickell, on the courageous assistance you lent your brother officers; was it twelve or twenty against one? They could scarcely have done without you. Cowards! And having assisted your friends in getting rid of the rightful claimant, you had no scruple in placing Mr. Beaton's money in your pocket, and, I presume, paying with it some of the more pressing debts which I understand you owed?"

The young gentleman winced, the lady's thrust had gone home.

"That's all I want from you, Mr. Tickell; I am obliged to you for the confession you have made. I advise you to consider your position, and to ask yourself, when you are dancing with your next partner, if a person who has behaved as you have done is entitled to show his face in such a house as this. Mr. Beaton cheated no one; he is incapable of such conduct as yours; you cheated him, having first joined yourself with some twelve or twenty of your friends to get him out of the way. Think over what I have said to you, Mr. Tickell, instead of whispering soft nothings to your partners, and remember that I shall be watching. Now you may go."

CHAPTER XIV
"Who is Simmons?"

Miss Forster was strolling by herself along the corridor; she had declined to permit Mr. Tickell to accompany her, and the youth had seemed glad enough to get away. She examined her programme; she had it in her mind to cut the next dance, not from one of the reasons which usually prompt that nefarious course of action, but because she had a strong feeling that for a few minutes she would like to be alone. She passed into the conservatory through a door which was at the end of the corridor. The music for the next dance had already commenced; the sitters-out, to whom the conservatory is a haven much to be desired, had gone. She moved to a couch which was flanked on either side by towering ferns. She had just sat down and was congratulating herself upon the prospect of remaining, for at least a brief period, undisturbed, when a voice addressed her.

"I am fortunate, Miss Forster, in finding you alone."

The speaker was Captain Anthony Dodwell. She said nothing, but, rising, made as if to go away. He treated her as she had just treated Mr. Tickell; he interposed himself so as to render it difficult for her to pass.

"Pardon me, Miss Forster, but, as you are aware, there is an explanation which you owe me, and which you will be so good as to let me have before you go."

"Stand aside, sir."

"A short time ago you more than suggested that I was not the kind of person with whom you cared to dance--with whom, indeed, any decent woman would care to dance. You did this publicly, in such a way that your treatment of me is, at this moment, a common topic of conversation in the ballroom. What explanation have you to give?"

"None; you are not the kind of person with whom any decent woman would care to dance, or talk. Are you going to stand on one side, or am I to call for assistance?"

"What grounds have you for what you just now said--what have I ever done to you that you should say it?"

"Captain Dodwell--it seems incredible, but I believe you still do hold that rank in the King's service--you are a liar, a coward, and, I believe, a thief. That you are not, in any sense, an honest man, is certain; to what extent your dishonesty goes, you know better than I do, though I hope to make the thing quite clear before very long. Do you really imagine that an explanation is required as to why a decent woman is unwilling to dance, to talk, or to be associated in any way whatever, with a person of that kind?"

"You are taking advantage of your being a woman, Miss Forster; can you give me the name of any man who will be willing to be associated with you in what you just now said?"

"On an infamous occasion, Captain Dodwell, you found one man, Mr. Noel Draycott, who, for reasons of his own, was so base as to be willing to be associated with a foul lie which you uttered; but before very long I confidently hope that every man who was then present will be associated with me against you. Will you let me pass, or would you prefer that I should repeat what I have just now said in the presence of the dancers who are now leaving the ballroom?"

He let her pass. The music had ceased, couples were streaming in; among the first was Lady Cantyre on the arm of her attendant cavalier. At sight of the girl she started.

"Haven't you been dancing?" She glanced towards Dodwell, whose attitude scarcely suggested riotous enjoyment. As her eye caught Violet's she seemed to have a glimmer of understanding. She turned to her partner. "That was a perfect dance she's missed, wasn't it?" Then, to Violet, "And, by the way, I think I heard a certain gentleman inquiring for you--with an air!"

Miss Forster danced through the rest of the programme--no other of her partners had occasion to complain of her in any way whatever. Her demeanour could not have been more orthodox; she behaved just as a young woman ought to who is having a first-rate time at a delightful ball. During the dances and in that more critical period between them, she was all that her partners could possibly have desired; lucky men! No one, to look at her, or to listen to her, would have guessed that anything had happened to crumple a single rose leaf, to mar in the least degree her night's enjoyment.

Only when dancing with one partner was a word said which was not, perhaps, altogether in keeping with the spirit of the hour. The partner was Major Reith, and, in the beginning, the words came from him. That scene in the woods, far from weakening, had rather strengthened their friendship. He was years older than she; what had passed between them on that occasion seemed to have produced in him the attitude, say, of an uncle, who was on the best terms with his niece. He said the word, after the dance was over, when they had settled themselves on chairs which were in full view of the whole assembly; there was evidently no thought of the privacy of the alcove for them.

"What's this I hear you've been saying to Anthony Dodwell and to Jackie Tickell?"

"How can I tell what you hear behind my back?"

"Exactly; how can you? And you can't guess either?"

"Did I ever pretend to be any good at guessing?"

"It seems that you said something to Dodwell, when he asked you for a dance, which has set people's tongues wagging; you alone know what you said to Jackie, but he's going about with a face as black as his shoes."

"My dear Major Reith, I understand that you are sleeping here to-night. If you ask me in the morning for information, I will give you all I can; but, while I may remark that I have said to both the persons you name only a little of what I propose to say, I would rather not tell you what I have said now. This is a ball; I want that to be the only fact in my mind for the remainder of the night."

"One more question and it shall. Have you heard anything of Beaton?"

"I haven't; but I may have. Something has happened that I don't understand, which puzzles me; but ask me about that also in the morning. As Mr. Tickell said when he wished to change the conversation, isn't it a capital floor?"

The major took the hint, which was more than she had done. The rest of the conversation was more in harmony with the moment; that is, they talked of nothing in which either took the slightest real interest.

The ball had come to the end to which all balls come at last, and Miss Forster, having retired to her room, had gone through, with her maid's assistance, the preliminary stages of unrobing, when, Lady Cantyre entering, she informed the maid that her services would no longer be required--and the friends were left alone. The countess, who was attired in a mysterious garment of sky-blue silk, which became her, if the thing were possible, even more than the dress which she had worn at the ball, had placed herself in an arm-chair, and was toasting her toes at the fire.

"Violet, I'm told that you've been going it."

"Haven't we all been going it?"

"Yes, but not quite, I hope, on the same lines as you. You practically, it seems, treated Captain Dodwell to a whipping in the middle of the ballroom. That is not exactly the sort of treatment that one expects one guest to mete out to another."

"Margaret, I am more than ever convinced that Sydney Beaton has been the victim of a conspiracy. Something which was on Captain Dodwell's face during the brief interview I had with him, which he forced on me, made me absolutely certain that, for some purpose of his own, which I intend to get at the bottom of very soon, he was guilty of a deliberate falsehood on that horrible night; that he's a liar and a coward, as I had the pleasure of telling him."

"Oh, you did. No wonder that I had a feeling that he looked as if he had not altogether enjoyed the night. That was not a pretty thing for you to say. Vi, take care; be very sure of what you do. Things, from your point of view, are pretty bad already, you don't want to make them worse."

"I'm not going to make them worse--I couldn't. Margaret, something has happened to Sydney--something dreadful; something which I don't understand. Look at this. Do you know anything about it?"

She handed the countess something which she had taken out of the leather case upon the table.

"Isn't it your locket, the one he gave you, with his picture? Why do you ask if I know anything about it?"

"It's the one I gave him. You remember that you came to see me before you went downstairs; when you went out, did you see anything lying on the floor just outside my room?"

"Not that I'm aware of. Why?"

"Did you see that locket?"

"I certainly didn't; why am I being cross-examined?"

"Do you know anything about a maid in your employ named Simmons?"

"I don't; is there such an one?"

"Almost directly after you had gone a maid, who said that her name was Simmons, came into the room with that locket in her hand, and said that she'd picked it up off the floor just outside my room. Margaret, how could that locket have got there?"

"I don't believe it was there when I went out; I remember, quite well, looking up and down to see who was about. I could hardly have helped seeing it if it was there. But what's the mystery?"

"When we became engaged, we gave each other a locket; here's the one he gave me, that's the one I gave him; he said that it should never leave him. The last time I saw him-- you know, I told you all about it--I showed him my locket, where it was; he put his finger inside his collar, he hooked up that chain, and on it was that locket; he declared it had never left him since he had had it, and that it never should. I am quite sure that he took it away with him that night; how came it to be on the floor outside my door?"

"It does seem odd."

"I should say it's as certain as anything could be, that that locket has been with him all the time he's been away. As you know, I've had no communication with him of any sort or kind, in spite of all my efforts; I've not had the faintest clue to his whereabouts. Isn't it an extraordinary thing that that locket--from which he was inseparable--should be picked up on the floor just outside my room by a complete stranger, especially as it couldn't have been there before she came on the scene, or you'd have noticed it?"

"Simmons? I don't remember the name; and I rather pride myself on the fact that I do know the names of all the maids. Perhaps she came with one of the other women."

"No, she told me that she had been here only a few days, and that she came with some other new servants last week from town. Margaret, I've a feeling that that woman brought the locket with her; that she'd never found it as she pretended, that she knows more about it than she chose to say--the feeling was strong on me as she stood there with her smiling face. This locket came into her possession in some queer way. I saw it on her face, although she kept on smiling. If I hadn't been going down to the dance, I'd have had it out of her."

"Had what out of her?"

"The truth! If you only knew how I feel that everything--everyone--is against us; against me, and against Sydney; if you only knew what I've had to bear at home, from uncle, and other ways--from myself. Sydney is in some desperate plight; I'm as convinced of it as if he himself had told me. If I could only get at him to help him! But I can't! I can't! I don't know where he is! And now that woman brings me his locket, from which I'm perfectly certain he would not allow himself to be parted unless he were at his last gasp--unless something worse than death stared him in the face. I do believe he'd stick to it--yes, Margaret, I mean it. I know Sydney, as no one else does, as no one else can; he has his faults--no one need tell me that, but I know he loves me, and that, having said what he did say about that locket, he'd stand to his word while the breath was in his body, unless--mind!--unless some awful thing has befallen him, and that's what I'm afraid of. You may laugh, but there's something here"--the girl pressed her hands to her side--"which tells me--if you only knew how afraid I am--oh, Margaret, if you only knew!"

The girl sank on to her knees at the countess's side, she hid her face on her ladyship's silken lap--and she cried.

CHAPTER XV
'Twixt the Dark and Daylight

The night had gone, the morning was well advanced, the day would soon break, the countess had long since gone, and still Miss Forster had not gone to bed. There was something which kept her from placing herself between the sheets; and now that at last she was beginning to have thoughts in that direction, something occurred which banished sleep still farther from her eyes.

She was just about to remove her dressing-gown, and really make herself ready for bed, when the silence of the night was broken by a sound.

"What was that? Wasn't it in my passage?"

She stood in an attitude of listening.

"There it is again. Isn't it just outside my door? I wonder if there's anyone there at this hour of the morning? I believe there is."

Altering her intention, she suffered her dressing-gown to remain where it was. Rapidly crossing the room, she stood close up to the door and listened.

"There is someone. Who can it be, at this hour of the morning? Whoever it is, is running away."

She suddenly opened the door and looked out. There was no one there. She went into the passage. Although the lights were out, she was still able to make out dimly that a figure, but whether of a man or a woman she could not be sure, was moving rapidly along the passage, to vanish round the corner.

"I wonder who that was?"

She hesitated, returned into her room, and shut the door.

"It might have been anyone. It certainly might not be any business of mine; people can move about the house at any hour they please without consulting me. What was that? It sounded as if someone was calling. There it is again. And there is someone running past my door again. I'm going to see what this means."

Reopening the door, she returned into the passage.

"There's someone running down the stairs as if in a very great hurry. What's that? That's a queer noise. Someone calling again; someone calling for help. There's something queer going on downstairs. Someone is quarrelling. I'm going to find out what it is. I don't care if it is no business of mine; people shouldn't make a noise like that at this time of night. It's everybody's business when they do."

She went a few steps down the darkened passage. When she got out of range of the electric light shining through her open door, it was not easy to find her way; she had to touch the wall with her outstretched fingers and feel it.

"I ought to have brought some matches, or something; the place is as dark as pitch. Shall I go back and fetch them? Whatever was that? There's a light downstairs; someone is still up. That's a man's voice. I seem to know it. Whose can it be? I know it quite well. And that's another man's voice. They're quarrelling. I believe they're fighting. What are they doing? They're making noise enough. Surely, I'm not the only person in the place who hears them--a noise like that; it sounds as if they were fighting like two mad dogs."

She had reached what she realised to be the head of the great staircase. A faint light streamed in through the stained-glass window. She hesitated; she might have been frightened by the noise that was going on below. A strange sound was coming through the darkness, as if furniture was being upset in all directions by persons who were chasing each other round the room; then--surely they were blows. Then a voice exclaimed, in a tone which suggested that the speaker, stricken with sudden, dreadful fear, was fighting for his life. The words which, in his agony, he uttered were destined to keep ringing in her ears:

"Beaton! My God!"

The sound of a blow, heavier than any of the others; the noise of a heavy body falling to the ground, and bringing articles of furniture down crashing with it. Silence, except for the light footsteps of the girl who was flying down the staircase as if for life. Beaton!--that was what he had said. Someone had called upon her lover's name in that terrible voice. What did it mean? She was rushing down to see. As she neared the bottom she caught her heel in her dressing-gown; striving to disentangle it in her haste, in the darkness she missed her footing, stumbled, went bungling to the foot of the staircase. Luckily, she had only a short distance to fall, but it was far enough; the thing was so unlooked for. She had fallen clumsily, heavily; the shock had nearly stunned her. For some moments she lay in doubt as to what really had befallen her; then, rising, not without difficulty, to her feet, she found that she was trembling, that her whole frame seemed to ache, that her right ankle pained her so that she could scarcely stand on it.

But it was no time to consider her bruises, what had happened to her; there was something else for her to do. She listened, but all was still; there was no sound of voices, of struggling, of falling furniture, or blows--no sound of anything. The silence, after what she had heard, in itself was ominous. Something terrible had happened.

She went limping across the hall, wincing each time her right foot touched the ground. All sorts of unseen things were in her way. The hall was used as a sitting-room; the household had its tea there. It was crowded with all kinds of impedimenta; it was not easy, by mere instinct, to find her way among them. She did not know until she had come in sometimes painful contact with them that the things were there. Presently she tripped, with her bad foot, over what doubtless was a footstool; she would have gone headlong to the ground had not an arm-chair saved her. It was an arm-chair; she was in doubt as to what it was at first, but when she perched herself upon its friendly arm she knew. She had been unable to keep back a cry of pain; the jerk to her twisted ankle had sent a shock all over her, as if red-hot needles were being driven into her limbs.

How it hurt her as she sat there; it really was excruciating agony. The foot was dangling in the air. How much worse it would be when, putting it back upon the ground, she would have to use it to stand and walk upon. She essayed a little experiment: putting it gingerly down, resting her weight upon it as lightly as she could. She flattered herself on her capacity to bear pain, but that was too much even for her. A sound, which was half wail, half sob, came from between her lips.

She had a feeling as, back again upon the arm of the chair, with an effort she held her breath, that someone had heard the cry which came from her lips. She peered about her; it was impossible to make things out, to see what was there and what wasn't. She might have been surrounded by a dozen people without her eyes even hinting that a soul was there. There was something which did her better service than her eyes--perhaps it was her ears--some subtle sense which she would have been unable to define. She felt sure that she had been overheard by--she did not know by whom or by what--by someone, something. It might have been a man, or a woman, or an animal--a dog. It could scarcely have been the latter; it is not the canine habit to preserve such silence when the sense of hearing is assailed. It was something human. She was not alone; someone else was with her in the hall.

She adopted the simplest way of finding out. She asked:

"Who's there?"

No answer. She had a feeling that her question had put the unseen person on his--or her--guard; that someone had withdrawn farther from her, and was awaiting a chance to effect a safe retreat. She was persuaded that there had been a just audible movement, that someone had been quite close to her, and had drawn away. While she waited, with straining ears and bated breath, uncertain whether to speak again or what to do--her foot was causing her such pain that walking was beyond her strength--there came what was undoubtedly a sound of an unmistakable kind. Someone had come hastening into the hall from the direction of the suite of rooms which was on the other side, someone who was pressed for time. Although he moved with a curious noiselessness, as if his feet had been shod with velvet, she felt sure that it was a man. She doubted if he was able to see any better than she could; the fashion of his progress suggested it. He seemed to be making for the side of the hall on which she was, and to be following her example by coming into contact with most of the objects which he met upon his way. She heard him mutter something beneath his breath which might have been an oath. She was sure it was a man. Plainly he was as blind as a bat; he was floundering closer and closer; he was nearly on her, came into actual contact with the chair on which she was perched. That was too much. She had to speak.

"Who are you? Take care--oh!"

This last was a cry of pain wrung from her much against her will. The chair on which she was resting had received a sudden push; she was precipitated forward, on to the bad foot. The result was anguish; her feelings escaped her in spite of herself. Whoever had done it was evidently as much taken by surprise as she was. There was a muttered, distinctly masculine ejaculation. Then, as she continued to wail--there can be few things more painful than a twisted ankle, and the pain of that was really unendurable--all at once a light was shining in her face. Her unintentional assailant was carrying a dark lantern; turning the shutter, he flashed it on her. For a second or two the effect it had on her was to make her blinder still; then the hand of the person who was holding it swerved, a pencil of light passed across his face so that she caught a glimpse of it--only one glimpse, but that was enough.

"Sydney!" she cried. "My darling! Thank God, it's you."

In the first wild rapture of the recognition she forgot everything--her foot, the singularity of the fact that her lover should be there at all; all she thought of was to reach him. Even while she was speaking she moved quickly towards him. That same instant the light was darkened, her foot gave way beneath her. As she sank to the floor she was conscious that the bearer of the lantern, instead of sharing her rapture, of coming to her assistance, of rushing to take her in his arms, was retreating with so much expedition that things were being overturned in all directions in his haste to get away. She had been aware that, as he started back instead of forward, something had fallen from his hand on to the seat of the chair on whose arm she had been resting. He had not stopped to retrieve it, whatever it was. Her hand came into contact with it as she tried to raise herself. It was a leather bag of some sort, so much she learnt from the sense of touch. She found the handle, tried to lift it; it was oddly heavy.

As she was still trying to lift it she became conscious that someone else was coming down the stairs. Her heart was heavy as lead within her. She was filled with a great fear; the presence of that bag had frightened her more than anything else. A cushion was on the ground beside her; she picked it up, using it to cover the bag to the best of her ability so that its presence on the chair need not be at once detected.

The person who had descended the stairs had paused at the bottom. A match was struck. If she had only brought a box of matches with her, how much might have been avoided! The holder of the match moved forward towards an electric switch; immediately a light was shining down at her. A voice addressed her:

"Miss Forster! What on earth are you doing here?"

She looked up at the kindly, friendly face which was bending over her.

"Major Reith!"

Then something came to her. All at once the world was whirling round; for the first time in her life she had fainted.

CHAPTER XVI
The Lacquered Club

There was a sort of self-consciousness in her brain, even though she swooned; something which told her that this was the moment in all her life in which it was most necessary that she should keep her wits about her--and here she was losing them. They were willing to slip still farther away; with comfort she could have remained, to all intents and purposes, unconscious for quite a considerable length of time; but she would not. So it came about that her faintness endured but for a moment.

Major Reith's ideas as to what to do with a young lady who had fainted were vague. His impulse was to return upstairs and alarm the household; but before he could put his impulse into practice the lady relieved him of his difficulties by sitting up and returning to life.

"Oh, Major Reith, I've hurt my foot."

He thought that he had never seen her looking prettier. He probably never had; that dressing-gown became her.

"I'm very sorry." His tone was gravity itself. "Is it very bad? Let me help you to get up."

He helped her; would have placed her on the chair on which was the cushion and, underneath, the bag, but she managed to make him understand that she preferred another. He was all sympathy.

"Can I do anything for it, or would you rather that I let the people know?"

"Thank you, I would rather that you didn't. It is painful for the moment, but I shall manage; it's the first twinge. Did you hear a strange noise upstairs?"

"I did, and wondered what it was; it was that which brought me down."

It was on the tip of his tongue to ask what had brought her down, but he refrained. Where she was concerned he was a man of quick perception. He was already conscious that there was something in the situation which he did not understand, which, possibly, she would rather that he did not understand.

"What did you hear?"

"I thought I heard someone in the hall just now, but I suppose it was you."

"I expect it was. I heard something, and I came down to see what it was, tripped on the stairs, and I've been behaving like a goose ever since."

"As I came round the corner from my room I saw a light flashing down in the hall. Was that you?"

"A light? What light?" She went on without giving him a chance to answer the questions she asked: "Did you hear a sound as if someone was quarrelling?"

"That's what roused me. First of all, I heard someone running up and down my passage----"

"So did I."

"I looked out to see what was up, thinking that someone might be ill; then I heard a din as if a free fight was taking place downstairs."

"Did you hear anyone call out?"

"I heard voices."

"More than one?"

"I should certainly say that there was more than one. I couldn't hear what they said, but it seemed to me that two men were slanging each other at the top of their voices for all they were worth. Then I heard something which brought me down."

"What was it? I don't know; it's no good your looking at me as if you thought I did. I've been able to get no farther than where you see me now. Like you, I heard what seemed to me to be two men quarrelling, so I came down hoping to prevent mischief being done."

"It was very plucky of you to come down all alone. And you don't know what's happened?"

"No more than you. I'm not very well up in the geography of the house, but I thought that the argument was taking place in one of the rooms on the other side; but before I could get down it had stopped. It was the sudden stopping I did not like."

"Nor I, to be frank. Shall I help you upstairs, or will you stay here while I go and see? We may both of us be false alarmists; let's hope we are."

She seemed to be considering.

"I think you had better leave me where I am, only--mind you're not long. It's very silly of me, but I don't feel as if I'd care to be left alone too long."

She watched his tall figure, shrouded in a long grey dressing-gown which covered his pyjamas, across the hall. Directly he was out of sight she rose from her chair; leaning on the back of it, standing on one foot, she looked eagerly about the hall. The one electric light illumined the spot on which she stood; it scarcely penetrated the shadows beyond. She hesitated whether to switch on other lights, to make sure that no hidden eyes were watching, but it was only with difficulty that she could move; there was not time, the major might be back at any moment. She took the bag from underneath the cushion; considering it was only a small, brown, brief bag, it was curiously heavy. All the time she had been talking to Major Reith she had been wondering what would be the nearest convenient place in which to hide it, if opportunity offered. Against the wall, within a few feet of where she was standing, was an old oak chest, which was sometimes used as a seat, which was covered with a piece of dark blue velvet, embroidered almost as if it had been an altar cloth. Lady Cantyre had told her that it was half-full of things, but she herself did not know what they were; no one ever looked inside. If the lid was open, there might be room for the bag; it would be the very place.

She managed to get as far as the chest, hopping, for the most part, on one foot. The lid was open. She raised it. Pressing back the velvet cover, she saw that there was room. She thrust in the bag, lowered the lid, and returned to where the major had left her. She would have liked to sink into the chair, only to relieve her foot; something stopped her. She might have been guilty of some crime, her bearing was so strange. She pressed her hand to her side, as if to calm the beating of her heart. She endeavoured to peer into all the shadowy places in the great hall; there were so many places in which, in that light, a spy might be hidden. Suppose she had been seen?

Why was the major so long? She had expressly requested him to be quick; it seemed to her to be a frightful time since he had gone. What could be keeping him? She would have liked to call to him, but she did not dare. Something must be keeping him which perhaps she ought to know. She was suddenly afraid of what the major might have learnt. She would go and see what it was. She hobbled across the hall, ignoring the pain which each movement gave her, bent on being stayed by nothing. She passed into the room through whose door the major had vanished. It was brightly lit. He had switched on the lights, but he was not there. She listened. All was so still. He might be in the room beyond.

She had walked thirty miles with much greater ease than she traversed those less than thirty feet. More than once she had to stop. It needed all her self-control to keep from crying out; she was conscious that beads of perspiration were on her brow, induced either by the effort or the pain. When she came to the door leading to the other room she had to lean against it on one foot, the agony of putting the other to the ground had become so great. She turned the handle and, somehow, went through.

That room was also lighted, the electrics serving to show that it was in a state of singular confusion. The fine old furniture was all anyhow; chairs, tables, ornaments were overturned; scarcely anything seemed in its place. But she had found the major. He was on his knees about the centre of the room, leaning over something which was recumbent on the floor, something by which he was so engrossed that, plainly, her entrance had gone unnoticed. His unconsciousness of her presence affected her unpleasantly.

When he continued to ignore her, her heart stood still. She stole closer towards him, again resolute to disregard her suffering foot. She came to a point at which she could see what he was looking at--and she saw.

On the floor, in the centre of a sort of circle formed by ill-used articles of furniture, a man was lying--very quietly. It was Mr. Noel Draycott.

"Is he dead?"

Although she asked the question in a whisper, it seemed to be more audible than if she had shouted it. Major Reith looked up at her, showing no signs of being startled or of being taken unawares. His eyes met hers steadily.

"I'm afraid he is."

He could hardly have spoken in more even tones, yet one knew that it was not because he was unmoved. There was silence. Her glance was wandering round the room. What she saw was eloquent; its condition so plainly showed what a scene of violence it had witnessed. She pressed her hand again to her side. She tried to speak, but the words would not come. He saw something of what she was enduring.

"You can do nothing. You are in pain. Let me take you to your room."

She shook her head. Then words came; she spoke as if her throat had all at once grown dry and husky.

"How did it happen?"

"He was killed with this."

He picked up from the floor what looked like a lacquered Oriental club; there was something gleaming on the end of it.

"Could it have been that I heard?"

"Who can say?"

"Was he like that when you came in?"

"He was lying a little more over on his face; I turned him over to see if there were any signs of life left in him."

"You are sure--that no one else--was in the room?"

For some reason there was a perceptible interval before he answered; they looked at each other, as if each were reading something which was in the other's eyes; then his glance dropped, and he said:

"There was no one else in the room when I came in."

Somehow she felt that his words conveyed much more than was on the surface; neither spoke; it was as if each were occupied with thoughts which would not be denied.

All at once the stillness was broken in a manner which was sufficiently startling; what sounded like the report of a firearm rang through the silent room. The major sprang to his feet. Her face was turned in the direction from which the sound had come.

"What was that?" she asked.

"That was a revolver--someone fired a revolver."

"Where?"

"I should say in the next room; it was certainly very close."

He started to move towards the adjoining apartment. She stopped him. "Where are you going?" He turned to her.

"I'm going to see who fired that shot."

"Let me come with you; don't leave me here--with him. If you let me lean upon your arm, I can get along quite well."

He stood eyeing her, as if in doubt what was the right thing for him to do. His tone was stern, perhaps unconsciously so.

"You know you ought not to be here; this is no place for you--you ought to be in bed."

"I know, but what's the use of talking like that? You're not going to leave me here--alone? You shall take me with you. Give me your arm; I don't believe I can move without it, or I would; give me your arm."

He did as she asked, crossing the open space in which Mr. Noel Draycott lay to do it. Not only did he give her his arm, he put it round her, so that she was supported rather by his shoulder. Together they made what haste they could.

This was a suite of rooms opening one into the other; they passed into the next. It was in darkness.

"I fancy the switches are against the wall by the door here."

The surmise was correct, he switched the light on. When he had done so, they were conscious of two things; one was an open window, the other was the smell of powder.

"It was in here that the shot was fired."

"But by whom? The room is empty; who fired it? And why?"

"Whoever fired it may have gone through the open window. Sit down on that chair; I must look into this."

He withdrew the support of his arm, but she did not sit down on the chair, she leaned on the back of it; perhaps she feared that if she sat she would not be able to rise unaided. He advanced towards the open window, then gave an exclamation, stooping as he did so.

"Here, at least, is the revolver." He held up the weapon for her to see, and examined it. "One of the chambers has been discharged, that was the shot we heard; the others are still loaded."

He seemed to be about to say something else, but all at once, stopping, he stood at attention. It was she who spoke.

"You heard?"

"Wasn't that someone moving?"

"It was someone in the next room--there's someone in there now--listen!"

"Good gracious!"

There unmistakably was someone--a woman's scream rang out. There still seemed to be another room beyond, or, at any rate, there was another door. The major dashed towards it; this time he was through before the girl had a chance of stopping him.

She was left alone--to listen. And, clinging to the chair, she stood on one foot, and she listened. She never forgot those few moments. There was the dead man behind her; some strange thing had happened where she was; what was taking place in front? Her helplessness rendered her position so much worse than it need have been. She tried to move, but she had done too much of that already; the moment she put her injured foot to the floor a shock went all over her which made her shut her eyes, and the room swam round. She could not even get to a bell to summon assistance if it were needed; all she could do was to stand--and wait.

She was aware that she was in that state of mind and body in which it was quite possible that her imagination might play her tricks. Was it her imagination which made her fancy that such strange things were going on about her; which made her think, as she glanced towards it, that a face had been looking through the open window, which had been quickly withdrawn as she turned her head? The sounds she heard--were none of them real? The footsteps outside the window; the mutterings--surely they were mutterings--was that not someone speaking in whispers? She felt sure that they were footsteps, that someone was speaking. The horror of it--but she was too incapable of movement to make sure.

And then, in the room behind her, where he lay, with the lacquered club beside him, amid the broken furniture--was this another trick her imagination played her? Were those not real movements which she heard; was it only that she fancied that voices were speaking? Again she felt convinced that it was not imagination only; there was something going on which it behoved her to see--in the room behind her, outside the window--she knew not where besides. What was Major Reith doing? Had he not found the woman who had screamed? He pretended to be her friend, to care for her--did he not understand what she must be enduring, in that room, helpless, alone?

If he was much longer, she would have to scream, as that woman had screamed. Flesh and blood has its limits; she had really reached them. She would either have to scream, or go mad--or something would happen to her; she had never felt like that before, never.

In the nick of time, when it seemed to her that something would have to go, that she must break down, Major Reith returned.

"I am very sorry to have kept you waiting so long, but I can't help thinking that someone has been playing tricks with me."

"Haven't you found her--the woman who screamed?"

It sounded so strangely in her ears that she did not know her own voice.

"I found no one. I believe my attention has been diverted with some ulterior purpose. Have you heard nothing?"

"What haven't I heard? I believe there has been someone in the next room."

"We will soon see about that--come. I'm going to take you into that room on the road to bed; and I shall have to rouse the house, but first I shall see you safe to your own chamber."

Only with the greatest difficulty, even with his support, could she return to the adjoining apartment. The instant the door was opened they made a discovery.

"You see," she cried, "it wasn't only imagination, someone has been here--the lights are out."

What she said was correct; the room, which they had left lighted, was in pitch darkness. There appeared to be switches by every door, and it took Reith but an instant to have the room as radiant as before. Both their glances travelled in the same direction. This time it was the major who exclaimed:

"Good God! Draycott's gone!"

CHAPTER XVII
Sleepers Awakened

It was a fact: the dead man's body had disappeared, in so brief a space of time that Major Reith and Miss Forster did not find it easy to credit the evidence of their own senses. They had been out of the room--how long? At the most, three or four minutes. They had gone into the next room, been there not more than a minute when the woman was heard screaming. Although circumstances had made the time during which Miss Forster had been left alone seem infinite, actually it was probably only a minute or two. During those fleeting minutes what had--what could have happened? Had the dead man come back to life and taken himself away?

There was nothing to show that anything had happened. There was the club, the furniture, apparently in exactly the same confusion in which they had left it; only a dark red stain, that was still wet and shiny, marked the place on the floor where something had been lying. And that stain was eloquent; the man from whom so much blood had come must have been in a parlous condition, certainly in no state to pick himself up and walk unassisted from the room. For he would probably have been bleeding still; his progress would quite possibly have been marked upon the carpet. Which way could he have gone? There were two windows and three doors--all of them were shut. Reith looked to see if there were signs of him on the other side of the doors. There was nothing.

It was while he was standing at the door looking out into the passage that there was, for the first time, anything to show that the happenings downstairs had been heard above. A gentleman in a dressing-gown came along with a candle in his hand, followed by another, in the same attire, without a candle. The one in front was the Earl of Cantyre; the other was Sir Gerrard Ackroyd. The earl broke into exclamation at the sight of the major.

"Hullo, Reith! Have the beggars woke you, too?" When he saw the girl, on his good-humoured face there came a comical expression. "What! Violet Forster! What on earth's the matter?" He was looking round the room. "Who has been knocking the furniture about like this?" He turned to Ackroyd: "That must have been the noise you heard."

"I told you it sounded as if somebody was throwing the furniture about. Somebody's been having a lark all over the house."

"Lark, you call it? If someone has been having a lark, I call it jolly bad form at this hour of the morning." His lordship's tone was one of grievance. "What's the meaning of all this? I suppose the beggars disturbed you, too--nice thing! Wasn't there a pistol-shot, and someone screaming, and I don't know what besides? Lark, indeed!"

"I wish," said the major, "that I could think that it was only what Ackroyd calls a lark. I'm afraid there's been something very like murder done."

"Murder! Reith--you're joking."

"Does this room look as if I were joking? You see this great patch upon the floor, still wet, and what's upon this club? When Miss Forster and I came into this room Noel Draycott was lying here--dead."

"Dead? Draycott--I say! How did that come about? What have you done with him?"

"What someone has done with him is what Miss Forster and I were trying to ascertain when you came along. He was here perhaps not five minutes ago, and now--where is he?"

"Where's who?"

"Hullo! Now here is the whole jolly crowd! I knew how it would be. Why do all you people want to come downstairs? You were just as well off in your beds, and a lot more comfortable."

The earl's words were prompted by the fact that through the door by which he had entered were coming a stream of people, his own wife in the van. It was she who had put that question. Behind her were all sorts and conditions of people, some of them in surprising costumes. There were ladies, old and young; some of them were guests, some servants. They had one thing in common: that they were all in a state of considerable excitement. There was the same miscellaneous collection of men. The guests, for the most part, seemed disposed to treat the affair as a jest. The male servants were more serious; it might be that under no circumstances could they see a jest in anything which involved their being roused from well-earned slumber.

It was the countess who was the first to reply to the earl:

"My good Rupert, did you imagine that, after your rushing out of the room like that, I was going to stop in bed to be murdered? What has been going on? What a state this room is in! And, my dear Violet, what is the matter with you? You look as if you'd seen, not one ghost, but several!" When the lady saw that there really was something the matter with the girl, her flippant tones became suddenly earnest. "Violet, are you ill?"

"I twisted my foot coming down the stairs, and--it is pretty bad."

"You poor child! It's plain you can't stand; and you oughtn't to. We'll have you carried upstairs. There's a carrying chair in the hall. But"--her ladyship's glance was wandering round--"whatever has been going on in here? Is that---- What's that on the floor?"

Major Reith spoke:

"If you'll forgive me, Countess, I don't think, at any rate, that you ladies ought to come in here."

"And, pray, why not, Major Reith; what has happened?"

The major signalled with his eyes to the earl; the countess caught him in the act.

"It's no good your trying to tell the earl that I'm to be got rid of. I insist, Major Reith, upon your telling me what that mark on the carpet means."

"I'm afraid, Lady Cantyre, that there's been foul play."

The major was plainly embarrassed.

"At Avonham? In my house? Foul play? What do you mean?"

The major's embarrassment did not grow less, which she seemed to resent.

"What is it you are trying to find words to hide? Violet, you at least are my friend. What is it that Major Reith does not wish me to know? Tell me, in two words, what has happened."

"Mr. Noel Draycott has been murdered."

There burst a chorus of exclamation from all the assembled people. One or two of the more sensitive feminine spirits shrieked. One elderly lady pressed boldly to the front, heedless of the fact that the state of deshabille that she was in disclosed an amazing absence of hair on her head:

"I don't know about anybody having been murdered, but I know that I've been robbed."

The hostess turned to her.

"Duchess!"

"Every bit of jewellery I brought with me has been stolen."

A feminine voice exclaimed:

"What! the Ditchling diamonds?"

"You saw that I was wearing them to-night at the ball? Well, they're gone--stolen--every one!"

"But--are you sure?" The hostess was regarding the hairless lady with a look of very genuine concern.

"I was fast asleep when something woke me. I couldn't think what it was. I always sleep with the lights out. I could see nothing, but I had a feeling that there was somebody in the room. There's an electric light over my bed; I tried to turn it on, but it wouldn't come. I suppose the noise I had made had been noticed. I heard someone moving quickly across the floor. I sat up in bed. 'Who's there?' I asked. The only answer was that the door was opened. I got out of bed--I'm not so young as I was, and I'm not built for rapid movement; getting out of bed takes me some time. By the time I was well planted on my feet I knew quite well that whoever had been in my room was gone. I turned on the light at the door. As I expected, the room was empty, the door was shut; and, also what I expected, my jewel-case was lying empty on the floor. I thought I had heard something fall, and that was it. Everything was taken out of it; from what I saw, not so much as a ring had been left. I was just going to ring the bell, though whether any good would come of it I doubted--I have rung an electric bell in the middle of the night for an hour at a time, and no one has paid the slightest attention--but just as I was going to do it someone went rushing past my door, and, of course, I opened it to see if it was the thief, and a gun went off somewhere downstairs, and all the other bedroom doors seemed to open at once, everyone came out of them, and there was a pretty to-do, and then they went downstairs, and I came with them. I don't know what it's all about; all I do know is that every bit of jewellery I had has been stolen."

The duchess's somewhat incoherent narrative was greeted by a chorus of feminine voices:

"I've been robbed, too!"

"So have I!"

"Everything I had has been taken!"

"I've been stripped of every single thing!"

It would seem as if all the guests at Avonham had suffered from a series of mishaps. The host thrust in his word:

"By George! Do you know, Margaret, I shouldn't wonder if you had been robbed."

"Rupert!"

"That's what woke me--the feeling that someone was in the room, or, rather, had just gone out of it. I had an idea the door had just been shut. I had it so strongly that I got up and went out into the passage to see if there was anyone about. Then I heard a fine how-d'ye-do going on downstairs, and I went back into the room and switched on the light, and you woke up."

"Of course. Do you think I'm one of the Seven Sleepers? You'd have woke the dead. I asked what was the matter, and, instead of answering, you kept cramming yourself into your dressing-gown, and I could hardly credit my senses when, without a word, you rushed out of the room, and left me all alone."

"I'll bet a penny that somebody had been in the room, and that it wasn't fancy my thinking that someone had just shut the door. Where were your jewels?"

"They were in the case on the table."

"I'll lay a trifle that they're not there now. It looks very much as if the place had been plundered on a wholesale scale. What's that you said about Noel Draycott?"

This inquiry was addressed to the major, who explained to the best of his ability. The earl continued:

"I heard what seemed a jolly row going on downstairs--that's what brought me. But--could it have been Draycott? What could he have been having a row about, and with whom?"

A suggestion came from Sir Gerrard Ackroyd.

"He might have heard the thief, chased him, and have brought him to bay, and in the row which followed he might have got the worst of it. That sort of chap doesn't stick at trifles."

"But this is the most extraordinary thing of which I have ever heard: that anyone should have had the audacity to go into the bedrooms, one after the other. In each case it looks as if he knew just where the jewels were kept; and look at the risks he ran! Then he comes downstairs, and meets Draycott. Could Draycott have fired that shot?"

Again the question was addressed to the major.

"It could not have been. It was after we had found him lying dead that the shot was fired, and it was while we had gone to see who fired the shot that the body vanished."

"His body? You talk as if you were sure that he was dead, but was he?"

"I've had some experience of dead men. I ought to know one when I see him. I had an opportunity of examining him before Miss Forster came in. I should have been prepared to assert positively that he was dead, and I'm prepared to do so still. I do not believe that in such a matter I could have been so mistaken."

"But, my dear man, if he was lying dead upon the floor, he could not have picked himself up and walked away, could he?"

"Presumably not."

"Presumably! Did you ever hear of a dead man that did? Very well, then. And you say there wasn't time for anyone to come in and carry him off; and, mind you, it would have taken a good many minutes. Someone would have seen them, wouldn't they? The whole house was up and about by then. Two people can't walk about carrying a corpse without being noticed; and, even granting it, they must have planked him down somewhere. The only question is, where?"

"I should say that the thing to do is to go up to Mr. Noel Draycott's room, and see if he is in it--alive or dead."

This practical suggestion, which came from Sir Gerrard Ackroyd, was acted on then and there. Noel Draycott's room was empty. More, it seemed that it had never been occupied; at least, since he had dressed for the ball. There was a tweed suit, which he had exchanged for dress, lying just as it was extremely likely he had placed it. It was the same with all his other garments. There was nothing whatever unusual about the appearance of the room, nothing to show that anybody had entered it since its occupant had gone down to dance at the ball.

CHAPTER XVIII
In Bed

"Violet!" The Countess of Cantyre came dashing into Miss Forster's bedroom--the word "dashing" fairly describes her method of entry. "I have been robbed."

Miss Forster was in bed, though very far from asleep, or even inclined to slumber. She had been borne upstairs in the carrying chair, her foot had been bathed and bandaged by sympathetic hands, and she had been placed between the sheets. She was given stern injunctions that she was on no account to move; the doctor would be sent for at the earliest reasonable hour, and until his arrival she was not to move. But when her ladyship made that announcement, she sat up immediately.

"Margaret, you don't mean it?"

"Don't tell me that I don't mean it when I know that I do. I went straight to my room when I left you----"

"That's only ten minutes ago."

"The first thing I saw when I entered my room was my jewel-case lying on the floor. I had clean forgotten all about what Rupert had said till I saw it; really, I am not sure that I quite believe the stories that those other women have been telling; but when I saw it--there, of all places--of course, I dashed at it and--Violet, it was open, and it was empty; practically all the Avonham jewels have been walked off with."

Her ladyship, flouncing down on to a chair, presented quite a charming picture of feminine agitation.

"So Rupert is right?"

"Of course he is--that's the worst of it. He seldom is right, but when he is, it is nearly always when it would have been much better if he wasn't. While we were fast asleep in our beds, some dreadful creature must have had the incredible impudence to come into our room, and, under our very noses, walk off with everything. He has taken, from my room alone, nearly a quarter of a million's worth of jewels."

"Margaret!"

"Oh, it's all very well to say 'Margaret,' but I know he has. And the most maddening part of it is that to a certain extent it's my fault--as I shall be told before I'm very much older. I would have all the jewels out of the bank; between ourselves, I knew the duchess was going to wear her diamonds, and I had heard tales of what other people were going to wear. I've got diamonds as well as other people, and if I didn't wear them I meant to let them know it."

"You hadn't them on to-night."

"My dear, was it likely? I left that sort of thing to other people. But I meant to have my case down in the morning, and let those other people see what was in it. Talk about the Ditchling diamonds! You've never seen the Avonham diamonds, not the whole lot of them together, but they are--well, now they aren't, because they're stolen. And shan't I hear of it! Cantyre was quite unpleasant when I told him about having them all down here; in fact, he doesn't know that I did have them, and that's another thing. Oh, won't there be things said! I know I shall have to take to my bed for a month; it's only when I take to my bed that Cantyre thinks he's gone too far."

The excitable lady bounced up out of her chair and was trotting about the room--she was so very short that her longest steps could hardly be described as strides. Suddenly she stood still, and she turned to her friend.

"Violet--honour bright! What do you know about all this?"

Possibly it was because the assault was so unexpected that such a very singular look came on the young lady's face.

"Margaret! Whatever do you mean?"

"Oh, don't let's humbug each other any more, my dear! I was watching you downstairs, and I've been watching you all the while since, and I'm absolutely certain that before the duchess said a word about her having been robbed you knew she had been. Now, what do you know? I don't want to be horrid, and I'm not going to be, but you and I have been friends ever since we were tiny mites. You see what an awful hole I'm in. Not only have I been robbed myself, but practically all my guests--I do think if you can do anything to help me, you ought to. Now, don't trouble yourself to go in for denying; I know you through and through, just as you know me, but I'm perfectly convinced that you have some inkling into the meaning of what has taken place to-night--haven't you? On your honour. I know that your honour is as dear to you as to a man, and that what you say upon your honour that's the truth. You are silent."

And, indeed, the young lady was. Her excited hostess's sudden appeal seemed to have taken her singularly aback. The countess was quick to draw her own conclusions.

"My dear--you've answered me; I can see it on your face, in your eyes, as I've seen it all along--you do know something. Now, what do you know? I've helped you in more than one tight place, now you help me--a clean breast, my dear."

Thus assailed, the young lady made an obvious effort to evade the direct issue which the other was presenting, as if she were aiming a pistol at her head.

"Really, Margaret, to listen to you, one would think that I had stolen the jewels myself. Are you suggesting that I'm a thief? If so, pray don't beat about the bush; do be candid."

"No, Vi, you don't. I know how difficult it is to get from you a plain answer to a plain question, if you choose, but I'm going to get one now. It's not necessary for me to say that I don't think you stole the jewels yourself, but I do think that you've some sort of knowledge as to who did."

"Margaret!"

"It's no use your saying 'Margaret'--out with it."

"Out with what?"

"Vi, shall I have to shake you in spite of your bad foot? Have you any suspicion as to who stole my jewels? Answer me now--yes or no--on your honour."

"I shan't answer you."

"Thank you, you have answered me."

"I've not answered you, and I'm not going to. Margaret, will you please go away?"

The young lady laid herself down in bed, drew the clothes up over her shoulders, and turned her face from her friend. The countess observed her proceedings with something in her eyes, the meaning of which it was not easy to understand.

"Yes, my dear, I will go away, but that will make no difference to you--you'll feel as if I were at your bedside all the time; it will be worse for you than if I were. But I don't at all mind giving you an opportunity to think things over. You've told me something of what I want to know, and I rather fancy that when I see you again, you will tell me all the rest. Good-night, Vi; pleasant dreams; I hope that your foot won't keep you from sleeping. Shall I turn out these lights? You won't be able to sleep amidst all this illumination, and you've got that one over your bed."

The girl said nothing, but the lights went out; the one above her was not on, so that when the visitor had departed the room was in darkness.

Something kept Miss Forster from sleeping, and it was not her foot; it was her thoughts. The countess had prophesied truly: her going made no difference; she might as well have stayed, for all the peace she had left behind. What, the girl asked herself, as she lay there wrestling with the thoughts which banished sleep--what had she said; what had she admitted; what would she be made to admit when the countess could get at her again, before she was allowed to quit Avonham? What was more to the point--what had she to admit; what did she know?

That was where the iron entered into her soul, so that she hid her face on the pillow, and would have sobbed, only the tears refused to come. What did she not know? And, from what she knew, what did she not surmise? The leather bag in the old oak chest--what was in it? Did she not know as well as if the contents had been spread out in front of her? And it had been in Sydney's hand!

It was Sydney. She had tried to tell herself that it was not; that she had made a mistake; that there was a doubt about it; she could not be sure--how could she be sure when she had only seen him for an instant in a light which, after all, was no light at all? It was absurd to suppose that anyone could be certain, under such conditions, of another person's personality. Yet she was certain; she was sure.

It was Sydney; and it was he who was the thief. It was at this point that she dug her nails into the palms of her hands, and would have liked to tear her own heart out, and to have died.

It was Sydney who was the thief; it was his footstep she had heard hurrying past her room. By what odd chance had he not visited her? He had visited so many of the others. Could he have known which rooms it would be worth his while to visit, and which to leave alone?

Had he come to her--if he had!--with the leather bag in his hand, he would have found her still up. What a meeting that would have been!

It was not easy for her to reflect, but it was borne in upon her presently that this act of which he had been guilty was one of astounding daring. She had not gone to bed; others might have still been up; it was extraordinary that he had only gone to the rooms in which the people were asleep. How had he known--that they were asleep? The problem set her thinking.

She recalled the feeling she had had that she had not been the only person in the hall. If that was the case, who could that other person have been? It was not Sydney; she had distinctly heard him, as she believed, rushing from one of the rooms beyond. What had he been doing in there, and what was the explanation of the voice which, in its anguish, she had heard addressing him by name? Could it be he who had been quarrelling with Noel Draycott?

She did not dare to try to find an answer to that question; it had come upon her unawares--she did not dare to put it to herself again. She was a young woman of strong will--with all her might she put it from her. As it were, she passed her mind into another channel--she thought of the bag.

Two things occurred to her; the one was the almost uncanny feeling that she had had that she was being observed as she hid it in the chest; the other was a sudden hideous terror that if the bag was found, there might be something about it, in it, which would associate it with--its owner. This fear became all at once such a terrible, mastering obsession that it possessed her whole being; all else was banished from her tortured brain but that one thing--the bag. Suppose--suppose--something happened to the bag?

She would not risk it, she could not. The only chance she might have of getting it into her own keeping, where it would be safe, was--now. In the morning, in an hour or two, it would be too late. Servants would be about, then members of the household; she would never dare to go to that chest for the bag while a single soul was about. That would be impossible; that might be--to bring ruin to Sydney. She could not take the risk--she would not; the only thing to be done was that she should go and get it now.

She got out of bed to get it. She did not switch on the light. A grey gleam was coming through the sides of her blinds; the morning was come; there would be light enough for her to see. Her foot hurt, but it was not so painful as it had been; she could move on it, enough to serve her purpose. She got into her dressing-gown and she went to the door of her room.

CHAPTER XIX
The Two Women

Curiously quiet the house seemed to be as, in the cold, grey light, Violet Forster made the best of her way along the passage. At the head of the great staircase she paused; now it was possible to see; she wondered which was the stair on which, in the darkness, she had caught her heel in her draperies and stumbled. Her ankle was better, yet, in spite of the caution with which she descended, it gave her a twinge at every tread. How comfortless, how even ghostly the great hall seemed, as the first glimmer of the day came shimmeringly through the painted windows!

At the foot of the stairs she stopped--to listen. A curious quality which was in the air seemed to affect her nerves, which were already sufficiently highly strung; she was affected by the feeling which she had had in the darkness that there was someone in the hall already. She went out into it to look about her; there was no one to be seen, certainly nothing to be heard; she told herself that it was utter nonsense to suppose that anybody was watching her. It was not yet broad day, but there was light enough to render it difficult for anyone to keep from being seen, unless someone was cowering down behind one of the tall chairs, or hiding behind a hanging. She had a mind to search behind each piece of furniture, behind each curtain; she might have done it, too, had it not been that her foot rendered movement very far from easy. Ordinarily she would have peered into every nook and cranny in a dozen seconds; it might take her minutes as things were.

Realising that her doubts meant waste of time, she moved towards the chest under its velvet cover. She lifted the cover, had it nearly off, was about to raise the lid when--was that a sound? With one hand upon the velvet, the other on the chest, she stood and listened; this time her fancy was not playing her tricks, it was a sound. Someone was coming down the stairs, quickly, yet quietly--who could it be? On the instant she let the cover fall back into its place; with a rapidity of which a moment before she had not thought she could have been capable, she slipped behind a long curtain which hung against the wall, suspended to a rod, which could be moved at will so as to form a sort of cosy corner; but quick though her movements had been, they had not been at all too fast. No sooner was she behind the curtain than she became conscious that someone had come down into the hall, and had done as she had done--stopped to take a good look round. Then the footsteps began again; they seemed to be moving directly towards where she was; they were--she was sure they were each instant coming closer. She held her breath; what did it mean? Could she have been observed? Even if she had been, it seemed impossible that her retreat behind the curtain could have been noticed. And yet--the footsteps were making straight for where she was. Her impulse was to come out before she was discovered; she was about to do it, when the footsteps again were still.

A thought all at once occurred to her which diverted her mind into very different channels; was it possible that the new-comer's errand was the same as hers had been, with the old chest as an objective? That would mean that someone had been in the hall when Major Reith had switched on the single light; that her suspicions had been well founded, that there had been some interested watcher who had seen what she had put in the chest.

In that case the person who was within a foot or two of her, on the other side of the curtain, was probably the interested watcher. Whoever it was must be standing very close to the chest; was possibly, at that very moment, raising the velvet cover; would in a second or two have lifted the lid, and taken out the bag. What was she to do? It was a very knotty problem which so suddenly confronted Miss Forster in her hiding-place.

One thing seemed clear--that it was in the highest degree essential that she should know who it was with whom she had to deal. As matters stood the position was too one-sided. If her proceedings with the bag had been witnessed, then she had been recognised; but while her identity was known to someone, she had not the dimmest notion who that someone was. Since, in a sense, she was at someone's mercy, it was surely of the first importance that she should know whose. It might be--in an instant half a dozen different names flashed through her mind; any one of half a dozen persons might hold her--should it be written reputation?--in the hollow of a hand. The thought was unbearable. She must know with whom she had to deal; she would.

This presentation of the problem to her mind occupied a scarcely appreciable space of time; thoughts move quickly. To her it seemed longer than it was, for while she considered the position, what was being done on the other side of the curtain?

She heard something; when she had begun to raise the lid, she had been conscious that it creaked, though ever so slightly; that was a creaking she heard, which meant----

She did not stop to tell herself what it meant; there was an end of thinking; she decided before she knew it. Brushing the curtain aside, she stepped from behind it.

Whom she had expected to see she could not have said; she had told herself that it might be any one of half a dozen; yet when she saw who was there she knew it was the one she had expected.

A woman was bending over the chest; she had the velvet cover raised, and the lid an inch or two; she had come on the scene at what had been delicate moment for Violet Forster, and that young lady had returned the compliment in kind. She retained her presence of mind in a very creditable manner. One felt as one looked at her that she might be used to being found in delicate positions. She said nothing, but she never moved--she kept just still, and she looked Miss Forster in the face with eyes which betrayed no hint of nervousness. Even the scornful something which was in Miss Forster's tone when she did speak, did not seem to cause her the least discomfort.

"I thought it was you."

"Did you really?"

The thing was said so demurely that it was hard to tell from the tone alone if the intention was to be impertinent.

"What are you doing there?"

"I was just going to see what it was that I saw you put in this chest last night."

"So you did see? I thought that also--I begin to understand."

There was something in the girl's tone which the other seemed to resent.

"I confess I don't; but I hope to presently. Pray, miss, what do you begin to understand?"

"You were in league with him last night; you were--his confederate."

"His confederate, Miss Forster! What do you mean? With whom was I in league?"

"Oh, you do it very well; I've no doubt that this is the sort of thing in which practice has made you perfect. Now I understand how you came to be in possession of my locket."

The woman seemed to have a trick of repeating the girl's words.

"How I came to be in possession of your locket? I don't understand, Miss Forster, what you are talking about; will you please to make yourself plainer? I never did like insinuations."

"Was he concealed in the house last night, or did you let him in? But you must have seen him earlier in the day, or you could hardly have had the locket when you did."

It was a second or two before the other answered; when she did, it was in a tone which hinted resentment at Miss Forster's manner.

"I don't understand you, Miss Forster, but I should like you to understand me clearly. I was awakened early this morning by hearing someone running along the passage outside my room. Thinking someone might be ill, I got up to see if I could be of any use; I just caught sight of the skirt of a woman, who seemed to be running for all she was worth. And I heard a queer noise coming from downstairs; I waited, thinking it would stop, but as it continued, and kept getting queerer, I thought I would go down and see what was the matter. I came down in the hall here, and it was pitch dark; there wasn't a sound, and I was more than half afraid, and told myself I was a fool for coming. Then I heard someone coming down the staircase as if he didn't want to be heard. I said to myself that what was going on was probably no business of mine, and I tried to get away; but before I had a chance, someone came down into the hall, passing me so close that her skirts touched me as she passed."

Miss Forster interposed.

"I had a feeling all the while that there was someone there, but my ankle was so painful that all I could think of was finding something to lean upon."

"Of course I didn't know who it was----"

"I suppose not."

"How could I? The feel of the skirts told me it was a woman, and I fancied from the way she moved, that she must have hurt herself; but I couldn't see, and though I don't mind owning that I wondered what was up, I didn't want to be caught in what looked like prying, though no idea of doing anything of the kind had entered my head, and my one wish was to get quietly away. Then something did happen which took my breath away."

"What was that? I should imagine you are not the kind of person whose breath is easily taken away."

"I heard someone, who, I had no doubt, was a man from the noise he made, come rushing along, though I couldn't think from where. I heard him go rushing towards the someone who had just passed me, and I heard him speak to her."

"That's a lie, not a word was spoken."

"Then if that's so, I must have dreamt it, and it's one of the funniest dreams I ever had; because I thought I heard him say, 'Here it is, take it. Look out--there's someone coming!' In my dream I heard him say it as plainly as I hear myself speaking now."

"Each word you utter makes me understand you more clearly."

"That's what I want you to do, miss; to understand me. Then off this whoever it was went tearing, and along came somebody else, who turned on one of the lights, and I saw it was a tall, middle-aged gentleman, with a moustache. I got down behind a chair, so that I couldn't hear quite all that you said to each other; then he went off, and you took something which was under a cushion on the seat of the chair by which you were. I could see that it was a leather bag, and I said to myself, 'That's what that other party gave her,' who I'd heard speaking in my dream. You put the bag in the chest by which I am standing, and when you went after that tall gentleman, I wondered what it was; but, as I've said, it wasn't any business of mine, and I didn't like to take the liberty of looking."

"I appreciate the feelings by which you were actuated."

"But when, as I did later, I heard about all that lot of jewellery which had been stolen from the different ladies' rooms, that set me thinking. Miss Forster, would you mind my seeing what is in the bag which you put inside this chest, which you came downstairs to give the man I never saw a chance of passing on to you? Do you mind?"

The woman stood with her hand resting on the chest as if she waited for the girl's permission to raise the lid.

"I perceive," said Miss Forster, "now, for the first time, what a dangerous woman you really are. Do you actually suppose me to be so simple as to be taken in by your acting?"

"Explain yourself, Miss Forster, as plainly as I've explained myself to you. If you'll excuse my saying so, I'm only a servant, but I've got my character to lose--there's something in your tone that I don't like."

"What was your last situation, Jane Simmons?"

"Never you mind what was my last situation, but I was in it for seven years, and a seven years' character is good enough for anyone."

"You expect me to believe that also?"

"I don't care what you believe. May I see what's in the bag that you put inside this chest?"

"Am I also expected to believe that you don't know from whom that bag came?"

"I know it was a man, but who he was I know no more than a babe unborn. Am I to see what's in it, or would you like me to ring the bell and let others have a look?"

"Can't you realise what a foolish game you're playing? You're seeming to suggest that I was associated with what I have no doubt was an act of wholesale robbery; I know that you were."

"You know that I was what?"

"You call yourself Jane Simmons, but I don't suppose that that's your name; you probably assumed it when you entered this house."

"Well, I never did."

"You talk about being seven years in one situation. I doubt if you ever did any honest work in your life. I believe you to be a thief, and the associate of thieves; I have no doubt that what took place last night was carefully planned by you and your confederates; and you have the assurance to stand there and pretend that you think that I was associated with it, in any way whatever."

"Oh, that's it, is it? Now you have spoken plain, now I do understand what you are driving at. Miss Forster, I will rouse the household, and I'm going to tell them what I saw you do; and you'll be able to explain, if you're as innocent as you're trying to make out, why you hid that there bag inside this chest, and who it was that gave it to you; then we'll see."

"We shall. My record is known to every person in this house; I'll have careful inquiries made into yours--you will be able to give details about that situation in which you stayed for seven years; how you will come out of such an inquiry, you know better than I. You foolish woman! To think that sheer impudence will enable you to win at such a game of bluff; don't you know perfectly well that the attempt to fasten your guilt on me will make matters much worse for you?"

For some seconds there was silence; the woman by the chest seemed to be summing Miss Forster up. She did not change countenance, the smile did not fade from her eyes; yet, somehow, something seemed to have fallen from her; she seemed to have ceased to play the part of servant, and to have become a different creature altogether. When she spoke again it was very quietly, coldly, as if she were measuring the meaning of each word before she allowed it to pass her lips.

"Suppose, Miss Forster, that I do not alarm the household, what then?"

"I am afraid that I don't quite grasp your meaning."

"Oh, I'll make it plain enough; you and I had better be plain with each other--it will be good for both of us. There's a leather bag inside this chest; what's going to become of it?"

"It depends on what it contains."

"Oh, you know what it contains; there's jewels in that bag worth fortunes."

"And you ask me what is to become of it; you have that courage?"

"I even have courage to ask it again; if I don't alarm the household, what is to become of that bag?"

"Its contents will be returned to their various owners."

"By whom?"

"By me."

"Oh, I see; and where do I come in?"

"I rather fancy that will be a point for the consideration of the police."

"Oh, that's what you fancy, is it? Now again we are beginning to understand each other. Does that mean that you're going to give me away? If it does, let me beg you to be careful; you'll be giving yourself away much more than you'll be giving me; just think."

"Are you now suggesting that I have been in collusion with you?"

The woman smiled as if the question had been a funny one; the girl could not but see that the smile became her, and that she was not ill-looking.

"Hardly; I can assure you that you are not the sort of person I should choose as a partner if I wanted one; but I was serious when I said to you 'Just think.' For instance, you saw the person who came rushing into the hall last night, and unwillingly left in your charge that leather bag; you have to think of that. You recognised him, didn't you?"

"Who told you so?"

"He did."

The girl started; for the first time something which the other had said had gone home.

"When did he tell you?"

"I didn't time it, but I should say about a minute afterwards."

"Then you saw him again?"

The woman raised her eyebrows, as if with a faint surprise.

"Of course I did. I went straight to where he was; I knew where to find him. The first thing he said to me was, 'Vi Forster saw me.'"

"He said that to you?"

"His very words. I said to him, 'You don't mean that she recognised you?' 'She did,' he said. 'Then,' I said, 'we're in the soup.' 'She's got the bag,' he groaned; I could see that that was what worried him more than the recognition. Then something happened which turned his attention in another direction. You know as well as I do that the man who came into the hall with the bag, which he dropped on to the seat of that chair in his surprise at the sight of you, was Sydney Beaton."

CHAPTER XX
The Leather Bag

The girl had known it, but there was something brutal in the way the woman said it which affected her almost as if she had thrown something in her face; she shrank back-- shivered. The woman seemed to be enjoying her obvious discomfiture; she smiled, as if the joke had grown still funnier.

"You see, that's what made me say that you had better think. Suppose you do give me away; after all, I'm not the person whom you saw in possession of the bag, and you did see someone. That someone was a gentleman friend, whose name, I am sure, you don't want to have shouted from the house-tops. Now do you?"

The girl seemed to be reflecting; her cheeks had grown whiter, trouble had come into her eyes; her bearing was in striking contrast to that of the woman in front of her, who could not have seemed to be more completely at her ease.

"How long have you known him?"

"Oh, some time. We've been in one or two little matters together, out of which we have done very well."

"You mean that this is not the first time, that he has done this sort of thing?"

"Gracious, no; he has been in the business quite a time; but I'm not going to give him away, never fear."

She laughed right out, while the girl winced.

"Where is he to be found?"

"I beg your pardon."

"I asked where is he to be found?"

"And you may ask; do you suppose I'd tell you? What, for you to give him away? He'd get--well, he'd get penal servitude for this alone; and then there's that Captain Draycott, or whatever is the name, to whom he owed one."

Again Miss Forster shivered; she glanced about her, as if fearful that the other's words had been overheard.

"What do you mean--about--Captain Draycott?"

"Why, of course you know it was he who did it; you don't want me to tell you that. You know what cause he had; it was he who put him in the cart at that little game of cards."

One could see that Violet Forster made an effort at self-control; but the hideous picture conjured up by the other's careless words was too much for her. She put her hands up to her face; she sank on to a chair, so helpless before the stress of emotion which seemed to be raging within that she sat swaying to and fro. The woman, still smiling, stood and watched; then she said, her voice seeming to be broken by laughter:

"Why, I never thought that you'd take on like this, if you really are taking on, and it isn't put on for my special benefit; it can't be any news to you, you must have known. You saw the man lying dead there; you knew the cause he'd given--the person whose name we won't mention--to out him. What's all the fuss about? This sort of thing won't improve your looks, you know."

If the woman paused expecting Miss Forster to speak, she paused in vain; the agony which seemed to be tearing at the very sources of her being had bereft her of the powers of speech. The spectacle she presented, instead of moving the other to sympathy, seemed to divert her thoughts into channels of bitterness. The smile passed from her face; her tone became hard.

"What has Sydney Beaton to do with you that you should take on like this about him? Let me tell you something about him, which may be a piece of genuine news. If anyone ought to take on about him, it is I, since I'm his wife."

There was silence; then the girl did begin to regain some vestiges of self-control. She ceased to sway to and fro; the dry sobs which seemed to be rending her bosom grew less insistent; she withdrew her hands from her eyes, she looked the speaker steadily in the face.

"That I do not believe."

The words were uttered with an air of quiet conviction which the other resented.

"What don't you believe?"

"I do not believe that you are Sydney Beaton's wife; your statement that you are makes me doubt all that you have said. I am sure that you are not his wife; I believe him to be incapable of marrying such a creature as you. He may have sunk low, but I do not think that he could ever fall quite so low as that. The fact that you have told me that one great lie makes it obvious that you have probably told me others; I doubt that he is the kind of person you make him out to be."

"Oh, you doubt it, do you? Very well. Then rouse the household; they'll soon be getting up without your doing anything to rouse them; hand over the bag and tell your story--give me into custody if you like. Unless you perjure yourself, and I don't think you'll do that, you haven't one shred of evidence against me, as you're perfectly aware. All the evidence you have is against my husband; you could send him to penal servitude. I daresay you could hang him if you set your heart on it; but--I really don't see what good that will do you. By the time the whole story is told, you'll be in almost as bad a mess as he will be, and you know it."

"You steal to get money; I'll give you an opportunity of getting money without stealing. I want to be placed in immediate communication with--the person you know; for what sum of money will you tell me where he is to be found?"

"How much will I take to sell him, that's what you mean!"

"I mean nothing of the kind--and you know it well enough. I simply wish to have an interview with him."

"What good do you expect to get from that?"

"That's my affair."

"Oh, is it? You seem to be forgetting that he is my husband."

"I'm not. No harm will come to him, or to you, even if he occupies the position towards you which you say he does."

"Tell me plainly just what it is you want me to do."

"Give me an opportunity of having an interview with him in the next twenty-four hours, or at the earliest possible moment, and I will give you any sum, in reason, you like to ask."

"You're a fool--you must excuse me speaking plainly, but you are. Even supposing your intentions are all that you pretend they are, can't you see for yourself what harm you'd be doing him? You don't know much about the ways and dodges of the police, that's pretty plain. Now--well, now, you know nothing--to speak of; and particularly you don't know where he is, if anyone was to ask you, and mind you, it's quite possible that someone will before very long. But if you were to see him, and were to get out of him anything of what I'm dead sure you would try to get, then the situation would be changed altogether. As things are, no one can do anything to you, even if you do hold your tongue, because you don't know anything, whatever you may--well, we'll say suspect. But have you ever heard of an accessory after the fact? If you got anything out of him of what you'd try to get, that's what you'd be, an accessory after the fact, if you didn't give him away straight off; and with the best will in the world you wouldn't find it so easy not to do that as you suppose. No, take my word for it, Miss Forster, this is a case, if you don't know it, in which your ignorance is his bliss, and, for both your sakes, it would be folly for you to be wise."

"All of which means----?"

"It means that you'll get no information out of me concerning a certain person who happens to be my husband, if you were to give me all the money you have. Now we'll drop the subject, if you please; time is passing. You don't want to have all Avonham interrupting our tête-à-tête. What's going to happen to this bag? It's his bag. As you pretend to have some sort of feeling about him, and I know he is an old friend of yours, why don't you go back upstairs to bed, and keep from interfering in what, after all, is no concern of yours? I give you my personal assurance that there isn't so much as a ha'p'orth of anything in that bag that belongs to you. For his sake what you don't want is a fuss; he'll never forget the debt he owes you if you keep from making one; you may be the death of him if you do; let me give you my arm to help you up the stairs."

"Let me invert the proposition--you go upstairs, and leave me here."

"And take the bag with me?"

"Empty."

"What will you do with what's inside?"

"The entire contents will be returned to the Countess of Cantyre."

"And if the Countess of Cantyre asks questions?"

"What is that that someone says about the Countess of Cantyre asking questions?"

The inquiry came from the staircase just above them. Before either of them could move, or speak, a small figure came running into the hall. It was the Countess of Cantyre herself.

"Violet!" she exclaimed, "what on earth are you doing here? And--who are you?" The last inquiry was addressed to the woman; but, without waiting for an answer, her ladyship continued: "Do you know, Violet, I couldn't sleep; I haven't had one single wink of sleep, and at last I couldn't stay in bed any longer, I had to come to you. I had a feeling that you mightn't be getting much sleep either; but I didn't expect to find your bed empty, especially considering the state that your foot was in when I saw you last. I prowled about to see what had become of you, and then I heard voices down here, and perhaps now, Violet, you will tell me what this new and most extraordinary behaviour of yours may mean, and who is this woman?"

"This woman," Miss Forster replied, "is the person who calls herself Jane Simmons."

"And pray what may Jane Simmons be doing here, at this hour of the morning, with you?"

"If you please, my lady," replied Jane Simmons, "I heard Miss Forster in the hall, and knowing that she had hurt her foot, I came down to see if I could be of any use to her."

Nothing could have been more becoming to a person of her station than her manner of saying this. Her ladyship eyed her askance.

"Is that so? Well, Violet, has she been of any use to you?"

"None whatever."

"Then, Jane Simmons, I should think that you could go."

The woman went, swiftly, noiselessly, with downcast eyes, across the hall, towards the service stairs. When she was out of sight, she turned towards the direction in which they were; she did not look pleased, and she said, quite loudly enough to have been audible to anyone who might have been standing near:

"I've as good as half a mind to get him hanged, to spite the two of you."

The countess, in the hall, regarded her friend; it was now much lighter, so that it was easy to see how white and worn the girl was looking. It is possible that the consciousness of the pallid face beside her softened the asperity which the lady had meant to mark her tone. She just spoke two words, in the form of a question.

"Well, Vi?"

Miss Forster's reply was still briefer; she merely echoed the other's first word. "Well?"

Her ladyship waited; the girl continued still.

"Is that all you have to say to me?"

Miss Forster sighed, the long-drawn sigh of the sick at heart. Her tone was in tune with the sigh.

"Margaret, if I were to start telling you all there is to tell--and I am so tired. I feel as if I hadn't slept for years, and as if I should never sleep again."

Her ladyship's tone was practical.

"That's all very well, my dear; I can see you're not feeling yourself, but don't you think you ought to tell me something?"

"I'll do better than tell you, since actions speak louder than words."

Miss Forster raised the blue velvet cover, and she opened the chest, this time without interruption; from within she took a brown leather bag and held it out to the countess, who observed it with doubtful eyes.

"What bag is that?"

"Take it and see."

The countess took it, a little gingerly, as if she feared that unpleasant consequences might come from touching it.

"Vi, what are you playing at? Whose is this bag, and how did it get into that chest, and why have you given it to me, and what is in the thing?"

"I cannot tell you quite, as I've only seen the outside of the bag, and that for a moment only, but I can guess what it contains."

"Then it's not yours?"

The girl shook her head.

"Then why have you given it to me?"

"I fancy, if you look inside, its contents will supply the answer."

"But whose bag is it?"

"That I cannot tell you."

"But what right have you to give me permission to look into a bag that certainly doesn't belong to you?"

"Don't be silly, Margaret; I fancy its contents will explain why you should not stand on foolish points of etiquette; open it."

The countess did as she was bid--then broke into exclamation.

"Why, Vi, whatever is all this?"

"That's what I want to know."

"It looks as if it were a diamond necklace."

"I shouldn't be surprised if there were more than one."

"Vi, it's stuffed with them!"

"I thought so; I fancy, when you come to make inquiries, that you will find all those precious things whose loss your guests are bemoaning."

"Was it Jane Simmons who took them?"

"That is a subject on which I would rather you asked me no questions; I cannot answer them."

"But, my dear child, what reason have you for screening her?" Miss Forster merely shook her head. "But in the face of this you can't expect to be allowed to take up an attitude of silence. What explanation am I to give?"

"Give any explanation you choose; you'll find that the people will be too glad to have their things restored to bother you with questions."

"That's all you know; each one of those women will insist on knowing how I was able to restore them, and if I can't give a satisfactory answer they'll begin to think unpleasant things of me. I must tell them something--what am I to tell them? Am I to tell them that I found them in a leather bag which you handed over as if it were a cup of tea? If I do, then for the history of the bag they'll refer to you."

"Then they'll not get it. I'm very sorry, Margaret, but if you knew how I feel you'd let me off, at least for a while; talk to me later on. Mayn't I go upstairs, and try to get a little sleep? I believe that if I could I'd be better able to talk to you than I am now."

Shutting her eyes, the girl pressed her fingers against the lids as if they ached with weariness. The countess did show some signs of sympathy.

"My poor dear Violet, do get between the sheets, and get all the sleep you can; sleep the clock round, if you like. Is your foot still bad? Shall I come up and help you into bed?"

"No, thank you, Margaret; my foot isn't all that I could wish it to be, but I think I can manage. If you only knew how much I want to be alone!"

There was a pathetic something in the girl's voice which touched the other's heart; there was such a ring of sincerity in the expression of her desire to be alone.

She suffered the girl to go, so conscious of her wish to escape the scrutiny of even friendly eyes that she did not turn to look at her. When the pit-pat of her slippered feet had died away, her ladyship said to herself, with rueful visage:

"That girl's in a mood for anything; I'm not sure that I was wise to let her go alone; but how could I thrust myself upon her craving for solitude? I only hope she'll do nothing worse than she's done already. Now, who's that? Is she coming back again, or is it Jane Simmons? Those steps belong to neither--that's Rupert; he's found out that I'm missing, and he's coming dashing after me."

The lady's surmise proved to be correct; someone was "dashing" after her, two or three stairs at a time--a gentleman who, rushing out into the hall, looked about him; then, espying her, exclaimed:

"Margaret! You little wretch! If you only knew what a fright you gave me. What the dickens made you get out of bed, out of the room, at this time of the morning and slip down here?"

"Business."

"Business! What in thunder do you mean by business?"

The gentleman approached close to the lady's side; she was looking up at him with the demurest smile.

"Rupert, I've had a dream."

"You've had a what? What's that you're holding?"

"That's the dream."

"The dream? What are you talking about--it's a bag."

"Precisely, it is a bag, and the bag's the dream."

She observed him with a look in her big, wide open eyes which made them seem almost as if they were a child's.

"Are you dreaming still, or am I?"

She replied to his question with another.

"Rupert, do you always believe every word I say?"

"Well"--he made a sound as if he might have been clearing his throat--"that depends."

"At least you must believe every word I am going to tell you now; you hear, Rupert, you must. You know what those people said last night about the things they had lost?"

"Am I likely to have forgotten? Am I ever likely to forget?"

"Rupert--now this is the part which you have to believe--I dreamt that all those things were in a leather bag which was in this chest."

"Great Cæsar's ghost!"

"The dream was so real that, when I woke, I had to come downstairs to see if it was true--and it was."

"You don't mean it!"

"There is the chest; in it was this bag; and in the bag I do believe are all the jewels which were lost--including my own. Isn't that--wonderful?"

"It's more than wonderful, young woman, it's----"

She put her small hand up to his lips and stopped him, commenting on his sentence as if it had been finished.

"I quite agree with you, Rupert, it is delightful; nothing more fortunate could possibly have happened."

CHAPTER XXI
An Envelope

What the various ladies who had spent the night at Avonham thought when their presence was desired in Lady Cantyre's boudoir, and they found spread out upon a table an amazing assemblage of triumphs of the jeweller's art, and the countess told them that story about the dream and the bag, was not quite clear. Because, in telling her tale, the countess made it plain, not only that criticism was not invited, but also that questions would be resented, and, more, not answered.

When each lady was requested to choose her own property there ensued an animated scene. It was a regrettable fact that discussion actually arose as to who was the owner of certain trinkets. There were three diamond brooches; three ladies had lost a diamond brooch; the question arose as to which of those brooches belonged to each of them; before it was solved some very undesirable things had been said, and worse had been hinted. Nor was that the only instance of the kind; there were a couple of diamond pendants over which two ladies nearly came to blows. As one of them was unmistakably much the better of the two, it is difficult to evade the conclusion that one of them must have been a conscious liar, and, it is to be feared, even more than that.

The countess, when her guests would let her, was content to look on and smile; only when she could not help it did she essay the part of peacemaker. Although the choosing of each one's property ought to have been the simplest thing in the world, it would seem, when the task of selection was done, as if no one lady was on the best of terms with any other; a fact on which it is inconceivable that the countess had calculated as likely to prevent any undesirable discussion of her story of the dream.

"They can talk as much as they like about it afterwards," the countess had said to her husband, "but they won't have a chance of talking to me; because you and I are going for a yachting cruise which will occupy us all the spring and summer."

"What! Aren't you going to spend the season in town?"

"I am not."

"But you've had the house done up, and--no end!"

"Rupert, my health will not permit it. You are going to wire to your captain man to have the yacht ready to-morrow. I am going to see Sir James Jeffreys, and he is going to order me on board at once, because I must have sea air, and Violet Forster is coming with us."

"Is she--is that because that ankle of hers must have sea air too?"

"Surely you must be aware that there is nothing so restful to an injured ankle as the sort of life one leads on board a yacht. Please send your wire, or shall I?"

This conversation took place before the lady and gentleman had yet quitted their own apartment; he was dressed, and she had dismissed her maid. When she said that about the wire he began to snap his thumb-nail against his teeth, which was a trick he had when he was worried.

"Aren't you forgetting one thing? It's all very well for you to have a dream about that blessed bag, but I can't have a dream about that fellow Draycott. I can't start off yachting while that's in the wind."

The lady was standing, with her hands behind her back, looking down with a contemplative air at the toe of her tiny shoe as it peeped from under the hem of her dress.

"I don't see why not. Our Easter ball has not been, in all respects, the success I had hoped it would be, and usually is; but I don't see what is to be gained by your hanging about while somebody is looking into that very unpleasant affair. Indeed, it seems in itself to be a sufficient reason why you should go yachting."

The gentleman was still worriedly clicking his thumb-nail.

"It's all very well for you to talk, but things are not going to be so easy for me as they've been for you. I tell you I can't dream about a bag; I don't at all suppose that I shall be able to get away with anything like decency--not what you would call get away--for, at any rate, some days to come."

"Very well, then Violet and I will go alone; we will chaperone each other; and you will join us when you can. I presume you don't suggest that it is necessary that I should stay?"

His lordship pulled a rueful face.

"It certainly isn't necessary, because I don't suppose you'll be able to do anything, but----" He gave a little groan. "Well, I expect you're right, and after all perhaps you'd better go, and, of course, if you like, take Vi with you; she'll be a companion. I shouldn't wonder--I've a feeling in my bones that there will be a fuss made about Noel Draycott; and if there is, you'd certainly better be out of it. Upon my word, I wish we'd never had this ball; I've a kind of a sort of a feeling that the Easter ball at Avonham is going to bulk rather largely in the public eye; I see myself figuring in the public prints, and I certainly don't want to have you there. I'll wire to Slocock right away."

Captain Slocock was the officer in command of the Earl of Cantyre's well-known steam yacht *Sea Bird*.

The prophet was justified, there was a fuss; nothing had yet been heard of Mr. Draycott. It became a moot point whether something ought not to have been done in the matter, even in the dead of the night; it might, more than one person in the establishment became presently aware, become a very awkward subject for unpleasant future comment.

His lordship's point of view was easy to grasp; there really had been nothing to show that anything serious had happened.

Scandal was the thing most to be avoided; if the police had been called in, there would have had to be a scandal, and nothing might have suited Noel Draycott less. There might, his lordship put it, have been a discussion between Noel Draycott and, say, someone else, of a strictly personal kind, in which Draycott might have got the worst of it. It was a most regrettable incident, that such a thing should have occurred at Avonham, on the night of the Easter ball. Mr. Draycott owed an apology to his hosts and their guests; he would be called to a severe account at the very first possible moment.

Of course, Major Reith had been under a misapprehension. In the first shock of his surprise at finding the man in such a dreadful condition on the floor, he jumped to the not unnatural conclusion that he was dead, which, though natural, was absurd. Who had ever heard of a dead man picking himself up and taking himself off? Which was what Noel Draycott had done.

Where he had taken himself to was another story. He was not at the barracks, as they had learned on the telephone, but then it was hardly likely that he would be there. In that discussion with someone else, he had been pretty badly knocked about; the major's story made that clear. He would doubtless be ashamed of himself; there was probably something not nice at the back of it all. He would probably have preferred to take his broken head somewhere where there was a chance of his wounds being healed without their ever coming to the knowledge of his brother officers. What had to be ascertained was the hiding-place in which he had taken shelter.

And here something a trifle awkward cropped up; it seemed possible that he had never been either at Avonham or in that part of the country before. Then, in his state, at that hour of the night, for what quarter could he have set out, and how?

The presumption was that he had got out of the window, and shut it after him, which was in itself to presume a good deal; but as it seemed impossible that he could have gone wandering about the house--they had searched it from cellar to basement, to make sure that he was not hidden in it somewhere--he could have gone no other way. But after he had got out of the window, what then? In his then state, in the darkness, in a strange place, for what goal could he have been aiming?

The obvious answer seemed to be, none. He could not have had any cut-and-dried scheme formulated in his brain. The probability was that he had gone wandering, aimlessly, on. Then, in that case, he could scarcely have gone far; not beyond the park which extended for vast spaces about the house; he would never have found the way, even if he had been able to go the distance.

The conclusion therefore was that Noel Draycott must be somewhere within the precincts of the park, so search parties were sent off in all directions to look for him. There were quite a number of houses in the park; inquiries were made at each of these without result. One small fact did leak out, if it could be called a fact. At one of the keepers' cottages, a small child, a girl of eleven or twelve, declared that she had been awakened in the night by the noise made by a motor-car. If the child's tale was true, then it must have been after half-past three in the morning, probably after four. Her father had been kept up by the ball at the house; he had had something to do with expediting the departing guests. It was half-past three when he went home; the child was then awake, had spoken to him. She said that after her father had left her she fell asleep, and was disturbed by the motor-car; the cars and carriages, she said, had been waking her up all through the night. No one could trace that motorcar, whose it was. At that hour what could it have been doing there? The last vehicle had borne away the latest guests long before then. No one seemed to have observed the hour, but it was probably about that time that Major Reith had found Noel Draycott lying on the floor--to lose him directly afterwards. Had the belated motor-car, which that small girl asserted she had heard, anything to do with the loss?

It was not an easy question to answer.

The problem which the Earl of Cantyre, and in a lesser degree, his friend, had to solve, was, what was to be done? Should they wait for news of Noel Draycott, emanating probably from himself, or should communication be made with the police? The latter all the parties seemed to be most unwilling to do. It meant publicity. The news that the police had been summoned to Avonham would be flashed all over England inside an hour. It was just the spicy sort of tale the public would like. "Strange Occurrence in a Nobleman's Mansion": the earl could see that sort of headline staring at him from the principal news-page of a dozen different journals. "The Avonham Mystery"--that was the kind of title which some inspired journalist would fit to a commonplace, vulgar, sordid incident.

No, thank you. His lordship decided that he would not risk that sort of thing until compelled by circumstances. He would have inquiries set on foot, in a quiet way, in every possible direction; if nothing came of them it would be time to speak to the police.

One small, yet curious occurrence did, however, induce in him a momentary qualm of doubt as to whether it was really the wisest course which he was pursuing.

They had been talking in the hall--the amount of talk which was got through at Avonham that morning was beyond credibility. The earl was just marching off to his own particular sanctum, wishing with all his heart that the people would go, and that there might be peace, when he saw in the hand of a bronze figure which stood on a pedestal--an envelope. It was so placed that he could not help but notice it; as he came along it caught him full in the eye. He had passed that figure only a minute or two before; the envelope had not been there then, or he would certainly have seen it. He took it from the fingers of the outstretched hand. It was inscribed, in Roman letters which had been formed with a soft pen, "To the Earl of Cantyre."

He glanced around; no one was in sight who seemed likely to have put it there. It struck him, even in that moment of irritation, as a little odd. He tore it open. Within was a sheet of his own notepaper. On it, again in Roman letters, formed with the same soft pen, was written:

"Who stole the Ditchling diamonds?
"Sydney Beaton.
"Who killed Noel Draycott?
"Sydney Beaton.
"If in doubt apply for information to Violet Forster."

His lordship had but time to get a cursory glance at these singular questions and answers, when his wife, coming along with the Duchess of Ditchling beside her, snatched the piece of paper from his hand; it was done with a laugh, but it was none the less a snatch.

"My dear boy," she cried, "what have you got there which makes you pull such faces?"

She glanced at the paper she had captured--and her countenance was changed. Something was flashed to each other by the married couple's two pairs of eyes. Then the countess crushed the sheet of paper in her hand, and, without a word to her husband, went on with the duchess.

CHAPTER XXII
The Countess and Violet

Miss Forster's bedroom door was gently opened, and the Countess of Cantyre went softly in. She closed the door as gently as she had opened it, and, remaining motionless, looked inquiringly about her. All was still. The curtains had not yet been drawn. In the apartment, despite its size, was the stuffy smell which comes to a bedroom when the windows have not been opened through the night. Her ladyship, crossing the room, drew the curtains and threw the windows wide open. It was a lovely day; the clean, fresh air came pouring in. The room looked on to the park, over a waving expanse of green which stretched as far as the eye could reach. She stood for a moment to enjoy the glory of the morning.

"That's better," she said out loud. Then she turned to the bed.

Miss Forster's form was dimly outlined beneath the clothes. She had not moved when her visitor entered, or even when the windows were thrown open. She was either sleeping very soundly or she refused to allow herself to notice what was going on.

The countess, going to the side of the bed towards which her face was turned, stood waiting for her to show some signs of life. Presently there was a slight movement beneath the clothes, and a faint voice inquired:

"Who's that?"

"You know very well who it is."

"Margaret, is that you?"

"You know very well it's me. Who but me would take the liberty of coming into your room, drawing the curtains and opening the windows and letting in the air? If you only knew what an atmosphere you've been living in! Do you always sleep with your windows closed?"

The only answer was a sound which might have meant anything, followed by a movement beneath the clothes.

"How's the foot?"

"It seems better." The words were whispered rather than spoken.

"How are you?"

"I'm all right."

"You don't sound as if you were all right. What's become of your voice? And, if you are all right, what are you doing in bed at this hour of the day?"

"I was just going to get up."

"Were you? That's good news. There were no immediate signs of it that I could see. Vi, you and I are going yachting."

"Going what?"

"Yachting. I said yachting. Do you want me to shout? We are leaving here to-day; we are starting on the *Sea Bird* to-morrow for wherever Captain Slocock likes to take us; you and I alone together."

"Are we?"

"Yes, we are. Is that the dying-duck-in-a-thunderstorm sort of fashion in which you take my surprising piece of information? Move some of those bedclothes and let me see your face, or, if you won't, I will."

Her ladyship did. It was a white, wan face which looked out at her from between the sheets, so white and so wan that her ladyship was quite startled.

"Vi, what do you mean by telling me you're all right? You look like a ghost."

"I wish I were."

"What does the child mean! Whatever for?"

"If I were a ghost I should be dead."

"I see, that's it; and a good, sound, healthy idea, especially for a young woman who is scarcely more than a child."

Her ladyship, drawing forward a big arm-chair, placed herself, not on the seat, but on the back; her feet she placed on the seat. She was such a small person that if she had occupied the position which people usually do upon a chair, Violet, on her high spring mattress, would have been above the level of her head, and she, for the purpose she had in view, at a disadvantage. Balanced on the top of the back of the chair, she was at least on a level with the girl in the bed.

"Vi, I am going to talk to you. I wish I'd been made a foot longer; then I shouldn't be forced to take positions on furniture which people were never meant to take. You're going to tell me all about it. You and I have had our share of troubles in our time, and we've always made a clean breast of them to each other. Now start confessing to me."

"It's easy for you to talk."

"Of course it is; and it will be easy for you when you've once got going."

"You don't understand."

"Oh, yes, I do. Sydney Beaton was here last night."

"Margaret! How do you know?" The girl threw the bedclothes off for herself, starting up from her pillow. "Has that wretch told you?"

Her ladyship regarded the girl attentively; then shook her dainty head.

"No one has told me anything. I just guessed, though perhaps you've told me as much as you very well could."

"I told you? What do you mean?"

"My dear Vi, consider. Could your conduct have been more suggestive? Don't I know you? Aren't I aware that you're the coolest, calmest, most levelheaded of young women? Do you suppose that you acted up to that character last night? My dear Vi, something was wrong with you, so wrong that it had turned the girl I knew into one I didn't. What could it be? We know all about each other that there is to know, so that I knew that there was only one thing which could have on you such a dire effect. How did you know that leather bag was in that chest? Mind you, I'm not asking a question; I'm not trying to force your confidence; I'm only putting it to you if it isn't obvious that there was only one conclusion I could draw?"

The girl was sitting up in bed, white-faced, wild-eyed.

"Then, now you know why I wished that I was a ghost."

Again her ladyship observed her closely, her head a little on one side.

"Aren't you--doesn't it occur to you as being just barely possible that you're a goose?"

"Why am I a goose?"

"May I speak?"

"I can't stop you. You've evidently come here for that express purpose."

"I know you will misunderstand me, and fly at me, and scratch me, and do all sorts of pretty things."

Her ladyship sighed; her tone breathed resignation.

"You needn't be afraid."

"I'm not; only--Vi, if you only knew how sorry I am for you."

"I don't want your sorrow."

"Vi, I am afraid that your Sydney Beaton is a bad lot."

"Don't you dare to say it--you!"

"You can't believe that he isn't."

"I can, and I do."

"Was he Jane Simmons's catspaw, or was Jane Simmons his? I presume they were confederates. Only that could explain the little talk you had with her."

The girl clenched her fists; she drew a great breath.

"Margaret, I want to tell you just how it is with me."

"Tell on."

"I'd give--I'd jump at the chance of marrying him to-morrow."

"I'll do you the justice to say that I don't believe you. Even if you're a lunatic, you can't be absolutely raving."

"Let me explain."

"With pleasure. Your remark will need all the explanation you can lay your hands on."

"Do you know what it is--to love a man?"

"I'm rather fond of mine."

"Fond!" Nothing could have exceeded the scorn which the girl's manner was meant to convey. "Do you know what it is for your love for a man to have become so part and parcel of your being that life means nothing without him?"

"I'm glad to say I don't."

"Then, I do. So that, you see, is where we differ."

"Poor Vi!"

"Don't talk nonsense, Margaret; there's no poverty in such a state as mine. I'm far richer than you, because I have the only thing which life has to offer worth having. Don't speak; let me continue. You've read the fairy tale in which the heroine gets the gift of sight--it's an allegory. She meets one person in whose nature there is nothing hidden from her; she can see into his very heart. Now start laughing: I can see into Sydney Beaton's very heart."

"My dear, I'm very far from laughing. You're not the only girl who has thought she had that gift where a particular man was concerned. What would the police have said if they had caught the gentleman you name in the very act? You know, they don't consider motives, or peer into hearts; they only deal with facts."

"You don't understand."

"Well, make me."

"Aren't I trying to? But you will keep interrupting. Sydney has never been exactly wise----"

"So you've told me."

The girl took no heed of the interruption; she only glared.

"But I will answer for his standard of honour, and honesty, as I would for my own."

"I wouldn't."

"That's because you don't know him, as I do. They lied when they said he cheated. I spoke to some of them last night. Mr. Tickell, who was playing against him, admitted that he knew nothing about it, that he saw no wrong in anything that Sydney did, nothing in the least suspicious in his behaviour. Captain Draycott as good as owned that, in supporting Anthony Dodwell's accusation, he might have been in error; I could see for myself that that consciousness was weighing on his mind. Major Reith tells me that it was all done in the hurry and whirl of a few mad moments. They talked it over after Sydney had gone; they were all agreed that they would have liked to have him back, to have questioned him when he was cooler and they also. I haven't seen Colonel Sandys, who, you know, was in command of the regiment. I haven't had a chance. He's been abroad ever since. But I've been given to understand that, although he wasn't present, he expressed himself on the matter in terms which were unflattering to all concerned; and I've a suspicion that his feeling on the subject had something to do with his retiring. Anthony Dodwell has not become more popular since; I believe, that if the mess was polled, they'd exchange him for Sydney to-morrow."

"Not after last night, my dear."

"I'm coming to that. Until now I've not felt that it became me to interfere. I felt that Sydney might resent my interfering; that he would prefer to take the matter up in his own way, at his own time. But after last night I see how mistaken I may have been. Margaret, if you were a man of honour, consider what your feelings would be if those whom you had esteemed your friends treated you as those men did Sydney."

"It's not easy for me to put myself into such a position; but if I had been in his place, and been innocent, I think I should have recognised the danger of my position, have kept calm, and have had the matter thrashed right out."

"My dear Margaret, you don't seem to realise that all these men were half beside themselves. I can quite fancy what men can be in such a moment. Sydney wanted to fly at Dodwell's throat. I'm sure that I can't blame him; I should have wanted to do the same, wouldn't you?"

"Well, that depends. I can't say that the little I have known of Captain Dodwell has moved me to affection. But, that apart, how do you explain last night?"

"Don't I tell you that I'm coming to that? Margaret, have patience. Sydney left the barracks that night with, it is nearly certain, very little money, and half mad with rage and shame and grief. Then the curtain falls; we know nothing of what happened to him afterwards. But, in the light of last night, can't you imagine?"

"That's the pity of it--I can."

"Yes; but from one point of view only. Can't you conceive of there being another? Can't you imagine what he may have suffered in what, to him, was a new and hideous world--hopeless, helpless, friendless, penniless, alone? I can't think of any way in which Sydney could have earned a farthing, circumstanced as he was. When his money was gone, which probably lasted only a very little time, he perhaps went hungry. Oh, you don't believe that men do go hungry! My dear, since Sydney went, I've seen crowds of men, in London streets and parks and public places, who, I am convinced, go hungry nearly all the time. Margaret--again I give you permission to laugh--as I've been lying here between the sheets I've seen Sydney starving in rags. I'm sure it has been like that. When a man of his position gets down to that, what is there for him to do?"

"That sort of thing would be pretty rough on him, I grant. But, you know, Vi, you're taking a very great deal for granted."

"I've admitted that Sydney was never the wisest or the strongest of men. It is quite possible that in those depths he met those who were even more desperate than himself, who pointed out to him a way of at least getting something to eat. There's something about that woman Simmons which convinces me that she has known something of the sort of thing of which I speak."

"Do you mean that she has known what it is to starve?"

"I shouldn't wonder. There was something about her when she came into this room last night which struck me. When I was talking to her this morning in the hall I saw what it was; it kept peeping out. Margaret, that woman has stood at despair's very gate; she has never forgotten it, and never will. It's taken from her something which you and I have, but which she will never have again; she is not a woman in the sense we are. Although she may not know it, she is as some wild creature which has its back against the wall, and which fights, straining every nerve and every faculty it has, against what must prevail."

The countess was regarding her with her eyes wide open.

"I always have credited you with imagination, but I certainly never guessed that it amounted to this. I must take a look at Simmons myself, and see what my imagination does for me. I don't want to be beaten in a game of that kind."

"I told you you could laugh, and so you can. If I had had my wits about me, I should have stopped Sydney last night; I should have stuck to him tight; I should have made him understand that, whether he would or wouldn't, I would stay by his side, lest worse befell him. I am going to do that now; I am going to leave no stone unturned to find him. When I have found him I'll not lose sight of him again. He has not been very wise; but the world has used him ill. I will stand by his side against the world."

"My dear, you talk as I've always fancied young women talk in plays I've never seen, the sort of plays which I have been given to understand were popular at the Adelphi once upon a time. It may be very beautiful, but it's frightfully silly. Suppose it gets generally known--and these things do get out--that the gentleman in question committed what was really an act of burglary last night, do you imagine that even the most catholic-minded people will want to cultivate his acquaintance, even with you at his side? And, Vi, you know there may be worse than burglary."

"What do you mean by that?"

"Hasn't it occurred to you as just possible that he may have had something to do with what happened to Captain Draycott, who, by the way, is still nowhere to be found? Rupert tries to pretend that he thinks everything is all right, but I can see that he is oppressed by a feeling that he is lying at the bottom of the lake."

"I'm not going to talk to you, Margaret; I can see that it's no use. I'm sure that if Sydney had anything to do with Captain Draycott, that gentleman brought it on himself."

"My dear girl! But will the police think that?"

"Margaret, I'm going to get up. It's no use our continuing the discussion. We not only look out of two different pairs of eyes; we look on two entirely different worlds. In yours it's roses, roses all the way; in mine it's thorns, thorns, thorns. Are you going, or must I dress while you're here?"

The girl, slipping out of the bed, stood before her in her night attire.

"My dear, you often have, but I'll go if you'd rather. Shall I send your maid?"

"Send no one. I'll dress myself; I will do all things for myself in future. And, while you're here, I'll say good-bye. While I've been lying there I've been planning what to do to find Sydney. We're not to see much of each other while I'm doing that, and when I've found him we're likely to see still less. As you put it, he and I are not the sort of persons with whom you and your friends might care to claim acquaintance."

"Then you won't come yachting?"

"Thank you, I will not."

"Vi, don't be a pig! I'm on your side."

"I doubt it, nor, under the circumstances, do I see how you could be."

"But I am, you idiot! I've something of the sort of feeling for you which it seems you have for him, and though I've no doubt whatever that you're more foolish than a goose-- because a goose is quite a wise bird--all the same, I'm going to stick as close to you as you talk of sticking to him. So perhaps, before I quit this room, you'll promise that you won't leave the house till you've had another talk with me."

"What will be the use of that?"

"Never mind; you promise."

"Oh, I'll promise; but I shall leave the house this morning all the same."

"You can, and my prayers will go with you; but you're not going in your present frame of mind towards me--that I tell you straight. You've had no breakfast, and it's lunch time. When you're dressed, suppose you come to my room and have something with me; I'll see that we're alone."

"If you like, I'll come, but it will be on the understanding that you will not even try to persuade me not to do what I am going to do."

"I won't try to persuade or dissuade you--only you come."

When the countess was again in the pretty sitting-room which she called her very own she took a sheet of paper from between the buttons of her blouse: it was the sheet of paper which had been contained in the envelope which had been presented to the earl by the bronze figure on the pedestal. The little lady read it carefully through; then she struck a match, and lit it at the corner, holding it in her fingers while it flamed, and she asked herself:

"I wonder who wrote it--could it have been Jane Simmons?"

When the paper had been utterly consumed, dropping the ash on to the floor, she pressed it into the carpet with her shoe, so that none of it remained. Then she rang the bell. To the man who answered it she said:

"There's a maid in the house named Simmons--Jane Simmons. Tell them to send her to me here at once."

Some minutes elapsed, during which the countess, taking her ease on a couch covered with pink satin, opened, one after the other, a number of envelopes which were in a tray upon a table. For the most part just glancing at their enclosures, she dropped them from her on to the floor, and was still engaged in doing this when the man returned.

"It appears, my lady, that Simmons has left the house."

"Indeed?" The countess just glanced up from still another enclosure she was dropping to put the question; no one would have supposed she was interested in the least.

"Yes, my lady. She was missed some time ago. Mrs. Ellis sent to her room, and it was found she was gone. It seems that one of the gardeners saw her walking towards the lake with a bag in her hand."

"Is that so? Tell them to serve lunch in my room--lunch for two--in, say, half an hour."

The man went. The lady continued to treat her correspondence with the same scant courtesy.

"So she has gone. I thought it would be found that she had gone. She was seen walking towards the lake, with a bag. I wonder why the lake, and what was in the bag. Poor Vi!"

CHAPTER XXIII
The Latest Story

Days became weeks, and the mystery of what had become of Noel Draycott was a mystery still. It had got into the papers; to the disgust of the Earl of Cantyre, it had become, in a sense, the topic of the hour. "Where is Noel Draycott?" was the question, set in staring capitals, which faced newspaper readers day after day. The usual things were said about the incapacity of Scotland Yard; and people were assured by the morning and evening Press that the whole affair was but another illustration of how ineffective our detective service really is.

The official methods of dealing with his house and grounds were bad enough, but when it came to the amateur detective, his lordship drew the line. It was a subject on which he expressed himself very freely.

"Think the professional is no good, do they? I can't say that I'm struck with him myself. But compared to these male and female creatures who are aping him----! There's a woman who has taken on the job of what she calls 'solving' the mystery for the *Daily Screecher*; they tell me they've had the greatest difficulty in keeping her out of the servants' hall, to say nothing of the butler's pantry; and the other day they found her under the dining-room table just as they were starting to lay the dinner. I've given instructions that all such persons are to be warned gently off the premises, and kept off. Of course, if any of them should stray by any unhappy accident into the lake, it will be a misfortune. Privacy is getting a thing of the past. From the tone some of these fellows take, you'd think it was their house, their grounds--not mine."

Miss Forster had gone her own way--her uncle and many of her friends put it, her own bad way. She had gone straight from Avonham to Nuthurst, her uncle's house, which had been her home for so many years. In an interview she had insisted on having with him a very few minutes after her arrival, she had given her uncle one of the surprises of his life.

"You wish me to marry Sir George Beaton?" she had informed him.

"I'm not particular about your marrying George Beaton," the distracted old man declared. "There are hundreds and thousands of men in the world besides. What's the matter with Harold Reith? I thought you liked him."

"I like him too much to marry him."

"Of course, there's that point of view. I said to him: 'If the girl does marry you, you'll want to drown her and yourself inside six weeks.' Well, that didn't seem to cheer him."

Miss Forster looked at the old gentleman with doubtful glance, as if she suspected him of malign intention.

"Such a remark on your part was quite unnecessary. Major Reith is not likely to find himself in such a situation. I am going to marry Sydney Beaton."

Had she actually dropped a live bomb at his feet, Mr. Hovenden could not have seemed more disturbed.

"That pestilent young scoundrel! Was there ever anything like a woman for sheer impossibility?"

"It is because I am conscious of what your sentiments are on the subject that I am going to leave Nuthurst."

"You're going to do--what?"

"I have an income of my own----"

"Five hundred a year."

"It's more than five hundred a year."

"How much more?"

"I'm going to take a small furnished flat in London, and I'm going to live in it. For that my income will be more than ample."

"Is the girl raving? What's the matter with my house--or with me? If it comes to that, can't I take a flat for you?"

She crossed the room, and she kissed him. Educated in the school of experience, he did not show himself so grateful as he might have done.

"What does that mean?"

"It means, my dear uncle, that it can't be done."

"What can't be done?"

"I'd better be candid with you."

"I'd sooner you weren't. Candour with you means saying something disagreeable."

"Circumstances have arisen which make me think that things are in a very bad way with Sydney."

"I shouldn't be surprised."

"You would be surprised if you knew how bad they are."

"Oh, no, I shouldn't. A young scamp like that must expect to feed on the husks which the swine have rejected. I know. Rogues sometimes do get punished even in this world."

"Does it not occur to you how impossible it is that I should remain in your house while you speak like that of my future husband?"

"Your future husband?"

"My future husband." She said it with an air of calmness which irritated the old gentleman more than any show of heat would have done.

"Violet, if ever you marry that young blackguard----"

"Stop, uncle, before you say something which I may find it hard to forgive." She spoke as if she wished him to understand that the discussion was closed; that all she had to do was to make an announcement. "I am leaving Nuthurst this afternoon; I am going up to town by the three-twenty-three. I have told Cleaver to send my things on after me and what things to send. I shan't want her. You may dismiss her or keep her on, as you please. I dare say she may be found useful in the house."

"Dismiss Cleaver! At a moment's notice! I catch myself at it. And she has waited upon you hand and foot since you wore your first pair of long stockings!"

As Geoffrey Hovenden growled the words out he surveyed her as a clean-bred old mastiff might an impertinent young lap-dog. She went calmly on, holding out to him a sheet of paper:

"My address in town will be 2A Cobden Mansions, York Place. I've written it on this piece of paper in case you should forget it. It is quite respectable; you need be under no apprehension. All the occupants of Cobden Mansions are women, who have to supply satisfactory references before they are accepted as tenants. Good-bye."

Ignoring the hand which she advanced, he glared at her as if he would like to treat her to a good shaking.

"Are you in earnest?"

"I am. I know, uncle, how much I have to thank you for; please don't think I'm ungrateful because I am leaving Nuthurst. If I had married any of those hundred thousand gentlemen you just spoke of, I should have had to leave your house for his, so it comes to the same thing, because I hope that my husband will soon have a home for me. I don't suppose we shall see much of each other in future----"

"Don't talk balderdash! I'm disappointed in you, Violet, disappointed."

"I'm sorry, uncle; but I shan't cease to love you, and I hope you won't cease to love me."

"Why should I? Though your whole conduct shows you don't care a snap of your fingers for me. I don't believe you're really quite right in your head; I've half a mind to have you certified as a lunatic."

"You might find that harder than you suppose. But don't let us talk about that. You'll think better of me when I've gone. If you won't shake hands, once more good-bye. Remember, 2A Cobden Mansions. I shall be always glad to have a visit from you."

She was gone from the room, and very shortly afterwards from the house. His inclination was to stop her by strong measures, but second thoughts prevailed. He chose what he flattered himself was the wisdom of the serpent.

"If I let her think that it is a matter of complete indifference to me whether she goes or stays, she'll soon be back again. When a woman thinks that you don't care if she does make a fool of herself, she'll soon give up trying. I never thought that the girl would be such an imbecile."

When, a few days later, Sir George Beaton called, and placed him in possession of certain information, he formed a still lower estimate of his niece's mental capacity. The young man burst in on the old one just as he had finished his usual daily interview with his steward.

"Hovenden," he began, without any preliminary greeting, "what's this idea about Violet having left Nuthurst and gone to live in town?"

The old gentleman looked up from a bundle of papers which the steward had left behind.

"I don't know what you hear, but she's gone." His glance returned to the papers. "So far as I can understand, she's gone to look for your brother Sydney."

Sir George displayed signs of acute perturbation.

"Good heavens! Do you know what's the latest tale they're telling?"

"How should I? How long is it since I saw you? The worst tales about your brother I've always heard from you."

"Is that meant for---- What do you mean by that?"

"It's the truth, any way. Ever since Sydney was a small boy you've been telling tales to his discredit."

"Have I? I'm going to cap them with another: he's been committing burglary--that's his latest performance."

"Tell that to the marines. You know, George, you overdo it where Sydney is concerned; you make of him 'an 'orrible tale'; the colours with which you paint him are invariably sanguinary."

Sir George Beaton punctuated his words by striking his hand on the table at which the old gentleman was sitting.

"On the night of the Easter ball at Avonham all the women's jewellery was taken from their rooms--by Sydney."

"Who told you that?"

"Never mind who told me; it's a fact. It's the topic among the people we know."

"He did it for a lark; he has a peculiar sense of humour."

"That's how you look at it; you may well call it peculiar. There's something else which is being said of him, still more peculiar."

"He has committed murder?"

"That's what's being said."

"George, do you know you're talking of your own brother?"

"Don't I know it? You've seen in the papers about this Noel Draycott who is missing; he's one of the men who accused him that night at poker. They say that after Sydney had made off with the women's jewels he came across Draycott, there was a row, and he killed him. And this is the man Violet has gone to London to look for! She's not the only person who is doing it. And I'll say this--I hope that neither she nor anyone else will find him. I don't want to have my name entered in the Newgate Calendar, nor to see my brother finish at the gallows."

"Is it possible, do you think, that Violet can know of this--of these charges which are alleged against him?"

"I'm told it's because she knows that she's gone to town. She's got some cranky notion in her head that this is a case in which, for love's sake, the world would be well lost. To associate love with a man like that!"

CHAPTER XXIV
2A Cobden Mansions

It was hard to see what Violet Forster had gained by her change of residence, even from her own point of view; she felt that herself. She was conscious that Cobden Mansions was not Nuthurst, and that her particular corner in that tall, ugly, red brick building left a deal to be desired. And so far as she could see, she had done no good by coming; she had learnt absolutely nothing of Sydney Beaton's whereabouts; she could not have learnt less had she chosen to stray in the woods at Nuthurst instead of the highways and by-ways of London.

She had never got over the difficulty which had beset her at the first, that she had not been able to decide which was the best way to carry on her search. She had always the one dreadful fact to remember, that she was not the only person who wanted to get within touch of Sydney. If she was not careful she might do him the worst possible turn, by placing him in the hands of his enemies. That, in the sense in which she used the word, he was an innocent man she had no doubt whatever; but whether that sense was one which would commend itself to the authorities was the problem which caused her many a sleepless night, which took the roses out of her cheeks, the light from her eyes, the spring from her steps; which had transformed the blooming, light-hearted, high-spirited maiden into a nervous, shrinking, white-faced woman. She who had never known what it was to have an hour's illness, had suddenly become the victim of headaches which would not go. Such headaches! It seemed as if some terrible weight were pressing on her brain, making it difficult even for her to open her eyes. Major Reith caught her one day while she was in the grip of one of the very worst of them. Coming unannounced into her little sitting-room, he found her lying face downwards on the couch. Starting up, turning towards him her pallid face, they regarded each other with mutual discomfiture.

He spoke first: "I beg your pardon, but--I did knock."

Assuming a more orthodox position, she conjured up--it seemed with difficulty--a faint, wan smile.

"I'm not surprised. It's I who should apologise; this absurd head of mine makes me feel so stupid that anyone might knock half a dozen times without my knowing it."

Her appearance startled him; to him she seemed genuinely ill; the change which had taken place in her hurt him more than he would have cared to say. He was so unwilling that she should see the concern on his face that he turned his face from her under the pretence of putting his hat upon a chair.

"Have you seen a doctor?"

"What's the use? Medicine won't cure me, at least the sort of stuff a doctor would prescribe."

"Suppose you get really bowled over, what then?" She did not answer; she shut her eyes and sat still. "Do you know you are beginning to strike me as an extremely obstinate person?"

"Are you only just beginning to find that out?"

"You'll be a case for the hospital before very long, and then what good will you have done, for yourself, for anyone?"

"That's a question which I put to myself--so often. Please don't bully me. You never have seen me cry, have you? But I shall cry if you do; and I feel that if I once start I shall never stop. Have you any news? That's the medicine I want, and a doctor who will give it me."

"I'm more than half disposed to telegraph to someone who'd pack you off to the sea; you'll brood yourself ill."

"The sea won't do me any good; I've told you the only medicine which will. Have you any?"

"News? Of a sort. The regiment is all at sixes and sevens; in the whole of its history there's never been such a state of things before."

"What's wrong now with your precious regiment?"

"Everything. There's a bad spirit abroad in the mess; there's continual friction, the fellows are all at loggerheads, there's something that jars."

"So there ought to be, amongst such a set of individuals as constitute your mess."

"I've something to tell which you may regard as some of that medicine you are looking for."

"Have you? That's good; what is it?"

"It depends upon the point of view whether it's good or whether it's bad; from one point of view it's uncommonly bad."

"I hope that's not mine."

"I dare say it won't be. You know that throughout I've declined to express a positive opinion about that poker business of Beaton's."

"I do; and I've hated you for it."

"I'm beginning to think that there may be something in your point of view after all."

"Really? That is condescension; and what has brought it about--you're beginning to think?"

"I know what you think, and I know why; you must forgive me if my thoughts are on a different plane. You consider one man only, there's nothing that matters except him; to me there's a very great deal. I'm a soldier; to me the service is first and last; my regiment is all in all."

"Do you think I don't know that?"

"That affair of Beaton's was bad enough in all conscience; it's a tale which will be told of the regiment for many a day; but if it's going to be reopened I don't know what will become of us--I honestly do not."

"You don't believe that justice should be done even if the heavens fall?"

"I'm not sure that it is not better that one man should suffer, even though unjustly, rather than that a great and glorious tradition should be dragged in the mud and made a mock of."

"Your sentiments do you infinite discredit; I wonder, since you hold them, that I ever let you speak to me."

"Yes--well, I do hold them, and I'm going to continue to speak to you whether you let me or not."

"You haven't got your medicine."

"Young Tickell has made an announcement to the mess which is likely to cause trouble. He laid a cheque on the table for the amount which was in the pool that night, and he said that, as circumstances had arisen which caused him to doubt, he felt that he would like the money to be held in trust till the point was finally decided."

"Bravo, Jackie! Conscience moves in a mysterious way; that really is medicine."

"Yes, I thought you'd think so; it doesn't occur to you to think what the young gentleman's action means for the rest of us."

"I'm hopeful that it will cause your consciences to move in a mysterious way; I've always insisted that the age of miracles is still with us."

"Tickell as good as said that he doubted that Dodwell and Draycott had said the thing which was not, and if we had not all of us behaved infamously."

"You prefer the French point of view of the *chose jugée*; isn't that the phrase with which they decline to let injustice be set right?"

"The thing's done--that was bad enough; but if it's all going to be reopened it may be made infinitely worse; Tickell's action practically laid an unpleasant imputation upon every one of us."

"I shall write to Mr. Tickell and tell him how glad I am to find that there is in him the making of an honest man."

"What did you say to him that night at the Avonham ball?" Although the major paused for an answer, none came. "I believe that what you said, whatever it was, was the direct cause of his present action. Now what did you say?"

The lady rose from the couch, with a smile which, this time, was childlike and bland.

"I say that your medicine has already done me some good, and I think that the fresh air of the heavens may do me more. Regent's Park is within easy distance. Would you favour me with your society if I were moved to stroll in it? I will go and put my hat on." She turned again just as she was leaving the room. "By the way, who is the correspondent who has favoured this morning's *Daily Screecher* with that mysterious communication; do you think it was manufactured in the office? I fancy that mysterious communications sometimes are."

"You credit me with a knowledge of journalistic methods which I don't possess."

"You saw it?" He nodded. "What do you think of it?"

"I would rather not think of it at all."

"That seems to be your attitude in all such matters; you're like the ostrich who thinks that he hides himself and escapes from an unpleasant predicament by hiding his head in the sand. You see, I've got to think."

"Then, if I were you, I shouldn't."

"The *Daily Screecher* says that a correspondent has favoured them with an account of certain extraordinary occurrences which took place at Avonham on the night of the Easter ball. If the statement is true, and it seems to bear on it the hall-mark of truth, then it throws a very lurid light on the continued mysterious disappearance of Captain Noel Draycott. It goes on to say that searching and exhaustive inquiries are being made into the statement, the result of which will be published in an early issue. In the meantime it assures its readers that sensational, and even astounding, developments may shortly be expected. I suppose you are capable of telling me if you think that that communication was manufactured in the office?"

The major showed a disposition to fidget, on which the lady commented.

"It's no use your shuffling your feet, or looking down at your boots, or fingering your tie; everything is quite all right. Will you please tell me what you think?"

"It's difficult to say."

"That means that you think there is a bona fide correspondent and that the communication is genuine."

"I'll put it this way--it's a wonder to me that something hasn't peeped out already. You and I know that the facts that the papers have got are not the real ones; there are--how many persons?--goodness only knows!--who are in a position to supply them with something which is a great deal nearer the truth--the whole truth, that is."

"And you think that one of those persons has?"

"Who knows? So far what struck me most about the matter is, that in spite of the boasted argus eyes of the newspapers, how easy it is to keep things from them. Even the approximate truth of what took place at Avonham would make--if they knew it--the fortunes of half a dozen journalists; and in America they would have got it, long ago; it's possible that here they're going to get it now."

The girl's smile had again become wan and faint.

"You're a comfortable counsellor; that paragraph in the *Screecher* gave me my headache; your medicine did it good; but now it's as bad again as ever. I don't think that I care to stroll in the park--even with you."

"Whether you care or not you are coming. Go and put on your hat; or am I to carry you off without it?"

The girl hesitated; then, without a word, quitted the room. She was absent some minutes; a hat is not put on in a second. When she returned there was something about her eyes which filled the major with uncomfortable suspicions. In silence she led the way downstairs, and he followed.

It did not promise to be a very agreeable stroll, although the weather was fine. He seemed to find it hard to make conversation; she certainly declined to help him. They were into the park before a dozen sentences had been exchanged. Then, when they had walked quite a little distance without a word being spoken, all at once, as if moved by a sudden impulse, she made an effort to relieve the situation.

"If we walk on much longer, mumchance, like two dumb statues, people will think one of two things; either that we are married--I've been given to understand that husbands and wives never speak to each other when they take their walks abroad--or else that we have quarrelled."

He bore himself as if he had a poker down his back, and his eyes were fixed straight in front of him as he replied:

"I've not the least objection to their thinking the first."

"I dare say; but I have. Will you please talk to me about the weather."

Before he had a chance to air his eloquence upon that well-worn subject, something happened which rendered it unnecessary for him to say anything at all. A taxicab had gone rushing past, and as it passed, its occupant, a lady, put out her head to look at them. The cab had not gone another fifty yards before she stopped it. As they approached she was standing on the footpath with the obvious intention of accosting them. Her tone as she did so was enthusiastic.

"Miss Forster! This is a pleasure."

Judging from the expression on the young lady's face she was more than doubtful if it was a pleasure which was common to them both.

"Jane Simmons!" she exclaimed.

The other shook her by no means ill-looking head, and she laughed.

"Not Simmons; my name is Spurrier, Julia Spurrier. Most fortunate my meeting you like this, Miss Forster; I have for some time been most anxious to have a talk with you. Is there anywhere where I can say a few words to you in private? I believe you will regard what I have to say as of the first importance--to you, Miss Forster. I know what I am saying."

CHAPTER XXV
Julia Spurrier

Miss Spurrier was very well dressed; as regards appearance she was really smarter than Miss Forster. All her extremely nice clothes looked as if they had come from the hands of artists, and her hat was a dream. She stood with one well-gloved hand resting on a long-handled parasol--it was a sunny afternoon; with one champagne-coloured shoe she seemed to be describing figures on the ground; her head was held a little back at an angle which became her. It was not easy to recognise in this elegant personage Jane Simmons in her cap and apron. Major Reith, who, with old-fashioned courtesy, stood with his hat in his hand, seemed as if he did not know what to make of her; while possibly the singularity of Miss Forster's bearing was owing to the fact that she was divided between anger and amazement, with possibly a touch of fear lurking in the corner of her heart. She seemed to be in doubt as to whether it would be better and wiser to enter into conversation with this disreputable person, or to pass contemptuously on. When, at last, she did speak, it was with the plain intention of giving the other to understand that she was to keep what Miss Forster considered her place.

"Have you anything to say to me? Can't you say it here?"

"In the presence of Major Reith?" The lady swung her parasol in that gentleman's direction, and she beamed at him. "Oh, I know you, Major--you're not the only officer in your regiment with whom I have the pleasure of being acquainted. With one of them I've been on quite intimate terms; ask Miss Forster. It's about him I wish to speak to her."

The major, noting his companion's distress, made a somewhat blundering attempt to come to her rescue.

"If I'm in the way, Miss Forster, pray command me; shall I walk on, or would you prefer that I should stay?"

Miss Forster still seemed to be in doubt; her words were scarcely friendly.

"Major Reith, I've only seen this person once in my life--she was a servant at Avonham on the night of the Easter ball--or she pretended to be. Her conduct on that occasion was of a kind which makes it amazing that she should have the assurance to address me now."

Miss Spurrier showed no signs of being hurt by the speaker's candour; she only laughed.

"It's hardly fair, Major Reith, for Miss Forster to put it like that. You will, of course, recollect the robbery of the ladies' jewels--actually from their bedrooms, when they were fast asleep. You remember how all the jewels were found again, in a leather bag? It was rather a funny story." She turned to the girl. "Miss Forster, shall I tell him all about it? I'm convinced that it would tickle him."

A flush had come over Violet Forster's face, her cheeks were as scarlet as they had just been white. Not only her lips, her whole frame seemed trembling from head to foot.

Miss Spurrier observed her with malicious amusement--she remained all smiles.

"Why, Miss Forster, how red you have all at once become, and only a moment ago I was thinking how pale you were. Doesn't a touch of colour become her, Major Reith?"

The major looked extremely uncomfortable, as if he did not know what to make of the position. Miss Forster relieved him of his perplexity.

"I think," she said to him, "that I will hear what this person has to say. She can come with me in this cab to my rooms; and may I ask you to accompany us? I have reasons for wishing you to do so. Get in."

She ordered Miss Spurrier to enter the cab very much as she might have done if she had still been Jane Simmons. Miss Spurrier laughingly complied.

"What funny ways you have, Miss Forster! If you would let me tell Major Reith that story, he'd think they were funnier still."

Miss Forster, following her into the cab, chose to sit with her back to the driver; the major, entering last, was placed in the seat of honour by Miss Spurrier's side. When the cab reached Cobden Mansions, and the passengers had alighted, Miss Forster said to the major, as she opened the door of a room which was just inside the hall:

"This is meant to be used as a reception room for visitors to tenants of the flats who do not wish to see them in their own apartments. I am going to take this person with me upstairs; will you wait here till she has gone, or till I send for you?"

The major expressed his perfect willingness to await the lady's pleasure; the two women ascended in the lift to Miss Forster's flat on one of the upper floors. So soon as they were in, Miss Forster's manner entirely changed. All signs of confusion or distress vanished; she assumed what was almost an air of truculence. Closing the door, she pointed to a seat.

"Sit down." The visitor obeyed. "Now, Jane Simmons, or whatever you call yourself, you say you've been looking for me; I don't know what truth there may be in that, but I do know that I've been looking for you; and now that I've found you, we're not going to part until we've come to an understanding."

"That's what I want, Miss Forster--an understanding."

"In the first place, before you leave this room, you're going to tell me where Sydney Beaton is now."

The visitor raised her grey-suede-covered hands with what was possibly meant to be a gesture of lady-like amazement.

"How odd! How extremely singular! What a coincidence!"

"What's a coincidence--and odd--and singular?"

Nothing could have been grimmer than the tone in which Miss Forster put her question. She had taken up an attitude before the empty fireplace which was almost masculine, and again there was something which was almost masculine in the curt, unceremonious fashion of her speech; nothing could have been in more striking contrast than the other's airs and graces of a fine lady.

"That you should have said such a thing as that to me about dear old Sydney."

Miss Forster bit her lip.

"Have the goodness not to speak of Mr. Beaton in my presence by his Christian name."

"My dear Miss Forster, why not? When he and I have been such friends; I've always called him Sydney."

"Whether that is or is not a lie I am not in a position to say; you'll speak of him as Mr. Beaton to me. Where is Mr. Beaton?"

"That's what I said was so odd, so singular, such a coincidence. That you should put such a question to me, when one of the chief reasons why I was so anxious to have a talk was because I wished to put exactly the same question to you--where is Mr. Beaton?"

"Do you mean to say that you don't know?"

"I've no more idea than the dead."

"You did know."

"Up to a certain point of course I knew."

"Where was he living when--I saw you last?"

The visitor looked at her before she answered, with a smile which grew more and more pronounced; there was a singular quality in the woman's smile. In repose her face was good to look at; her smile invested it with a charm, a tenderness, a something daintily malicious, which made it almost irresistible. Miss Forster admitted to herself that she would be easy for any man to fall in love with, and, when she chose, there was a winning something in her voice; she had one of those flexible voices which are capable of expressing so many, and such fine, shades of meaning.

"Where was he living when you saw me last? Well, that's rather a question. I needn't tell you that a good many people would like to know. But as I have every reason to believe that you really are his friend, and have no sympathy with those objectionable creatures, the police, I don't mind telling you. He had rooms at Notting Hill--78 Caversham Street. Mine were close to Brompton Road, and when he wasn't in my rooms I was in his."

Miss Forster was making a note on a sheet of paper.

"78 Caversham Street, Notting Hill. You say that was his address at the time of the Easter ball at Avonham?"

"Exactly, and after what occurred at Avonham I expected that he would return to that address; and I don't mind telling you that when I left I went straight there, to find that he hadn't returned. I was a little surprised, but, of course--in the profession in which he was then engaged, accidents do happen--there's no shutting our eyes to that, is there? There might have been all sorts of reasons why his return had been delayed; but when day after day went by, and still nothing was seen or heard of him, I did begin to wonder."

The lady, pausing, looking down, began to draw figures on the carpet with the end of her parasol, smiling to herself as if in enjoyment of some private joke.

"Most regular in his habits, was Mr. Beaton--you see, I adopt the Mr. in deference to you; I'm always so anxious not to wound people's feelings, especially yours. Everything in his rooms was in perfect order, the rent had been paid up, and the landlady, who was a most innocent creature, and quite attached to her lodger, whom she believed to be something in the commercial way, was not in the least concerned--but I was. You see, I knew. As time went on, and there were still no signs of him, I became positively anxious; I was almost as attached to him as his landlady."

Again--it is necessary to dwell upon the fact, to such an extent was it her most outstanding characteristic--her face was irradiated by her wonderful smile. She continued, with her eyes still cast down.

"I was really concerned; then it occurred to me that probably my distress was wasted, the explanation might be quite simple; seeing you that night had brought his thoughts back to the old channels, and--you knew where he was instead of me. I began to take it for granted that he had exchanged 78 Caversham Street for an address which would be more convenient for you, and less for me--isn't that the case?"

Miss Forster's manner, as she replied, was still ungenial.

"In dealing with persons such as you, one is confronted with the difficulty that one can never tell when you are telling the truth and when you are lying; I am quite sure that you can lie like truth. What I do gather is that you wish me to believe that you have seen and heard nothing of Mr. Beaton since that night; but though your tale sounds plausible, there is no reason why it should be true."

"It doesn't matter to me one pin's head whether you do or don't believe. Will you please answer me one question? Have you seen or heard anything of him?"

"I have not."

"I do believe you, and I'm very sorry to hear it." Nothing could have been sweeter than the smile with which Miss Spurrier said it, or nicer than her bearing. "I'm afraid, Miss Forster, that there's something wrong. If you do or don't believe it, I have heard nothing of Mr. Beaton, and if you haven't, then I don't like the look of things at all. Do you see"--the lady hesitated; looking down, she still described figures with the end of her parasol--"there's that business of Captain Draycott. It is, unfortunately, possible that Mr. Beaton may have had his reasons for not wishing to let me know his whereabouts, or you either. In matters of that kind it may be better--for the person who did it to keep himself to himself; it's safer for him, and for all concerned, because, of course, if one doesn't know, one can't tell."

The lady glanced at a gold watch set in a jewelled bangle.

"How the time does go--I must be off; I'm keeping Major Reith waiting. One moment--excuse me, Miss Forster, if I am interrupting you when you were about to speak--but please don't let us talk about that business of Captain Draycott; it's so much better not to."

"I don't agree with you; what do you know about it?"

"Suppose I know everything--what good will it do you, or him? You're not fool enough to suppose that I did it. Captain Draycott was an utter stranger to me; I had no grudge against him; you know how it was--with Mr. Beaton. You don't want to put the noose about his neck, do you? And you can't want me to do so. I've had one friend hung, and I certainly don't want to have another--it's a nasty business, I can assure you."

"I can't believe that, for what happened to Captain Draycott, Mr. Beaton was in any way to blame."

"Miss Forster, you really must forgive me if I say that now I don't believe you. I tell you again that I don't wish to talk about it, and it's better on all accounts that we shouldn't; but do you suppose that I can't see that your heart's as heavy as lead, and that you've worn yourself nearly to a shadow, because you've been worrying about what you pretend you don't believe? If you were to go down on your bended knees, and swear that you were quite certain that he had nothing to do with it, still I shouldn't believe you; your face, everything about you gives you away; I know better. Let me tell you something, and this is the last word you'll get on the subject from me. I don't know"--the lady suddenly lowered her voice--"who killed him, and I don't want, and I don't mean to know, but I have my doubts--so now you've got it."

CHAPTER XXVI
Happiness!

Miss Forster was silent. That her visitor's words had affected her disagreeably her behaviour showed. Showing Miss Spurrier her back, facing the mantelshelf, she pretended to be interested by the trifles which were on it, but to an observant eye few things can be more eloquent than a person's back; the twitching of her shoulders was in itself more than sufficiently eloquent. Even her speech betrayed her; it faltered.

"Do you think--that he's left England?"

"It's on the cards. It all depends on whether he's had the chance. If he has, let's hope he'll be able to cover his tracks. I suppose nobody does know anything."

"How can I tell?"

"Exactly, how can you? It's queer that nothing has been found--of the body." The girl said nothing, but again Miss Spurrier noticed the twitching shoulders. "There's one thing, nothing can be done till it is found; and as it looks as if it is in a sure place, he ought to have something like a start before trouble begins."

The girl still continued silent. The visitor, holding out her gorgeous parasol, began to fasten the elastic band.

"Miss Forster, I am going away. I don't mean only from this room, but out of the country; I'm leaving England."

"Are you?" The girl's tone could scarcely have been more void of interest, but the other still kept her eyes upon her back.

"I'm going to be married."

"Indeed."

"I am going to be married to an old friend with whom I have been associated in some rather successful--matters; so, as we've got quite a nice little capital together, we've decided to turn over a new leaf. We're going to America, to a town in one of the middle States, where we have, both of us, reason to believe that there's an opening for an enterprising couple. We are going to start in the dry goods--a store. It's a trade in which we may both of us be able to show even the Americans a thing or two. We hope, by strict attention to business, to do well."

The visitor paused, but the girl said nothing; she still kept her face turned away.

"Of course, my prospects and intentions don't interest you, but now that I'm going to put the old things behind me and begin a new life, and leave England for ever--for we both of us intend at the earliest possible moment to become American citizens; you do get such a pull on the other side if you are a citizen--since you and I are alone together for probably the last time in our lives, there are one or two things which I should like to tell you about Mr. Beaton. That's one of the reasons why I wanted to see you. Wouldn't you like to hear them?"

"It depends on what they are. I should advise you to be careful what you say of him."

"Oh, I'll be careful. To begin with, Mr. Beaton is a gentleman, as I dare say you know."

"What do you suppose?"

"Now, my experience of what is called a gentleman in England is, that so long as he has got plenty of money to spend, and everything's made smooth for him, he may be quite a decent sort; but he's the most helpless creature on God's earth when his pockets are empty and he has to trust to himself to fill them. So long as he has friends to give him a lift he may manage somehow, but when his only friend is himself he's scrambling for crusts in the gutter almost before he himself knows it. To one who has had to earn his bread all his life by the sweat of his brow it's nothing less than amazing how soon he gets there. Mr. Sydney Beaton was in the gutter, and worse than the gutter, when I first met him."

At last Miss Forster did turn, and looked the speaker in the face.

"Where did you first meet him?"

Miss Spurrier was settling her beautiful hat upon her well-groomed head.

"It's not a pretty story--not very much to his credit or mine. You don't know how little of a hero a man can be when his stomach's empty and he has nothing to put into it, especially when he's a gentleman."

Apparently the visitor got her hat all right. She rested both hands on the handle of her parasol and she smiled.

"I want to slur over the disagreeable places in my story, Miss Forster--I always do like to avoid as much as possible what is unpleasant--and I don't want to keep you any longer than I can help. I want to get to what I'm after by the shortest possible way. You know what my profession is?"

"I can form a shrewd guess."

"I shouldn't be surprised; circumstances have helped you. But the world in general, Miss Forster, treats me as in every respect your equal. I was on my beam ends when I adopted it. I dare say you don't know what it is to be on your beam ends."

"I am thankful to say that is a condition of which I have no personal knowledge."

"You have cause to be thankful. Well, I have, and so has Sydney Beaton. If it hadn't been for me he'd have been dead long ago, with cold, misery and hunger."

"Is that true?"

"If you doubt it, you can. Say you don't believe me. Well--don't. I taught him one way of keeping himself alive and of putting money in his pocket, and he managed to do both. But it was a way he never liked; there were times when, I believe, that after all he would have rather starved."

"So I should imagine."

"Oh, you can imagine a great deal, I shouldn't wonder, but do you think you've imagination enough to enable you to put yourself in the place of the woman who was peddling matches at the corner of the street as we came along, with odd boots on--such boots!--and no stockings, and probably little more on than a skirt which it would make you uncomfortable to think of touching even with your finger-tips? You say you never could be in the position of such a woman--but he was."

One could see that, in spite of herself, Miss Forster shivered.

"Is that absolutely a fact?"

"The second time I met him he was carrying a sandwich-board in the Strand--now it's out--in that cold weather we had last January; and he hadn't three-penn'orth of clothing on him--three-pennyworth! Why, a rag-man would have wanted to be paid for carrying away what he had on. He was perished with the cold; he was nothing but skin and bone; misery and hunger had made him half-witted. In that weather he had slept out of doors every night--in the streets. He hadn't had six-pennyworth of food in a week. You stand there, well-fed, well-housed, well-clothed, and you think yourself a paragon of all the virtues, entitled to look down on such as I am, on what he became. You've not yourself to thank for being what you are. If you were to be stripped naked, and put into the woman's rags who was peddling matches, and had to live her life, for only a month, what kind of a fine lady, with pretty sentiments, do you think you'd be by then?"

Miss Spurrier had become suddenly so much in earnest that there was no doubt about her having succeeded in interesting Violet Forster at last. A light seemed to have come into her face, and a glow into her eyes.

"Do you really mean--that he was a sandwichman--in the Strand, one of those men who carry boards upon their backs?"

The visitor laughed as if she regretted the warmth to which she had given way; but there was something in her laughter which did not ring altogether true.

"Oh, I didn't mean to give myself away--or him either. I don't suppose he's very proud of his little experiences, so if you ever meet him again don't let him know that I told you; I shouldn't like him to think that I'd given him away on a thing like that--especially to you, because I happen to know that there's nothing in the world for which he cares except your good opinion, and that makes it so funny."

"How do you know he cares for my good opinion?"

"As if I didn't know! Why, he bought a portrait of yours in a picture paper; he cut it out, he made a little case for it--a sort of little silk bag stiffened with cardboard--he bought the silk himself, shaped it, put every stitch in it with his own needle and thread; he carried it about with him inside his shirt; I believe he said his prayers to it."

The girl had all at once grown scarlet; what was almost like a flame seemed blazing in her eyes.

"If--if he so wanted my portrait, how did you come to be possessed of that locket with my likeness in it?"

"That's one of the things of which I am ashamed; and, as I'm going to turn over a new leaf and become a respectable married woman, it's one which I want to make a clean breast of--to you. That locket was stolen from him when he was trying to get some sleep on one of the steps of the tunnel under Hungerford Bridge by two men who knew he had got it on him. One of them sold it to--an acquaintance of mine; he showed it to me, I recognised you from the picture he had cut out of the paper, and I bought it."

"Why didn't you give it back to Mr. Beaton? You knew that it was his."

"Well, that's one of the peculiarities of human nature. I didn't. I couldn't tell you why; at least, it would take me a very long time to do it; human nature is such a mass of complications and contradictions. I gave it to you instead."

"As if that were the same thing!"

"As if I didn't know that it wasn't. Haven't I admitted that that is something for which you are entitled to throw bricks at my head, or articles of furniture, or anything that comes handy?"

As the girl showed no inclination to throw anything, but stood there with that light still flaming in her eyes and her cheeks all glowing, Miss Spurrier went on, with something in her bearing more than a trifle malicious.

"Well, now that I've told you everything that I came to tell you, and all you want to know, I'm going."

She made a movement towards the door. The girl found her tongue.

"But you haven't told me anything; at least, I don't understand what it is you have told me."

"I've told you the one thing you want to know: that the one thing he values in the world is your good opinion; that still, although he's been very near to the gate of hell, he loves you. Good day."

"You swear that you don't know where he is?"

"I've no more idea of where he is, or where he has been, since that night at Avonham than you; and, as things are turning out, I would much rather continue in complete ignorance of his whereabouts until that business of Captain Draycott has blown over, which is a consummation devoutly to be hoped for. Is there any other question you would like to ask me?"

She stood by the door, presenting a sufficiently appetising picture of a pretty woman, fitly and gaily apparelled to take her walks abroad on a sunny day. Something which she perhaps saw in her face moved the girl to what, coming from her, was an unexpected confession.

"I'm not sure that I haven't been doing you an injustice."

The woman laughed.

"I shouldn't wonder. I've been doing the same to you. We are all of us continually doing each other an injustice; that sort of thing depends a good deal on the mood you're in and on whether the world is going well with us. I hope that, for both of us, in the future it will go very well indeed. Good-bye."

The woman was gone and the door was closed, and almost before she knew it the girl was left alone. Some few minutes later there came a tapping at the door; it was opened, and Major Reith came in. He found Violet Forster sitting on the floor beside the couch, her face pillowed on a cushion. When she raised it he saw that she was crying. The sight moved him to sympathy and anger.

"Miss Forster!" he exclaimed. "What has that abominable woman been saying--or doing?"

Her answer filled him with amazement.

"I'm not sure," she said, "that she is an abominable woman, and--I'm not sure that I'm not the happiest girl in the world."

It seemed such an astounding thing for her to say that he appeared to be in doubt as to whether he ought to credit the evidence of his own ears. But there was such a light upon her face, which was no longer white, and such a smile was shining from behind the tears that, almost incredible though he deemed it, he was forced to the conclusion that he must have heard aright, especially when, rising to her feet, she came close to him and laughed in his face.

"Yes," she told him, "you may stare; but at least I am not sure that I am not much happier than I deserve. And now I'll wash my face and dry my eyes, and I'll put my hat on straight; I know it's all lop-sided--you've no idea how easy it is for a woman's hat to get lop-sided--and then you can take me for that stroll in the park."

CHAPTER XXVII
A Game of Billiards

The officers' mess of the Guards--the billiard-room. Dinner was over, coffee was being drunk while the diners played a game of snooker pool, that is, some of them. There had been something in the atmosphere during the meal which was hardly genial. It is essential that all the members of a regimental mess should be as a band of brothers, as it were, a big and perfectly happy family. Unless they are on the best of terms with each other, that easy atmosphere is absent, and things become impossible; there must not be even a suspicion of a rift in the lute, if that complete harmony is to reign without which the position becomes unbearable.

In the officers' mess of a British regiment, as a rule, the conditions which make for comfort are not to seek; in that famous regiment, in the whole history of its mess, they never had been to seek until quite recently. Now something had crept in which jarred. First there had been the deplorable business of Sydney Beaton. They were just beginning to recover from that when there came the peculiar conduct of Jackie Tickell, his own version of which we have heard Major Reith tell Miss Forster. Mr. Tickel's action had had an even more deplorable effect upon the morals of the mess than the major had cared to admit. This had been to a large extent owing to the position taken up by Anthony Dodwell. He had declared that what Mr. Tickell had done was a slur upon himself, and had gone so far as to demand that the whole affair should be referred to a court of honour.

Than that sort of thing nothing could have been more foreign to the regimental traditions. It had always been regarded as a matter of course that among the officers of the Guards there should be no differences of opinion; if there were, they were certainly not to make themselves heard in public. The regiment never had been concerned in any such inquiry as that which Dodwell suggested. If his suggestion was acted upon, all sorts of unpleasant consequences would follow. Not only would the whole disreputable business have to be made officially public, but outsiders would have to be called in to adjudicate in what after all was a family quarrel; which, in effect, would mean that other regiments would sit in judgment on the Guards. In the eyes of authority, than that a more inconceivable state of affairs there could scarcely be.

What was to be done to restore the harmony that had heretofore reigned it was not easy to see; a single jarring note is so apt to keep on ringing in the ears. Sydney Beaton had gone--where, no one, not even his nearest and dearest, seemed to know. He had been one of the most popular persons in the regiment, not only with his brother officers, but with the rank and file; his own company adored him. Not only was the one hideous scandal still fresh in men's memories, but now still worse stories were being whispered about it.

It was difficult to say how they had first gained currency. Someone must have been the first to whisper something, but who that someone was no one seemed to know. Two stories had gone right through the regiment; one, that Sydney Beaton had turned professional thief; the other, that he had murdered Noel Draycott.

Why Mr. Tickell had chosen the moment when these stories filled all the air to take up the position he had done, his friends and acquaintances were quite at a loss to determine. The thing was over and done with; Beaton had admitted his guilt by running away; what on earth possessed Tickell, they demanded, that he should want to start muddying the water all over again? If he had had any doubts on the matter, he might have kept them to himself; it was too late to declare them in public now; he ought to have done it ages ago; the thing was all settled and done with. Then there was the absence of Draycott. If Draycott had been about, and he had said what he had said, Mr. Tickell would soon have been disposed of; Draycott would have agreed with Dodwell, there would have been two to one, Tickell would have been compelled to bow to the weight of evidence. As things were, the case against Beaton rested on one man's word only--Anthony Dodwell's. Tickell had not directly impugned it; but he had done almost as bad. He had stood up to Dodwell in a quite unexpected fashion. Jackie Tickell was an easy-going, good-natured youngster, who in general preferred to do anything rather than come to an open rupture with anyone; yet he had stood up to Dodwell; and all the regiment knew that there was no more unpleasant man to quarrel with. He had said to him in the hearing of them all:

"You know, Dodwell, I'm not saying for a moment that you didn't see what you thought you saw."

Dodwell interposed.

"It's not a question of what I thought I saw; I should not have made an accusation of that sort had I not been certain. Just as you see me strike this match"--he struck one to illustrate his words--"as certainly I saw Beaton cheat."

"I'm not denying that in the least, but, you see, I didn't."

"What has that to do with the matter? If I tell you that I did strike this match, are you to be at liberty to doubt it merely because you didn't happen to see me do it?"

"The things ain't the same; you can't compare them. Because you're satisfied that you saw Sydney Beaton cheat, it doesn't follow that I am; and until I am I'm not going to keep the money which was his if he played fair."

"You seem to be altogether forgetting," put in Frank Clifford, "that Dodwell wasn't the only person who saw. What about Draycott? And look at the way in which Beaton did a bunk!"

"I'm not so sure, if I'd been treated as we treated him, that I shouldn't have acted as Beaton did; we had all of us had as much as was good for us to drink--and that's where it was. As for Draycott, I had a chat or two with him, and it isn't so clear to me as it might be, that he wasn't rather sorry that he spoke."

Anthony Dodwell had looked very black, and he then and there publicly announced that if that was the way in which Tickell chose to look at it, he would insist on having the whole business referred to arbitrators, who would act as members of a court of honour.

So far Dodwell had not gone any farther; that is, he had not brought the matter before his official superiors in a form which would render it impossible for them to continue to ignore it. It is possible that he had been given the hint not to, and that words had been spoken both to him and to Mr. Tickell which had been meant to be not only words of healing, but also of warning.

That night, at the mess dinner, Dodwell had seemed to be in a curious frame of mind; nor, when they were in the billiard-room, did his mood seem to have sweetened. He had what is apt to be a very unpopular possession--a biting tongue; under the guise of a smiling exterior he could, when he liked, set a whole room by the ears. Jackie Tickell not only never said willingly a thing which could wound either the present or the absent, but there were not infrequent occasions when it was only with difficulty that he said anything at all; his tongue was certainly not the readiest part of him, a fact of which Dodwell, apparently relying on his notorious good temper, had more than once taken advantage. Dodwell played all games well; the different varieties of billiards he played almost as well as a professional. Tickell played very few games well; at billiards he was a notorious duffer; why he ever played snooker-- which, for a poor performer, in good company, at anything like points, is apt to be an expensive amusement--he alone could tell. What amusement he derived from it was a mystery; at the end of a game he was almost invariably the one player who had to pay all the others. Yet there never was a game of snooker from which he was willingly left out.

That evening he was, if possible, playing worse than usual, missing easy shots, leaving certainties for the man who followed--who happened to be Dodwell. Thanks partly to his own skill, and almost as much to Jackie's generosity, Anthony Dodwell was piling up a huge score, and nearly every time he put a ball down he returned sarcastic thanks to Jackie. As a bad player of snooker pool not only loses himself, but is the cause of loss to others, Jackie's misdemeanours gratified no one but Dodwell.

"Really, Jackie," declared Cyril Harding, when on one occasion he had managed to leave a white ball over one pocket and, in some mysterious fashion, the black over another, "you might be doing it on purpose. I wonder how many that is you've given Dodwell?"

"I do seem to be making rather a mess of it tonight," admitted Jackie.

"I sometimes wonder," persisted Payne, "if it ever occurs to you that you are not the only person who has to pay. If there's anything to which I personally object, it is to seeing Dodwell get that assistance that he does not stand in need of; as if he couldn't put the lot of us in the cart without help from anyone."

Dodwell, putting down both the white and the black, proceeded to make a break, for which he professed himself grateful to Jackie at the end.

"Thank you, Tickell; these gifts which you persist in making me are really rather overwhelming. Every time I come to the table I find that you have left me everything you possibly can; I hope the victims of your unnatural generosity will not think that we are in collusion. Do you know, I myself am almost moved to wonder if you are doing it on purpose?"

Mr. Tickell looked unhappy, but he said nothing; his tongue, as was its wont, seemed to be tied in a knot. He moved away from Dodwell's neighbourhood; but the other's sarcasm followed him.

"I'm in rather a difficult position; if I don't take advantage of your leaves they'll think that I'm not trying; and if I do, since they are so regular, they'll wonder."

As the victim continued silent, and something in the bearing of the others more than hinted that in their opinion he was going too far, some contrary spirit seemed to push Dodwell farther still.

"At bridge, I've heard it maintained that a bad player ought to pay his partner's losses; if that was the rule at snooker, Tickell, it would be awkward for you; you might have to break in on that little pot of money of which we have heard so much, and which you so chivalrously refused to put into your pocket because, as I understand the matter, some friend of yours put Noel Draycott away."

At this Major Reith, who was the senior officer present, interposed.

"Dodwell, you have no right to say that sort of thing."

"In your opinion? Thank you for its expression."

Jackie Tickell came towards the speaker.

"I didn't quite catch what you said, Dodwell--at least, I hope I didn't. Did I understand you to say that a friend of mine had put Noel Draycott away?"

"It would at least appear--I won't say at a convenient moment for you--that someone has--would you prefer that I should use another form of words, and say--murdered Noel Draycott?"

"Who says that someone has murdered Noel Draycott?"

The words did not come from one of the previous speakers; they were uttered by someone who had just come into the room; in a voice which was startlingly familiar to all those who heard it. With one accord each man in the room turned round to stare in the direction from which the words had come. Just standing inside the doorway was the man who had first been spoken of as having been put out of the way, and then as having been murdered--Noel Draycott.

CHAPTER XXVIII
An Irregular Visitor

It was probably some moments before the occupants of the billiard-room realised what had happened; it was certainly some little time before they even dimly perceived what the advent of the new-comer must mean.

It was George Payne's turn to play; he was just about to make his stroke when the door had opened. Leaning over the table, his cue in position, he stared at the man who had just come in at the door. The other players, each with his cue in his hand, stared too.

Noel Draycott was something to stare at. He seemed to have grown thinner since they had seen him last; he looked as if he had been ill. There was a recently healed scar on his forehead, another right across his left cheek. His hair had been cut very close to his head, a strip of plaster came from the back to the front. The fact was unmistakable that he must have been pretty considerably in the wars. He had on a dinner-jacket. In his right hand was an ebony cane with a crook handle, on which he seemed to lean as if in need of its support.

He stood looking round the room as if searching for individual faces. His eyes rested first on one and then on another with a glance as of pleased recognition. When they reached Dodwell they rested on him rather longer than on any of the others, with, this time, something in them which was hardly pleasure.

It was he who broke the silence which had followed his appearance with a question:

"Playing snooker? Don't let me interrupt you. Go on playing. You look as though you had got an easy one. How's the family--all all right?"

As he came farther into the room they broke into speech; they came crowding round him.

"Noel, old man!" exclaimed Clifford, "is this a little game which you've been playing? To spring a surprise on us like this when we were all thinking---- Why, on my word, I was very nearly on the point of going into mourning. I'd sooner see you--I don't know that there is anything I'd rather see."

A hearty chorus of welcome greeted him from all sides.

"Draycott," declared Major Reith, "you may laugh at me, but as I look at you I hardly know whether I am standing on my head or my heels. Do you know that when last I saw you I would have been willing to swear before a jury of medical men that you were dead? My dear, dear man, if you only knew how glad I am to see you--what a weight you are lifting off my mind. You're sure you're not a ghost?"

Draycott's smile was a little pale and wan, as if the major's suggestion was hardly as much of a joke as he would have liked it to be.

"I've always understood that ghosts are unsubstantial things. If you'll have a prod at me with your cue, you'll find that I'm solid enough; only go easy--I'm not yet as firm on my pins as I mean to be soon."

"But, my dear fellow, where on earth have you been hiding all this time? Do you know that all the papers are full of what they call the mysterious disappearance of Captain Draycott? All sorts of theories have been started, but none of them has ever come to anything. People were beginning to wonder if you had been snatched up by a flying machine, and carried above the clouds; and now you drop in in this unexpected fashion as if we'd only seen you half an hour ago! Do you realise the fact that you'll have to give a realistic account of what you've been up to, and why you've been keeping the readers of the halfpenny papers all gaping with wonder?"

"As it happens, I do recognise that some sort of explanation is required; and it is to give it, after a fashion, that I've come. Captain Dodwell, may I trouble you not to leave the room?"

Anthony Dodwell had not been among those who had crowded round to bid the new-comer welcome. His demeanour had been singular. The major had spoken of Draycott as a possible ghost. Captain Dodwell was regarding him not only as if he were an actual ghost, but almost, as it seemed, with the unreasonable terror with which people are supposed to regard spectral visitants in tales and legends. At the sound of Draycott's voice he had started as if someone had struck him a heavy blow; when, turning, he saw him standing in the flesh, he gazed at him as if he were the most horrible sight he had ever seen. So far from showing any inclination to join the others in their cries of welcome, he had drawn himself farther and farther away from the object of so much attention, until, having at last reached the neighbourhood of the door, he seemed inclined to take himself through it.

It was this disposition which Noel Draycott's words were intended to check. Their immediate result was to divert general attention to Captain Dodwell. To judge from the look which came upon the different men's faces, the peculiarity of his bearing seemed to occasion them almost as much surprise as Draycott's original unexpected appearance. There was no cooler person in the regiment than Anthony Dodwell. In a community in which sangfroid had been raised to the dignity of a fetish, his calmness had become a byword. That you could never take Anthony Dodwell by surprise; that under no conceivable conditions would he ever turn a hair; that he would continue wholly at his ease under all sorts of unpromising conditions; that he would meet difficulty, danger, death, with a smile--these were axioms among those who knew him.

How far removed from fact these judgments of his friends were, it needed at that moment only one glance at Anthony Dodwell to show. Something, stirring him to the very sources of his being, had upset his equilibrium so entirely that it almost seemed to them as if they looked upon a stranger. When Draycott uttered his quietly spoken request that he would not leave the room, he stood for a second motionless; then, as he glanced at the speaker over his shoulder, they could see that his face had been transfigured by some violent emotion which was beyond their comprehension. It was with an effort which was obvious to all of them that at last he managed to speak.

"Why shouldn't I leave the room?"

It was an instant or two before Draycott, looking steadily at him, answered question with question.

"Do you require me to tell you?"

There was something in the quietly uttered words which made Dodwell wince as if they had pricked him. He seemed in doubt how to treat the challenge which they conveyed;

that they did convey a challenge was plain; his reply, when it came, was both sullen and undignified.

"If I want to go I shall go, and you shan't stop me."

Draycott's rejoinder was so curt as to be contemptuous.

"You know better than that."

"Why should I know better? I have taught you one lesson already. Shall I teach you another? I'll be hanged if I'll stay in a room in which you are."

"Dodwell!"

The sharp utterance of his name conveyed both a command and a threat, as the other seemed to perceive. He had made a half-movement towards the door, and had already stretched out his hand to open it--the tone in which Draycott pronounced his name seemed all at once to check him.

"Are you speaking to me," he demanded with what was almost a snarl, "or to a dog? Hang your impudence! Do you suppose I'm going to allow you to dictate to me whether I am to go or stay?"

Ignoring the speaker, Noel Draycott turned to the others.

"Will you men be so good as to see that Captain Dodwell doesn't leave the room until I've given the explanation which I am going to give? I am not very fit at present; in fact, it's against the doctor's orders that I'm here at all; but, as matters were going, I felt I had to come. If I were fit, I shouldn't trouble you; I should make it my own particular business to see that Captain Dodwell didn't leave the room until I'd finished; as it is, I'm afraid I must."

Clifford voiced the general feeling by the question which he put.

"Why do you want to go, Dodwell--what's up?"

Anthony Dodwell made an unsuccessful effort to treat the speaker with the air of insolence which they knew so well.

"Really, Mr. Clifford, I have yet to learn that I am to be called to account for my goings and comings by you."

"All the same, there's no reason why you shouldn't answer my question. Here's Noel come back out of the grave, as it were. It's pretty plain that he's been in the wars, and you know well enough what a pother there's been; especially when he asks you, why can't you stop and hear whatever he has to say?"

"Because I'd sooner go. If that doesn't appear to be a sufficient reason, I'm sorry."

"One moment, Captain Dodwell, if you please."

The interpolation came from Major Reith. Dodwell already had the door partly open.

"Well, major, what can I do for you--with your one moment?"

"To begin with, you can shut that door."

Striding forward with unexpected rapidity, the major, wresting the door from his grasp, shut it sharply.

"Reith! Do you imagine that I am going to take my orders, in such a manner, from you?"

"Only the other day you were throwing out some very uncomfortable hints about Draycott here; I'm not going to recur to them now, but you know very well what they were, but here is Draycott to answer for himself. In view of those hints which you threw out, I'm going to make it my business to see that you stay and hear what his answer is."

Confronted by the major, Anthony Dodwell drew himself up; there had been something hang-dog in his attitude just now. "By force?" he asked.

"Yes, if necessary, by force. You were one of those who resorted to force on an occasion which it is not necessary for me to recall to your memory, and in this very room. I may tell you that there is something in your attitude which makes me wonder if, in this business, you have not been guilty of conduct which is not altogether to your credit. If I am wrong, the fault is yours; I can conceive of no creditable reason why it should be necessary to resort to force to compel you to listen, in the very remarkable circumstances, to what Noel Draycott has to say."

"I may tell you, Dodwell, that I quite agree with Reith."

This remark came from Payne; it was more than echoed by Jackie Tickell. Mr. Tickell went bursting towards the pair at the door, still with his cue in his hand; he trailed it after him as if unconscious that he still had it.

"Considering how you've been throwing out hints about my taking advantage of Draycott's absence to doubt if Syd Beaton cheated as you say he did, it seems jolly rummy now Draycott has turned up to give me the dressing-down which only half an hour ago you seemed to think I needed, that instead of calling on him to do it, you want to what looks like take to your heels and run."

Dodwell looked at him very much as a bad-tempered big dog is apt to regard a courageous little one.

"If you're not very careful I shall whip you, Jackie Tickell; I don't intend to stand more than a certain amount of impertinence, even from an ass."

Instead of showing signs of trepidation, the little man seemed to grow more heated.

"We'll see what you will or won't do when we've heard what Draycott has to say. Until he has said it, you'll do nothing; you won't even run away. Draycott, do you remember that poker business? I've been thinking a lot about it since; I'd have had a jaw with you about it if you'd been here----"

Noel Draycott cut him short.

"That's all right, Tickell, you can have all the jaw with me you like a little later on, if you want to talk to me at all after what I am going to say; but in the meanwhile, if you don't mind, I'd rather get off my chest what's on it, in my own way."

Major Reith was standing with his back to the door. In front of him on one side was Anthony Dodwell, on the other Jackie Tickell.

"Hullo!" he suddenly exclaimed, "there's someone outside who wants to come in; who's there?"

The door had been opened by someone without sufficiently far to come into contact with his broad back, which acted as an effectual buffer.

As he moved it was open wide enough to admit one of the orderlies of the evening, Private Henry Barnes.

"Well, Barnes," inquired the major, "what is it you want?"

"If you please, sir--a lady."

Holding the door open at its widest the orderly ushered in--Miss Forster.

CHAPTER XXIX
The Visitor Remains

Had the billiard-table taken to itself wings and commenced to waltz about the room, those present could scarcely have been more amazed. That a lady could be introduced in that haphazard, unlooked-for, bewildering fashion by one of their own servants, who knew the written and unwritten rules as well as anyone living--it was a crime almost equivalent to high treason. It was all done before they had really time to recover their breath--the lady was in, the orderly had gone, the door was closed; there they were, gaping at her, and she was looking at them. They seemed to have lost their presence of mind, to say nothing of their manners.

Presently her attention became centred on Noel Draycott.

"You!"

The monosyllable seemed to burst from her in the fullness of her surprise. Plainly he was as much of a ghost to her as he had been to his colleagues of the mess. Major Reith stammeringly took upon himself the task of endeavouring to make it clear to her that the position was unusual.

"Miss Forster, I--I'm afraid it's rather contrary to regimental custom to receive ladies in this apartment. Some mistake has been made. Let me take you to where you will feel more at home."

A surprising interruption came from Noel Draycott.

"No mistake has been made. It is by my instructions that Miss Forster has been shown in here. She has a right to be present at what I am about to say; you will see that, Reith, yourself, before I have finished."

It was said with an air of authority which caused the others to look at him askance. Miss Forster turned to Major Reith, holding out something in her hand.

"I received," she said, "this card." She read out what was written on it: "'If Miss Forster will present herself at the main entrance to the officers' mess to-night about ten o'clock, and will hand this card to the orderly whom she will find in attendance, she will learn the whole truth about Sydney Beaton.'"

"May I look at that card?" inquired the major. She gave it to him. "This is the most extraordinary thing to receive. May I ask how it reached you?"

"I found it awaiting me on my return home this afternoon. I was told that a man had brought it who said that there was no answer."

Captain Draycott carried the lady's explanation several stages farther.

"That card came from me; I wrote it. I gave Barnes directions to show Miss Forster in here directly she arrived. As Miss Forster is at least as much interested in Sydney Beaton as any of us, and has heard one story, I consider that the least we can do is to give her the first opportunity which offers to become acquainted with the truth."

The major still seemed uncomfortably conscious of the irregularity of the position.

"Really I hardly know what to say; but if it is the general wish that this lady shall remain----"

Mr. Tickell took upon himself to answer before the sentence was concluded.

"Of course it's the general wish; we are only too glad to have Miss Forster among us. Miss Forster, won't you have a chair?"

The lady declined; she said she would rather stand. One person declared himself to be in disagreement with Mr. Tickell--Anthony Dodwell.

"Without intending the least discourtesy, I cannot admit that Draycott is entitled to introduce his lady friends where no ladies are allowed, even if the intruder is Miss Forster."

111

"Then in that case you are one against all the rest of us, so you don't count. Now, Noel, what is it all about? Cut it as short as you can, old man, and then, as Reith puts it, if Miss Forster will allow us, we will take her somewhere where she will feel more at home."

Thus urged, Mr. Draycott prefaced his story with a few outspoken, candid words; every eye was fixed upon him, and all was still.

"The story which I am about to tell you is not very much to my credit, nor to that of others; I don't propose to try to excuse myself in any way whatever; I'll just say my say straight out."

He paused for a second as if to get his words into proper sequence.

"I can tell you the first part in half a dozen sentences; in fact, in one: That night when Sydney Beaton was accused of cheating, he never did cheat, and we behaved as we did to an innocent man."

Mr. Tickell broke out the moment the words were uttered.

"If I haven't felt it in my bones; the very next morning in bed I began to feel it; I've not been easy in my mind ever since. Now, Dodwell, what do you say to that?"

"I say that, for reasons of his own, Draycott says the thing which is not; you all heard what he said that night."

"What I said then was a lie; one for which I deserve all that I am likely to get. I behaved all through like a blackguard--that's what I want to tell you."

"You may put it either way you like," sneered Anthony Dodwell; "it is plain to the meanest intelligence that you behaved like a blackguard whichever way you put it. Either you were lying then, or you're lying now; from neither predicament do you come out nicely."

Draycott ignored the other's words.

"Dodwell owed Beaton a grudge, and I owed Dodwell money, or at least, he said I did."

"You're a pretty bounder--I said you did!"

"He said I did. As a matter of fact, I don't believe that I owed him a farthing; but he made out that I owed him a lot, more than I could pay without going to the Jews, which I had promised my father I never would do. I didn't want to have a row, or a scandal; I've seen since what a fool I was, but it seemed to me then that he had got me under his thumb. He had, as I said, a grudge against Beaton; that was about some money which he said Beaton owed him and which Beaton wouldn't pay."

"If I had posted Mr. Beaton, as I ought to have done, that would have brought him to his senses, and then Mr. Draycott wouldn't have been standing there, stuffed with the lies he's going to tell."

Still Draycott continued to ignore the other's words; he went on with his story as if Dodwell was not persistently interrupting.

"Dodwell said to me that if I would help him to get even with Beaton, he would say no more about the money which he made out I owed him, and as I was tired of his perpetual dunning, I was cad enough to listen."

"You were a cad first, last, and altogether, Mr. Draycott."

"Then that night we played poker, and Dodwell said that he had seen Beaton cheating; then he looked at me, and he winked; I knew what he meant, and I said that I had too--but I hadn't."

There arose an outcry from those who heard him; all the men began speaking at once. Major Reith called them to order.

"Gently, gentlemen, gently; let us know where we are standing."

"You are standing," cried Anthony Dodwell, "in the presence of an infamous animal whom only the fact that Miss Forster is here, prevents me from characterising as he deserves. I don't wish to assert that he took care that the lady was here before he began what he calls his story; but when the lady has gone he will receive from me the treatment from which her presence saves him."

"If you will take my advice," the excited gentleman was told by Major Reith, "you will let Draycott tell his story without comment or interruption; when he has finished you will be able, if you think it necessary, to tell yours; but you will not improve your case by doing your best to keep him from stating his. Draycott, do we understand you to say that you did not see Sydney Beaton cheat?"

"I did not."

"You did not see him exchange one card for another?"

"I did not."

"You did not see him do anything irregular, or indulge in malpractices of any kind?"

"Absolutely no; nor do I believe that he did. I did not believe it then; I believe it still less now. I believe he played as straight a game as anyone else, and Dodwell knew it."

Three or four men interposed to prevent Anthony Dodwell venting his wrath upon the speaker then and there.

"I'll break every bone there is in your body," he declared, "before I've done with you, you libellous hound."

Suffering his threat to go unheeded, Draycott looked him steadily in the face. Clifford, the biggest and most powerful man in the regiment, addressed himself to the infuriated Dodwell.

"Let me tell you something frankly. I've had doubts about you from the first; and I've not been the only doubter. I for one have regretted the part I played that night; I only hope that one day I shall be able to forget it. I'm not saying a word for Draycott, he's given himself away with every word he's said; but he'd better do that than continue to play the cur to Beaton in the way he owns he has done. Your case, Dodwell, is safer in our hands than in your own. After what has happened we'll sift his story to the bottom before we pronounce judgment on it either way; I'm afraid the time has gone by when his mere 'Yes' or 'No' would be accepted. But if you want to force us to the conclusion that you are the kind of person he says you are, you can't do better than continue your present behaviour. If you weren't afraid of what he has to say, you'd let him say it; that, to us, is as plain as the nose upon your face. Draycott, I'm going to take the liberty of asking you one or two questions. Do you seriously wish us to understand that merely because Dodwell winked at you, you charged Beaton with being a cheat when you knew he wasn't?"

"That's what it comes to."

"Then it comes to a very ugly thing."

"That I realise. Dodwell said to me that if I helped him to get even with Beaton he'd say no more about that money. I took the wink to mean that that was the moment in which he wanted me to help him--and I did. The next day he gave me a quittance for the whole amount; I had not misunderstood him."

"Do you mean to tell us that the next day you talked Beaton over between you, and that each of you admitted to the other that he had lied?"

"The next morning Dodwell came to my room and told me that after all he had found out that he was wrong in supposing that I owed him money, and he gave me a sort of friendly note admitting it in so many words."

"So you got your price?"

"I did."

"Then what was said about the night before?"

"Very little--in words; but he knew I hadn't seen Beaton cheat, and I knew he hadn't."

"How did you know he hadn't?"

"Because Beaton hadn't cheated; I'd been watching him all the time, he was seated next to me, and I was sure of it."

"Dodwell charged him with substituting one card for another. There was a card upon the floor; Dodwell said he had dropped it and taken the other in its place."

"The card upon the floor was mine."

"Do you mean that you had dropped it intentionally?"

"I didn't know I had dropped it till it was picked up. I recognised it as mine when I saw it--it was a nine of spades. I had two pairs in my hand--nine high; the nine of spades was one of them."

"And you, knowing the nine of spades was yours, had allowed us to think that Beaton had dropped it from his hand to take another, and a better one, in its place; in fact, one which gave him a full. You allowed us to think that?"

"I did."

"You admit that you never for a moment supposed that Beaton had cheated, having sufficient reasons for knowing otherwise; but it's possible that Dodwell may have thought he did."

"He never thought it."

"What grounds have you for saying that? Now, Dodwell, don't you interfere; you shall have your turn presently, when you'll have every opportunity of making Draycott out even blacker than he has painted himself. Consider, Draycott, before you speak; it's a very queer story you're asking us to swallow, much queerer than your first. What grounds have you for saying that Dodwell never thought, even at the moment of making his accusation, that Beaton had cheated?"

"He told me so."

"Weren't you surprised at his making to you such a remarkable admission?"

Draycott paused before he answered.

"I was inclined to think at first that he might have made a mistake, though I couldn't see how he had done it; but before very long I knew he hadn't. That nine of spades was on the floor. I didn't know I'd dropped it, but as I threw down my hand he saw me brush it off the table with my elbow. He knew that it never had anything to do with Beaton."

"When did he make you these frank confessions?"

"That belongs to the part of the story that I haven't come to yet."

"Oh, there is a part of the story that you haven't come to? What part's that? You seem to have been bottling up a good deal inside yourself, Draycott."

"It's the story of what took place on the night of the Easter ball at Avonham."

CHAPTER XXX
The Story of what Happened after the Easter Ball

So far the only sounds heard in the billiard-room had been the questions and the answers. The listeners had been so still; particularly had this seemed to be the case with Violet Forster. She gripped with her gloved hand the back of the chair as if from the very intensity of the grip she derived moral support. She stood very straight, with her lips tightly pressed together, and with a strained look on her white face, as if with her every faculty she was bent on following the words, without missing a syllable or an accent, and, if possible, reading any hidden meaning which might lie behind them. Her immobility was so continuous as to be almost unnatural.

But when Mr. Draycott made that reference to what had happened on the occasion of the Easter ball at Avonham her whole being seemed to undergo a sudden transformation. Her hands fell to her side; a faint flush came into her cheeks; her lips parted; she moved a little forward with an air of odd expectancy, as if she longed, and feared, to hear what was coming.

Before Draycott was allowed to continue there was an interposition from Anthony Dodwell, addressed directly to him.

"Let me warn you, Draycott, that for every lie you're going to utter--and I can see from the look of you that you're going to tell nothing else but lies--I'll call you to an account; and don't flatter yourself that, however your friends may try to cover you, you'll escape me."

As he answered, Draycott looked Anthony Dodwell very straight in the face.

"I shall never be afraid of you again--never! Don't you suppose it!"

"Don't you be so sure. You were afraid of me once; and, when you and I are again alone together, you'll be just as much afraid of me as you ever were. Gentlemen of your habits of body are only courageous when they know themselves to be in a position in which they are sure of being protected by their friends."

"I don't think I ever was afraid of you, Dodwell; but you were a mystery to me, I didn't understand you, and I was a fool. But now I do understand you; if you were holding a revolver to my throat I shouldn't be afraid of the kind of man you are. I know you."

Draycott turned to the girl.

"You remember, Miss Forster, that on the night of the Easter ball you said something to me about that poker business?"

"I remember quite well."

"I'd been ashamed of myself a long time before that; but what you said to me made my shame greater than I could bear. All along I had had a feeling that if Beaton had gone under because of what had happened, of what I had said, then I was directly responsible for his undoing; although he had never done me a bad turn--I had done that to him. I understood that nothing had been heard of him, that he had disappeared. He might have committed suicide; I was haunted by a feeling that he had. If so, his blood was on my head."

"From whom have you been learning all this fine language, Draycott?"

The question came from Dodwell; it went unanswered.

"I told myself, over and over again, that I would make a clean breast of it, that I would let everybody know that Beaton was a man of honour, and that I was not. But I had not found it easy, when it came to the point; in the first place, there was Dodwell; and then there was my--I suppose it was cowardice."

"In anything in which you were concerned one can always count on your playing the coward."

"But that night, after what you had said to me, I made up my mind that I could stand it no longer. I looked up Dodwell and I told him so. He laughed, as he always did; then when he saw I was in earnest----"

"I saw you were drunk."

"When he saw I was in earnest, he said that if I would turn up after the dance he would talk things over with me then."

"I warn you once more--look after that tongue of yours."

"I should advise you, Dodwell," struck in Clifford, "to begin by looking after your own. You keep on talking about Draycott's cowardice, while all the time you seem to be in mortal terror of what he is going to say."

Noel Draycott continued as if he had not been interrupted.

"When the others went upstairs I stayed behind."

"But where were you?"

The question, eagerly asked, came from Violet Forster.

"At first I was in the conservatory."

"But weren't the lights out?"

"They had been; I turned some of them on again. Dodwell came to me. We started quarrelling right away."

"You were quarrelling drunk." This was Dodwell.

"I told him that I meant to tell you, Miss Forster, the whole truth about that poker business in the morning; I knew you were interested in Beaton, and that you had a right to be the first to hear. Afterwards, I informed him, I should make it known in the regiment. When he saw that I meant what I said, he threatened me."

"You miserable animal--threatened you!"

"When, in spite of his threats, I made it clear that nothing would keep me from doing what I said, he got worse. He would not let me leave him. I didn't want to have a row with him; I knew there would be more than enough scandal anyhow; I was in a house in which I was a stranger. As you know, the whole lot of us were asked to the dance, and I had no acquaintance with either my host or hostess; but it was only after a sort of rough and tumble that I managed to slip away."

He paused, as if to enable himself to recall quite clearly what had occurred. Dodwell, seizing a billiard cue which rested against a chair, glared at him as if he would have liked to continue the quarrel where it had left off.

"He followed me; I don't know the geography of the house, but I know that we came to what seemed to be a sort of drawing-room in which there was a lot of gilded chairs and furniture."

"I know," said Miss Forster. She glanced at Major Reith. "You remember?"

"Perfectly--am I ever likely to forget?"

Draycott went on.

"In the scrimmage we had we knocked the things all over the place. We made such an awful din that I kept on wondering how it was that nobody heard us."

"Someone did hear you--I did. And Major Reith heard you also."

This again was Miss Forster.

"He wouldn't let me leave the room until I'd promised that I wouldn't say a word about what I said I would, and I wouldn't promise. I was no match for him; he's a bigger and a stronger man than I am; he hammered me a good deal, and I told him what I thought of him. There was a sort of a club lying on a table; he sent me flying against the table, the table went over, and I with it; the club fell on to the floor. I told him again what I thought of him as I was going over. I suppose that made him madder than ever. He picked up the club, and he struck at me with it. I put up my left arm to ward off the blow, and he broke it--just there."

Mr. Draycott held up his left arm, touching it between the wrist and the elbow.

"I heard the bone snap. I was trying to get up from the floor when he hit me a second time; that time I think it must have got me on the head--down I went again, for good. Yet I was conscious that he kept on hitting me as I lay motionless. What is still queerer--I can't explain it, but I had an extraordinary feeling that Sydney Beaton had come into the room, that he saw Dodwell raining blows down on me, that he said something, that Dodwell gave a yell at the sight of him, and ran away. That's all I can remember of what took place at Avonham."

"It seems to be a pretty good deal." This was Clifford. He turned to Dodwell. "What do you think?"

"It's a farrago of lies."

"Somehow, Dodwell, you don't look as if it were a farrago of lies. I don't want to prejudice the minds of the judge and jury before whom you will possibly be brought, but if I were betting I should be inclined to lay odds--against you. Do you deny that you did meet Draycott in the conservatory after the rest of us had gone to bed?"

"What right have you to ask me questions?"

"I see; that's the tone you take! What right has anyone to ask you questions? As I expected--you deny that you quarrelled with Draycott?"

"What have my private affairs to do with you?"

"Your private affairs? It has come to that! You call attempted murder your private affair? Do you deny that you did strike Draycott as he says?"

"I deny everything."

"I see--a general denial. You know, Dodwell, you should have started denying at the first. When you tacitly admit that you did meet Draycott, and that you did quarrel with him, you have already reached the point at which a general denial only tells against you. What I don't understand, Draycott, is, where have you been since that night? I don't know if you are aware that the British public has been taking a most lively interest in your private affairs, and that all sorts of more or less interested persons have been searching for you high and low. It's a good time ago, you know, since the Easter ball. The puzzle is, in what unfindable place have you been hidden all this while?"

"I've been with Beaton."

"You've been--where? Pardon me, Miss Forster, you were going to speak."

"I--I was only going to ask him what he meant by--by saying that he has been with Mr. Beaton."

"It is not altogether easy to explain; you will get a fuller explanation from someone else; I can only tell you what I know. The last thing I remembered at Avonham was, as I have told you, that Dodwell was beating me about the head with a club as I lay on the floor."

"You delightful person, Mr. Dodwell." The interruption came from Frank Clifford. "Mixed up with it was the feeling that Beaton was in the room. Then, I suppose, I lost consciousness. When I came to myself again I couldn't make out what had happened, or where I was. Then by degrees I began to understand that I was in bed, in a strange room, and that Beaton was leaning over me. 'Why, Syd!' I said--it wasn't a very brilliant remark to make, but I remember that I did make it. What he said I don't know, I fancy I must have slipped back into unconsciousness again. To make a long story short, when I did come really to myself again, I found that I was in Beaton's rooms."

"But how on earth did you get there?" demanded Major Reith. "When I last saw you I could have sworn that you were lying dead on the floor of that room at Avonham. Directly my back was turned, did you get up and walk to Beaton's rooms?"

"That's a part of the story with which I'm not very well posted. It wasn't only imagination when, while Dodwell was clubbing me, I felt that Beaton had come into the room; he had, and Dodwell had seen him--and he saw what Dodwell was doing to me. He will be able to bear witness to that part of my story, as Dodwell is probably aware."

Suddenly, it seemed, that Mr. Dodwell had decided to take up a new position as regarded the last part of Noel Draycott's story.

"I don't deny that I did strike him, I never have denied it, but what I did was only done in self-defence."

"While a man was lying on the floor you struck him, with a club, in self-defence?"

"He had been threatening me, and telling all sorts of lies, and I was half beside myself with rage, and I meant to give him the thrashing he deserved, and if I went a little too far it was because I had been drinking, as he had, and was mad with fury, and didn't know what I was doing--and there you are."

"And all this time the world has been wondering what became of Draycott, and you never so much as hinted that you knew."

"I didn't know; I was just as much in the dark as anyone--I wondered."

"You thought you had killed him?"

Dodwell was silent; Clifford went on. "You thought you had killed him, and that was why you never said a word."

"I knew I hadn't killed him."

"How did you know?"

"If I had he'd have been where I left him; he wouldn't have got up and walked away."

"It didn't occur to you that what you had done to him that night had anything to do with his disappearance?"

"I don't know what you mean."

"You didn't think it advisable, or necessary, to come forward and throw some sort of light on what seemed an insoluble mystery by telling your story of what took place that night?"

"I wished to avoid a scandal."

"What a thoughtful man you are, Mr. Dodwell! It did not occur to you, I suppose, that if you did tell your story you'd be in the hands of the police immediately after--that had nothing to do with your silence?"

Anthony Dodwell was silent. Clifford, who seemed to be taking on himself the office of examiner-in-chief, put a question to Draycott:

"How came Beaton to be at Avonham that night? Was he an invited guest?"

"That I cannot tell you; I only know it was lucky for me that he was there."

"You say he saw Dodwell clubbing you, and that when Dodwell saw him he ran away. Why didn't Beaton, knowing that crime had been committed--because you must have been in a pretty bad state, or Reith wouldn't have thought you dead----?"

"I believe I was; I believe that for ever so long nobody thought I should live; indeed, it's only by a miracle that I'm alive now, and owing to Beaton's care of me."

"Then, as I was saying, knowing that a crime had been committed, why ever didn't Beaton rouse the house?"

"That again I cannot tell you. I fancy that, as Dodwell put it, he also wished to avoid causing a scandal."

"From, however, I presume, a different motive; he couldn't have been afraid of the police. Then are we to understand that you have remained in Beaton's quarters all this time?"

"Exactly; he did everything for me; I owe everything to him--life, all."

"And what does he owe to you?"

"That's just it; what doesn't he owe to me? It's the consciousness of what he owes that's driven me here to-night; which made me feel that I must take the first chance that offered to clear him in the eyes of all you fellows--and that I must do it, too, in the presence of Miss Forster. That's why I arranged that she should be here; and now you fellows will see why I wanted her to stay. Only recently I recovered consciousness--what you could call consciousness--and since then I've been hanging between life and death; I know I couldn't lift a finger. I fancy that Dodwell must have hit me on some peculiar spot, because I believe the doctor fellows never thought I should regain my reason; I must have been a handful to Syd Beaton. I had done him the worst turn possible, and he knew what I'd done, but he treated me as if I'd been the best and truest friend that ever was. I'm convinced that if it hadn't been for him I shouldn't be here talking to you now. A better, a finer, a nobler fellow than he never lived--and that's what I want you fellows to know. You may do what you like to me; I deserve any punishment; but you ought to beg Sydney Beaton's pardon--and you've got to do it, too."

"Have we? You rush your fences. And, pray, where is Mr. Beaton, if, as you say, we have to beg his pardon?"

"I believe that, by now, he ought to be outside."

CHAPTER XXXI
Asking Forgiveness

"Outside!"

The word came from Violet Forster as if it were an echo. Turning, she made a wavering and, as it seemed, almost involuntary movement towards the door; then, as if suddenly remembering, shrank back and went all red. If there were any there who smiled, it was with sympathy; as if they saw how, even against her will, the girl's heart was being drawn towards the man who was on the other side of the door.

It was Major Reith who spoke, and it seemed with unnecessary sternness.

"Do you mean that Sydney Beaton is in the building? How do you know it?"

The reply was simple.

"He promised me that he would come."

"Promised you? When?"

"He came with me as far as the barracks. I'm afraid I'm not yet very good at getting about alone, but I shall be all right soon; he knew what I was coming for, and he promised me he would wait, and that, if he heard nothing, in about half an hour he would come in."

The girl asked an eager question.

"Was he in a taxicab? There was one waiting as I came in, by the pavement a little way down--I passed it. It was open; there was a man sitting inside whom I had the strangest feeling that I knew, although it was dark and I could not see; perhaps it was Sydney."

"I shouldn't wonder. He said he'd wait in the cab; but he ought to be here by now."

Facing round, Frank Clifford, as it were, addressed the meeting:

"Gentlemen, shall I go out and see if Sydney Beaton is still waiting in the cab?" There was an instant chorus of affirmatives. He turned to Violet. "Miss Forster, with your permission I will go and ask Mr. Beaton to do us the favour to come in here."

"I--I shall be very glad to see him."

"So shall we." He opened the door, but he was not yet through it when he broke into exclamations. "Why, Beaton, you're a sight worth seeing. I cannot tell you how glad I am to see you. We have only just heard from Draycott that you were outside; I'm acting as a deputation to ask you to come in. Gentlemen, Captain Beaton."

Sydney Beaton appeared in the doorway of the room from which, when he was last in it, he had been thrown out. There was a great difference between that man and this; so great that all those who were there, who had known the man that was so well, looked at him and wondered, and were ashamed. The few months which had elapsed since they had seen him last might have been years, so much was he changed; it needed the evidence of their own eyes to assure them that in so short a space of time a man could have so aged. The Sydney Beaton they had known was young, debonair, careless, incapable of looking seriously upon either life or death. This man was serious above and before all else; the burden of life weighed heavily on him; he was hollow-eyed; great lines seamed both his cheeks and forehead; his hair was grey; he had become an old man.

Their surprise at his appearance hushed them into silence. Beaton, as if not knowing what to make of their speechlessness, seemed disposed to draw back. But Draycott reassured him.

"It's all right, old man, I've told them; they know all about it; I think the sight of you has rather bowled them over."

Then they did speak, and the first was Jackie Tickell.

"Beaton, of course you can knock me down and jump on me if you like; I shan't say a word if you do, but it's an absolute fact that I never really doubted you; I knew you were a white man, although I did treat you like a pig. You know that pool--there was a pot of money in that pool--I haven't touched a farthing of it from that day to this, although there have been times when I've badly wanted it, but I knew all along that it was yours. I handed it over to the keeping of the mess--they'll tell you all about it; we've got it all right. And I say, you chaps, here's an idea. What do you say to giving Beaton a feed, a real tip-topper, and, at it, presenting him with the pool, as a--you know--not as a testimonial, but you know what I do mean?"

They laughed at Tickell as they crowded round Beaton. Major Reith spoke.

"Beaton, I have done you a serious injustice; how serious I did not realise until now--that I see you. I am more--more ashamed than I can tell you; to ask your pardon is to do nothing. Can you ever forgive me? I shall never be able to forgive myself; my punishment will be as great as yours."

Then Beaton spoke.

"Reith, I hope not; you don't know what my punishment has been."

"Looking at you, I can guess."

"I suppose you can; I believe it's printed pretty plain."

There came a chorus from the others--all asking for pardon.

"We didn't understand each other, that was what it was," said Beaton. "You never could have done what you did if we had. Yet I'm not sure that the lesson I've been taught wasn't worth learning even at the price I paid. I'm not the man you knew. I can see by the look that's on your faces that you've found that out for yourselves. I shall never be that man again; but don't take to yourselves any blame for that. I wouldn't, if I could."

"Will you also forgive me, Beaton? I admit that I, too, may have been mistaken."

This was Anthony Dodwell; there was something in the eyes which looked at him out of their hollow caverns which seemed to make him shrivel up.

"In your case it's not a question of forgiveness. You see, Dodwell, I know you. Since I was last in this room I've been in some strange company; I've met one or two men like you, and I haven't liked them. I know how you treated me; I saw how you treated Draycott that night at Avonham; you would treat me, and Draycott, exactly the same again tomorrow--if you had the chance. You can't like the man whom you know is that kind of person; you avoid him, if you can; you are on your guard against him, if you can't. If you are even superficially sorry for what you did to me you will take care that I never see or hear of you again. I am afraid that's as far as I'm prepared to go."

"And that's quite far enough. Now, Dodwell, you have our unanimous permission to do what you were so anxious to do at first--go."

Frank Clifford held the door wide open, with a significance it was impossible for the other to misunderstand. Anthony Dodwell showed how plainly he did understand by marching through it without a word.

Miss Forster had drawn back as Beaton entered the room, so that she had been behind him, where she had stayed. Now she came forward and touched him on the arm.

"Sydney!"

He was silent; he did not even pronounce her name; he took the hand which she offered, and bowed his head before her. Frank Clifford said:

"Miss Forster, I trust that I am neither presumptuous nor impertinent in suggesting that I think it possible that you are not over-anxious to stay with us much longer; if that is the case--I don't know how to put it, but--if you'd like to take Beaton with you, you can."

CHAPTER XXXII
In the Taxicab

They were alone together in the taxicab, the one which had been waiting. Draycott had been left behind. There had been a brief discussion as to the address to which the man was to be told to drive.

"Where are we going?" she had asked him.

"You are perfectly well aware," he had told her in the grave tones which had seemed to have become habitual, "that I'm not a fit person for you to consort with. Let us say to each other all that there is to be said here; it shouldn't take very long, there is so little to be said; then let us part company--for ever."

"That is your opinion, is it? It's very nice of you to express it. Where are you living?"

"In a road near Clapham Junction--Lavender Sweep; a name which suggests possibilities--which don't go any farther than the name. It's a street of little houses."

"What is your number?"

"A hundred and ninety-seven."

She spoke to the cabman.

"Drive us to 197 Lavender Sweep, Clapham Junction." Then to Beaton: "Will you open the door for me?"

She entered. He spoke to her still standing on the pavement.

"You know you ought not to go there; it's not the sort of place to which you're accustomed."

"Then the sooner I become accustomed the better. Will you please get in?"

He got in; the cab started; as it has been written, they were alone in the cab together. Their conversation, especially at the beginning, was of a distinctly singular sort; as a matter of fact, she was enjoying herself immensely. It was many a day since she had even supposed it possible that she could enjoy herself so much.

"You don't seem to be particularly glad to see me."

"What right have I to be glad?"

"That's it--what right have you? That's a particularly sensible inquiry, which makes it the more awkward--for me--that I should be rather glad to see you. I imagine that these things are an affair of temperament."

"You are laughing at me."

"I don't know what else to do, since you certainly aren't laughing at me. You might be an owl for gravity. You sit screwed up there in your corner as if you were afraid you might be infected with something if you came within a quarter of a mile of me."

"Put it the other way. I don't wish to carry infection to you."

"Don't you? How nice! What sort of infection do you think you'd carry? I'd like, if I did ask you to come nearer, to know the risk I'd run."

"You know the kind of creature I am."

"The ignorance is on your side; you don't know the kind of creature I am. Do you know this is the very first time you and I have been alone together in a taxicab?" He was silent. A sound came from her which might have been a laugh. "You're full of conversation."

"I am so oppressed by the hideous consciousness of being in a false position."

"Are you? We'll talk about all that kind of thing when we get to 197 Lavender Sweep."

"You don't know what kind of place it is I live in."

"I soon shall."

"What would your uncle say if he knew you were coming alone with me to my wretched rooms?"

"My uncle and I are two; he lives at Nuthurst, and I live in town. I also have what you call wretched rooms--of my own. I would have asked the man to drive us there, only I thought I would prefer to go to yours, and I should; and I'm going. Is anything very terrible about your wretched rooms?"

"A person of my sort ought to be glad to live anywhere; especially after some of the places in which I have resided."

"I know all about it."

"What do you mean?"

"Oh, I've been told; but would you mind leaving all that sort of thing until we get to your--wretched rooms? Let us, while we are in the cab, be frivolous; couldn't you be frivolous?"

"I've forgotten how to be."

"I believe you smiled."

"If I did it was the sort of smile with which you meet the dentist when he's going to play tricks with your teeth."

"It's some time since I was frivolous; it's rather hard that now, after all this time, I'm in a mood to frivol, you won't. Couldn't you try? For instance, you seem to have forgotten that I possess a name; couldn't you start by calling me Violet? I suppose it would be too much to expect you to get as far, at the start, as Vi?" There was silence. "Well, are you trying?"

"I'm trying not to."

"Thank you very much; does it require much effort?"

"All my strength."

"Have you got much?"

"Very little."

"Indeed? Then, if you're going to use it in that direction, I hope you've none at all. It's rather fine weather for the time of the year, isn't it? Is that the sort of remark you would like me to make? Will it need all your strength to enable you to answer that?"

"I wish you'd let me stop the cab and get out."

"I shall do nothing of the sort. How dare you suggest it? I suppose you think you're going to keep on behaving to me like this. My dear Sydney--you see, I call you by your Christian name, and it doesn't need much trying--my darling Sydney, my well-beloved Sydney--I'm going to be Mary Janeish--do you think I don't know what is going on inside you? You'd give--shall I say twopence?--to put out your hand and touch mine which is lying there upon the seat. You can see it, although you're not looking and you pretend you can't. Sydney, won't you touch it--just once?"

"I won't."

"Thank you; that is frank, and so sweet of you. You think you are as hard--oh, harder than that; and I believe that you have got much harder than you used to be, but when I've really made up my mind you shall, you'll melt and become--oh, yes, much softer than that. How far is Lavender Sweep? I don't seem to find it easy to get much out of you in this silly cab; perhaps I may have better fortune when we get to your wretched rooms. Is it much farther?"

"Let's say all that there is to be said now. I wanted to say it before we got into the cab; it will only make it worse for both of us if we wait till we get to my rooms. You shan't go there. I won't have you."

"Won't you? How are you going to stop me?"

"By giving myself up to the next policeman we meet, if there is no other way; he'd think himself in luck to get me."

"Sydney!"

"It's the truth, and you know it. What's the good of either of us pretending that you don't?"

"Will you please say nothing else until we reach your rooms? I won't, and I'd rather you didn't either. I'm going with you to your rooms, and nothing you can say or do will stop me. Now will you please be silent till we get to 97 Lavender Sweep? I think that, while we're in this cab, I prefer your silence to your conversation."

She had her way; not a word was spoken on either side until the cab drew up in front of one of a long terrace of houses.

CHAPTER XXXIII
"Vi!"

Miss Forster looked about the room into which he had ushered her, the first room on the right when you had come through the front door. It was the usual ground-floor front apartment of the £45 a year suburban "modern residence," a fair size, as a habitation for a "single gentleman," with a sufficiency of light, and air, and space.

"If this is one of your 'wretched rooms,' I don't think it's very wretched, don't you know; it compares not at all unfavourably with my best parlour."

Standing before the empty fireplace, he was observing her with singular intentness, brows knit, head bowed between his shoulders.

"You understand where the money to pay for this palatial apartment has come from; how it has been--earned? You saw me engaged in the practice of my profession that night at Avonham."

"Did I? Dear me! How terrible! Why should I mind?"

"You ought to mind; you do mind; at least it is certain that you would mind if you understood."

"It is because I do understand that I don't mind; unfortunately the understanding is all on one side; you do seem to be so slow in grasping the true inwardness of things. I want you to answer me one or two questions--will you?"

She had placed herself in an old arm-chair, and was looking up at him with the tip of a first finger touching either cheek. Her pallor had given way to a faint pink flush, which kept coming and going. Her whole face was lighted with laughter, as if challenging the persistent gravity which was on his.

"I will answer any questions you like to put, to the best of my ability."

"That's right, that's the proper tone in which to speak; as if you were faced by the rack and the thumb-screw, and similar pretty things. To begin with--I will make a statement; I was at Avonham that night."

"As if I didn't know it."

"I was wondering if you might have forgotten it." This was said with a little air of malice. "I saw poor Mr. Draycott lying on the floor, and I, as well as Major Reith, thought that he was dead. I've been asking myself how, during the very few minutes I was out of the room, you managed to take him away."

"You remember that I ran up against you in the hall?"

"Am I likely to forget? You did surprise me."

"And you surprised me; I hadn't a notion that you were in the house, or I shouldn't have been there."

"You might have stayed to say good-night, or ask me how I was; I had hurt my foot most frightfully. You didn't show the slightest sympathy."

"How was I to know?"

"That's just it. If you'd only said how-do-you-do, you'd have known. In your hurry you even left your bag behind you."

One could see the man wince; the woman's pause was perhaps to enable him to recover himself.

"Did you see what was in it?"

"The countess did--as probably Jane Simmons told you."

"That woman!"

"That woman! She came to see me the other day."

"What?"

"We had rather an interesting conversation. She's going to be married."

"Going to be married? To----"

He left the sentence unfinished, and the name unspoken; she smiled and nodded, as if she understood.

"I shouldn't be surprised; it's as likely to be him as anybody else. She's going to turn over a new leaf."

"Is she?"

"She's going to America with her husband."

"Are you sure of that?"

"I think she must have got married the very next day, and started the day after, because only the other morning a little box came through the post, postmarked Pittsburg, and in it was a piece of wedding cake, with a card on which was written, 'With the compliments of Julia Spurrier and her husband.'"

"Who was Julia Spurrier?"

"She was Jane Simmons; I dare say she had one or two other names besides, within your knowledge."

"She had. You understood what kind of person she was?"

"Perfectly; she made me understand."

"And I dare say she told you one or two things about me."

"She did--one or two; but we're coming to that presently. I want you first to explain to me how you got Mr. Draycott out of the house that night."

"I was rushing off to get something to wrap him in when I met you. I heard you and Reith go into that room, and I heard you both go out--I was outside the window. Directly you left it, I opened the window, picked up Draycott, carried him out, closed the window again--and it was done."

"I see--you call that done. But how did you manage to get him away from the neighbourhood of the house?"

"There was a motor-car a little way along the path, about as silent a one as there is made; I put him in that and off I went."

"Nothing could be simpler, could it? But why did you trouble to take him at all? What affair was he of yours? It wasn't as though he had treated you very nicely."

"Don't you see that it was the chance of my life?"

"The chance of your life? Good gracious! How?"

"That poker business--they said I cheated; it was a lie--an infernal lie."

"They've admitted it themselves to-night."

"They hadn't admitted it then, and I never thought I should have a chance of making them do it, until I saw that dear man Dodwell doing his best to murder Draycott as he lay there on the floor. Well, then, it was a wild-cat idea, but it was an idea. I thought that if I could get hold of Draycott, and he wasn't quite dead, and I could bring him back to life, he might feel some--some sort of gratitude. It was Draycott who supported Dodwell; I don't think they would ever have believed him if it hadn't been for Draycott. I fancy there wasn't a man in the regiment who hadn't a sort of feeling that Dodwell was a liar; it was Draycott's endorsement of his lie that did it."

She could see, when he paused, how the muscles of his face were working, and how his fingers twitched as he clenched and unclenched his hands.

"When I started to think afterwards, when hell was all about me, at first it was all a blur, I couldn't think how it could have happened--all of it; it was so--so impossible that they could have thought such a thing of me. Then, by degrees, I began to put trifles together, and to get some sort of a vague idea how--how it had all come about."

He pressed his hands to his temples; she fancied it must have become a trick with him; he had done it once or twice before, even when they were in the cab.

"I'd had a row with Dodwell about some money which he said I owed him; as you know, I owed pretty nearly everybody money, but I was quite sure I didn't owe him any. The way in which he made out that I did, did credit to something besides his financial genius. I had a suspicion that Draycott had had a row with him of the same kind. He had told me that he would be even with me for the position which I had taken up; and I began to see, afterwards, when I--I was looking for crusts in the gutter, that that lie he had told was his way of getting even, and I began to wonder if Draycott had backed it because Dodwell had got him under his thumb."

He gave a great sigh, which was the most eloquent thing he had done yet; there was something about the matter-of-fact way in which he did it which showed that, at any rate, that was an habitual trick of his. The abomination of desolation which, it suggested, was in his very soul, moved the girl with a sudden pain which seemed to go right through her.

"When, as I've said, I saw Dodwell hammering Draycott, the wild-cat idea came to me that, if I did Draycott a good turn, he might be disposed to do me another; Dodwell would have killed him if it hadn't been for me, so he did owe me something, if he was to owe me nothing more. If he would only own to me, between ourselves, that he hadn't seen me do what he said he had, that would be some satisfaction. I didn't like to feel that there was any possibility that he really believed that I was--that kind of thing; if he would admit to me, in private, that he had spoken in haste, that he might have been in error, I should have been a happier man. The reality surpassed all my expectations."

A wintry smile passed over his face; he stood up straighter; but he continued to speak in the halftones of the man from whose life all the salt has gone.

"Draycott turned out a perfect trump. We had a pretty tough time--the landlady here, who's a dear, good old soul, the doctor, and I between us--in pulling him through; Dodwell had used him cruelly, he will carry some of the scars with him to the grave--but it was a labour of love. I hadn't been so happy for I don't know how long; I had never thought I should be so happy again, as I was as I sat by Draycott's bedside, sometimes all night and sometimes all day, watching him, slowly, come back to life again. You see, it was the first thing I had done of which I hadn't cause to be ashamed for ever so long. Directly he was safe he told me the whole story, which I expect you heard to-night. He's behaved like a trump."

"I suppose it doesn't strike you that, in any degree, or in any sense, you've behaved like a trump?"

"I had a motive for what I did. Draycott's father is a big bug over in New South Wales. They've been telegraphing to each other, he and his father, spending no end of money on wires. It seems that the old man heard that he was missing and got flurried; but they've made that all right by telegram. Draycott's going back to his father; he is the only son, his father has big interests, and wants him, and he hasn't made a very good thing of soldiering; so Draycott's going back. And, what is much more--to me--I'm going with him."

"Sydney! Really?"

"Very really--thanks to Draycott. I couldn't stay in England--now; and I wouldn't. I've made such a mess of things that I shouldn't be able to breathe if I stayed. I want to put the old things behind me, and to get into a new world, and a new life."

There was silence; he seemed to be straining his eyes with the effort to see the new life for which he longed.

"And that means?"

"That means that the man you knew is dead."

"Is he? I wonder! Sydney?" He did not speak, but he looked at her. "Have you ever thought of me during all you've gone through?"

"Before I answer your question, as I will do presently, let me say what I've got to say. I'm a criminal."

The girl rose quickly from her seat.

"And let me tell you that I won't let you say it--I will not. You answer my question, and then we'll say something to each other. Answer me--did you ever think of me when, as you put it yourself, you were picking crusts out of the gutter?"

"It's not a fair question."

"Why?"

"Because you'll draw deductions from my answer which you must not draw."

"What is your answer? We'll talk about deductions afterwards. Answer me--did you ever think of me when you were picking crusts out of the gutter?"

The man closed his eyes and turned his face away. She pressed her question home.

"Answer me!"

"There was a time when I was so hungry, and so cold, and so deep down in hell, that I tried to stop thinking of you--and I couldn't."

"They stole the locket from you which I gave you."

"They did--the devils! Who told you?"

"You cut my picture out of one of the papers, and you made a case for it with a piece of silk with your own hands, and you carried it next your bosom."

"It's there now. Who told you all these things?"

"And if you go to New South Wales you'll take that picture with you?"

"I did mean to."

"And why shouldn't you take me with it? Oh, you needn't if you don't want; but unless you take a whole ship to yourself you can't prevent my travelling by the same boat, which I shall do, with or without your leave. You say you're going with Noel Draycott. I'll soon find out from Mr. Draycott the ship he's going by, if I can't get the information from you, and, as I don't suppose that my money will be refused by the people who own that ship, we'll make a party of three. Of course, you needn't speak to me while we're on the voyage, but I dare say Mr. Draycott will, when he's a moment to spare. And I hope so to find favour in Mr. Draycott's eyes that he will be able to persuade his father to invite me to pay him a little visit--so we'll all three of us be together there."

"You don't understand what it is you're proposing."

"Do credit me with some perception, please; I do understand, quite well. What you don't understand is that if you go to New South Wales, and leave me here, I shall die--yes, Sydney, I shall die."

"Violet!"

"That's the first time you've called me by my Christian name--you wretch! And now you haven't made it Vi. Hasn't a man any imagination? A girl can project herself into his mind, even when he's miles and miles away, and she doesn't even know where he is; is he absolutely incapable of projecting himself into hers? I know you've been thinking about me--thinking, thinking, thinking! And it's been bread and meat and life to me, and morning, noon, and night, all the long weary time, I've been thinking, thinking of you, and you pretend that you don't know it. You know it perfectly well! Don't you know it?"

She went and stood close up to him.

"What would all the world think of me if I took you at your word? What would you yourself think in the time to come?"

"Isn't every drop of blood in your body burning with the desire to take me in your arms?"

"If I did--afterwards--what then? When I had the consciousness that with my shame I had sullied you?"

"Can't you feel, as I stand here close to you, that I'm all on fire with the longing that you should kiss me as the man kisses the woman who loves him? Do that first--do it first, I tell you! Then, when you've kissed some of the craving out of me--if you only knew how I longed for you to kiss me, you wouldn't keep your lips from the refreshment for which, I believe, they're dying. Kiss me!"

The limit of his powers of resistance had been reached; he did what, from the first, with the whole force of his being, he had longed to do; he took her in his arms.

"Vi!"

"Vi! That's better; say it again, my dear--just like that; say it again, and again, and again! Now, wasn't that worth while?"

She drew herself a little away from him, so that, standing face to face, they held each other's hands.

"Wasn't that worth waiting for?" Her voice dropped to a whisper; she looked at him with eyes which seemed to make him tremble. "Are you going to New South Wales without me?"

The street door was heard to open; someone came along the passage.

"Is that someone coming to your room?"

"I think it's Draycott."

"Is it? That's all right. You needn't take your hands away. Sydney! of course he knows."

The door opened, to admit Noel Draycott. He paused when he saw them.

"I beg your pardon, I had no idea----"

"Oh, yes, you had, you had every idea; so you can come right straight in--because you understand. Mr. Draycott, I am coming with you to New South Wales."

"Are you? I'm delighted to hear it; I thought you would."

She turned to Beaton.

"There, Sydney, you see? He thought I would."

CHAPTER XXXIV
Some Letters and a Telegram

Mrs. Sydney Beaton sat reading a letter. By her, in a bassinette, was a baby; every now and then, half unconsciously, she would move the bassinette to and fro, as if to make sure that the baby should go on sleeping. At a little distance two children were playing, a boy and a girl; sometimes the boy called the girl Violet, and she called him Sydney. It was a glorious day; the clear champagne-like air of New South Wales in spring time.

Mrs. Beaton was at home, and a lovely home it seemed to be; a pretty picture of happiness and health its mistress would have made. Though, plainly, she was troubled by the letter. Although it had only arrived that morning, she knew its contents almost by heart, yet she read it again; when she had read it she let it lie upon her knee, while, with something wistful in her glance, she seemed to be looking at some picture which the eye of her imagination conjured up before her. Then, with the faintest little sigh, she took up other letters that were lying on her lap, and glanced through them. Then she reverted to that picture of her imagination; and she sighed again, and this time it was obviously a sigh.

As if conscience-stricken, as if guilty of at least some impropriety, she rose abruptly from her seat, and, with a startled air, looked round her, the letters bundled together in her hand. All at once firm footsteps came hurrying towards her. Turning, a tall, upright, sinewy, wiry man, without an ounce of superfluous flesh about him, his face and neck and hands bronzed by the sun, greeted her with hands outstretched.

"Sydney!" she cried, "you're earlier than I expected. I was coming over to meet you."

"Yes, I came by the earlier train. Hullo, you people!"

The boy and the girl had come rushing to him with boisterous glee. He picked them up, one on either arm; they were full of questions which had to be answered, and news which required his instant attention. It was some minutes before husband and wife were alone together.

"What made you come by the earlier train without letting me know? I can see there was something."

Her quick eyes were skilled in reading the signs of the weather on her husband's face; she could see that on it there was something like a cloud, though no larger than a man's hand.

"Yes," he said, "you are right, there was; I've had a telegram from home. I've been turning it over in my mind as I came along."

"That's rather odd, because this morning I had quite a packet of English letters. Just look at them. From whom is your telegram?"

"From Carr and Phillips, the Aversham lawyers. George is dead."

"Your brother--dead! Sydney! When did he die?"

"The telegram says--here it is--'Your brother, Sir George Beaton, died suddenly this morning. Letter follows.' That's all, except their name; it's rather a facer. I haven't seen George for----"

He paused, as if searching in his mind for an exact date.

"It's more than seven years since we left England."

"Yes, nearly eight years. You remember, we were talking about it only the other day. More than once lately I've had a feeling that I should like to see him again; and now he's gone. He wasn't exactly the most affectionate of brothers, though I dare say he would have said the same of me; but he was all I had; the last Beaton of them all."

"What will become of Adisham?"

"It's mine, since he never married; that's another facer; the old house is mine, and it will be our Sydney's when I'm gone. The whole property, such as it is, goes to the next male heir; under the old entail women don't count. No feminine thing has ever had Adisham, or ever will."

"It seems as if this were going to be a day of coincidences, one of those days on which if it rains it pours. You've had news--and such news, and I've had letters--such letters, from home. There's one from Nuthurst."

"From your uncle?"

"Yes, from uncle. It's the sweetest letter. I can see him sitting down to write it, at his big table in the justice room, with his eyes, as it were, across the sea, trying with all his might not to put a word on paper which could hurt."

"He wants you to go home?"

"He doesn't say so. In every word he has written I can read what is in his mind; he feels that there are reasons which might make it difficult for me to go, and he doesn't want to hurt me by asking me to do what I mightn't be able to; he thinks it might hurt me to have to refuse. But, Sydney, all through his letter, although he doesn't know it, he's telling me that he is a very old man, and he's crying out for me to come--before he goes."

"Does he speak of me?"

"Does he! He speaks more of you than of me, and he's full of the children. His body is in England, but his spirit is with us in New South Wales. If he weren't such an old man, and so little of a traveller, I'm sure he would come to us; he would have come long ago."

"I wonder what it would feel like to go back to England on a visit?"

"I wonder? I hardly dare to."

"Vi! Is it so bad with you as that?"

"Oh, Sydney, if you only knew how I'd love to go--with you and with the children. Why, the children never have seen England."

"That's certainly a fact."

He was regarding her with something quizzical in his eyes.

"Just think of it! Though they pray for the dear homeland every night in their prayers, and for the friends who are at home."

"Are there any friends at home? Do you think any of them would speak to us--to me?"

"Why, Sydney, what a goose you are! They'd be tumbling over each other to get a chance."

"Would they? I shouldn't want them to do that, if only from the point of view of dignity, to say nothing of their getting hurt."

"Just think of the letters I'm always having, and which you get; just look at this heap! There's another from Major Reith; he says that if we won't go to him, the next long leave he gets he'll come here."

"We might bring him back with us."

"And there's one from Margaret, Countess of Cantyre; she's longing to make your acquaintance."

"Is she?" His tone was more than a trifle dry.

"You know she is! Only in her last letter she said she never would believe you were a real creature till she'd met you in the flesh; she has heard all sorts of tales about you; you've been the hero of all kinds of wonderful stories, but she's never seen you once. She has the impertinence to say in this very letter that she is still convinced that you're only a person out of a novel, a mere fiction; and that, though I pretend that you're my husband, she never will believe it till you tell her so, in person, to her face. What do you think of that?"

"Vi, I think I'll wire to Carr and Phillips."

"Haven't you sent an answer to their telegram?"

"No, that's it; that's one reason why I came by the earlier train; I wanted to see you first, to know what answer I was to send."

"I see."

In her voice, although she spoke so quietly, there was a tremor, a catching of her breath, a suspicion of eagerness; all these things in those two little words, which probably did not go unnoticed.

"It's a matter on which I wished to consult you before I did anything; so much may hinge on the reply I send. The question is, what steamer could we catch?"

"Sydney!" His name burst from her rather than was uttered; her whole face was lighted up.

"When could you be ready?"

"Why--when could I be ready? Why--Sydney, I haven't thought; what a question to spring on one; as though--as though one could decide upon a thing like that, without a moment's notice."

"I have been talking to Draycott, and he says that if we were to go by the next boat----"

"The next boat!"

She seemed to be springing out of her shoes.

"And were to stay in England, say, a year----"

"Stay in England--say, a year!"

"Everything would go on all right here, and he'd look after things. The question is, could you and the children be ready for the next boat?"

"When does it go?"

"In ten days. I don't want to hustle you; if you want time for consideration--why, take it."

"Of course I don't want time for consideration, you absurd creature; of course we can be ready."

"You think so?"

"I don't think, I'm sure--silly!"

"I don't want to have you worried or hustled----"

"Sydney, if you don't take care----!"

"Then, before it comes to threats, I may as well send a wire to them to let them know we're coming, and to the steamship people to secure our berths. I happen to know that there's a nice suite vacant, just the very thing we want; and, as regards the telegrams, I may mention that I've both forms in my pocket--already written out."

"Sydney--you--darling wretch!"

THE END

Printed in Great Britain
by Amazon